SOMEONE'S LISTENING . . .

My phone rang. I checked the display but didn't recognize the number. Still, it could be Jamie trying to reach Tim again, who might have turned off his phone or set it to Do Not Disturb for the night. I didn't know her number by sight, and these days the first three digits in a cell number—the area code—didn't necessarily tie that number to a specific region, so people didn't have to change their number when they moved.

I'd better get this, in case it was her. I connected and said hello.

No one spoke, but it wasn't dead air. The faint sound of breathing came over the line.

"Hello?" I asked. "Who's there?"

Crickets.

"Hello?" I pressed. "Who is this?"

Silence.

I jabbed at the phone to disconnect the call. The hair on my arms stood up. My neck prickled, and a shiver ran through me . . .

Books by Maddie Day

Country Store Mysteries
FLIPPED FOR MURDER
GRILLED FOR MURDER
WHEN THE GRITS HIT THE FAN
BISCUITS AND SLASHED BROWNS
DEATH OVER EASY
STRANGLED EGGS AND HAM
NACHO AVERAGE MURDER
CANDY SLAIN MURDER
NO GRATER CRIME
BATTER OFF DEAD
FOUR LEAF CLEAVER
DEEP FRIED DEATH
CHRISTMAS COCOA MURDER
(with Carlene O'Connor and Alex Erickson)
CHRISTMAS SCARF MURDER
(with Carlene O'Connor and Peggy Ehrhart)

Cozy Capers Book Group Mysteries
MURDER ON CAPE COD
MURDER AT THE TAFFY SHOP
MURDER AT THE LOBSTAH SHACK
MURDER IN A CAPE COTTAGE
MURDER AT A CAPE BOOKSTORE
MURDER AT THE RUSTY ANCHOR

Local Foods Mysteries
A TINE TO LIVE, A TINE TO DIE
'TIL DIRT DO US PART
FARMED AND DANGEROUS
MURDER MOST FOWL
MULCH ADO ABOUT MURDER

Cece Barton Mysteries
MURDER UNCORKED
CHRISTMAS MITTENS MURDER
(with Lee Hollis and Lynn Cahoon)

Published by Kensington Publishing Corp.

MURDER AT THE RUSTY ANCHOR

Maddie Day

A Cozy Capers Book Group Mystery

Kensington Publishing Corp.

www.kensingtonbooks.com

For my author-chef pals at Mystery Lovers' Kitchen, who inspire me to devise recipes and stories as good as theirs: Leslie Budewitz, Lucy Burdette, VM Burns, Peg Cochran, Maya Corrigan, Cleo Coyle, Vicki Delany, Leslie Karst, Tina Kashian, Libby Klein, and Molly MacRae (and all their pen names).

Acknowledgments

Many thanks, once again, to pharmacologist Luci Zahray, aka The Poison Lady, for her presentation to the New England chapter of Sisters in Crime about the toxicity of certain botanicals. She has led me to various other commonly available poisons, but this is my first time killing someone in this series with a poison derived from a common perennial shrub. You rock, Luci!

The daughter of longtime friends is named Sita, and I shameless borrowed that beautiful moniker. The Raleigh, North Carolina, arboretum, however, is entirely fictional, with apologies to the two actual ones in that area.

A note on dialect: where I come from (California), those metal boxes on wheels at the supermarket that you fill with your groceries are called shopping carts. In Massachusetts, they're carriages. Mac's a native of the Commonwealth, so that's how she and the locals around her refer to them.

I'm grateful to Amy Glaser for her eagle eye and insightful comments on this manuscript. Among other observations, she made sure Mac was as sensitive to others as she should be. You rock, Amy.

Huge thanks to Jennifer McKee for saving me from having to create my own graphics. She also ably assists with various other non-writing aspects of my business.

Note to readers: the ideas and words in this novel were generated entirely by the author without contribution from an AI application. I wish I didn't have to include that statement, but you should know where your fiction comes from.

No book of mine can go out without thanking my Wicked Authors blogmates—Jessie Crockett, Sherry Harris, Julie Hennrikus, Liz Mugavero, and Barbara Ross (and all their pseudonyms)—for their ongoing support and friendship. Please also visit me on the second and fourth Fridays and the eleven other talented author-cooks at Mystery Lovers' Kitchen, where you can find an original recipe (and quite a few giveaways) every day of the week.

I'm grateful, always, to John Scognamiglio, my editor at Kensington Publishing, and the expert team of publicists, artists, production staff, salespeople, and everybody else who makes the process of getting my books into print seem nearly seamless. Many thanks to my agent, John Talbot, for making it all possible.

To my sons, Allan and John David, and their fabulous wives; to my sisters, Barbara and Janet; to my partner in life, Hugh: I'm deeply grateful for your support. I'm a lucky woman.

And I always feel blessed for enthusiastic librarians, book bloggers, and readers. I wouldn't be on this path without you.

Chapter 1

Hurrying to open my bike shop on time during yet another day of pouring rain might seem like madness. Nobody wanted to rent bikes while a mid-July downpour drenched the beaches and the rail trail. The only Westham, Massachusetts, businesses doing well this week—at the height of the year's tourist season—were retail shops and restaurants.

But hurry I did. At eight thirty on a Monday morning, I was running late to open Mac's Bikes at nine. I didn't like to be late.

Part of our business was retail, after all. My shop covered the three Rs: rental, retail, and repair. And maybe an optimist or two would want to buy a new bicycle for whenever the heck the rain stopped.

My hurrying didn't actually extend to running. Hunching into the hood of my rain jacket, I trudged as fast as I could. I slowed a bit in front of Greta's, the bakery my gentle and talented husband, Tim Brunelle, owned. The aroma of fresh baked bread and brioche lured me into being even later, but I resisted and kept going.

The door of the Rusty Anchor pub in the same block flew open and nearly hit me in the face.

"Careful," I warned whoever had been so heedless as I sidestepped.

Yvonne Flora, the pub's head cook and manager, burst out. She cast wild looks right and left.

"Yvonne?" I asked. "What's the matter?"

"Mac! You have to help me." Her normally pale face was now ashen. Her brows pulled together, and her mouth turned down at the corners. Her eyes looked haunted. She grabbed my hand and tugged.

"Wait," I began. "Are you okay?"

"No. Not at all. Mac, there's a . . ." Her hand flew to her mouth. She swallowed and dropped her hand. "He's . . . just come with me, please."

My heart chilled as I followed her inside. I didn't like the sound of this. Not one bit.

Even though it hadn't been open since last night's closing time of nine o'clock, the pub still smelled of hops and hamburgers, chowder and coffee, beer and brats, fries and fillet of fish. But the dark wood of the rustic booths, the cold gas fireplace, and the dim lighting gave the place a spooky vibe. And the background scents had an additional component I couldn't identify—except that it wasn't a pleasant one.

Yvonne stopped so abruptly I bumped into her.

"Sorry," I murmured.

She'd paused at the open end of the horseshoe-shaped bar. Other than the red glow of the EXIT sign above the door to the kitchen, the only illumination was from a row of pendant lights. They shone onto the lower workspace on the other side of the bar's shiny maple surface, its gleaming layers of finish impermeable to spilled drinks or careless customers.

Yvonne pointed behind the bar. Her hand shook. Her nostrils flared as she shook her head, slowly, with what looked like sorrow.

At first, a black leather shoe was all I saw. A shoe with a brown sock wrapped around an ankle. Which emerged from a gray polyester pants leg. *No.* My breath rushed in. I edged past her. A man lay crumpled on the floor on his side, his pale-green shirt ghostly against the black mat. His hands, now clawlike, were at his stomach, as if he'd clenched it in pain.

The side of his face, all that showed, was stained around the mouth. A string of gray hair hung across a waxen and yellowing cheek. His chest didn't move. The bad smell I'd detected was way worse back here and seemed to come from a drying pool near his mouth.

I whipped my face around to stare at Yvonne. "Did you check for a pulse?"

She nodded. "Nothing. He's dead, Mac. And his skin is cold."

A memory of a circled red *D* on a double-spaced typed page flashed into my mind. I gazed at the dead man.

"Is this Mr. Byrne?"

"Yes," she whispered.

My long-ago freshman English teacher had aged in the twenty years since I'd graduated. I hadn't seen him since then. What was left of his essence remained,

right down to the shirt pocket holding index cards
and two pens. One black, one red.

"We have to call the police." I slid my phone out of
my jacket pocket.

She again nodded, her eyes now brimming with
tears.

I had so many questions. How had Mr. Byrne been
left, dead, inside the pub? Was that dark pool blood
or vomit? Was this suicide, homicide, or a natural
death? And why was Yvonne here so early?

Calling 911 came first.

Chapter 2

I asked Yvonne to sit at a table near the front door so she could let the police in when they arrived. The Westham station was a block away on Main Street. It wouldn't take them long.

Then I sent a quick text to my bike mechanic, Orlean Brown, saying I was unavoidably detained and to please open for the day. Should I tell her to take the rainy morning off, instead? No, she was likely already on the road from Falmouth, where she lived. And I knew she had repairs lined up for the day. Orlean, like me, appreciated a set routine.

Yvonne, who didn't object to being directed what to do, selected a chair as far from the bar as possible. *Good.* She sank into it shakily and kept her gaze pointed in the opposite direction from where Mr. Byrne lay. The two of us had already contaminated the crime scene by being nearby, but that couldn't be helped.

While it was hard to believe I even knew that much about crime scenes, the several—well, four or five— murders in our town in the last couple of years had educated me in ways I'd never dreamed of. My small successes in helping track down killers, assisted by the members of the Cozy Capers book group, had also earned me more than one caution from the Westham PD, as well as the state police detective, to stay well away from investigating homicides.

I tried. But when a person I was close to was a suspect—as my bestie, Gin, had been one time—I truly had no choice. I switched on my phone's flashlight app and approached the body. I had to admit, my native curiosity also drove me. That, and my intense dislike for messy situations.

Mr. Byrne lying dead behind the Rusty Anchor bar was nothing if not messy.

I didn't touch him, but I squatted and shined the light on his face even while breathing through my mouth. It wasn't blood that stained his mouth and was drying on the floor mat. Something had caused him to vomit.

Scanning the teacher's head and shirt with the light, I didn't see blood anywhere. No gunshot wounds. No marks on the wrinkled skin of his neck, at least the part of it not covered by his shirt's open collar. The skin on his age-spotted hands was like parchment but didn't bear marks or stains. Even though he lay on his left side, his left hand was visible at his collar. No wedding band adorned the ring finger, nor a pale line indicating he'd worn one recently.

He'd seemed old twenty years ago, and he had to be close to retirement age by now. As a young teen, I hadn't even thought about Mr. Byrne's personal life. What had he loved doing when classes were over for the day? How had he spent his weekends? All I knew was that he'd been strict to the point of petty and unfair. I had not deserved a big red *D* on my paper about Ruth Bader Ginsburg. Still, the sight of those old-man hands about did me in. Mr. Byrne did not deserve to die on the floor of a bar, and especially not in questionable circumstances.

"What did you find?" Yvonne asked.

At the same time, a knock on the front door sounded. I stood and stepped out from behind the bar, trying to thumb the flashlight app closed. I failed, dropping the phone in a fit of nerves.

August Jenkins stepped inside. "Westham Police. Ms. Flora, you have an emergency?" He was an officer about ten years younger than my thirty-seven. He usually patrolled on bicycle, but not during a frog strangler—my grandma's term—like today's downpour.

Yvonne pointed to me. And the bar. At least it was August responding and not Victoria Laitinen. The Westham PD chief and I had been at loggerheads back in high school and had never really mended the relationship.

"You called this in, Mac?" August asked.

"I did." I scooped my phone off the floor and pocketed it, gleaming light and all.

"What's the nature of the emergency?" he asked.

All I'd told the dispatcher was that we had an emergency and were not in danger. I'd thought the "body" part could wait.

"Sadly, there's a dead man behind the bar." I tilted my head in Mr. Byrne's direction.

August blinked. Swallowed. Squared his shoulders. He pulled on a pair of nitrile gloves and headed toward the body. He squatted, laid two fingers on Mr. Byrne's neck, and waited, then touched the mike in his shirt and mumbled into it.

All I could make out was "death."

"Who discovered the remains?" He stood, glancing from me to Yvonne.

She raised her hand, still staying silent.

August gazed at me. "Do either of you know who—"

The door pushed open again. State police detective Lincoln Haskins stood backlit, his large frame filling the entrance. He pushed back the hood on his raincoat.

"What's this about a body?"

Chapter 3

I nodded as I pointed behind the bar. "He's here."

"And so are you, I see," Lincoln said.

"I am." Was he going to give me a hard time about once again being at the scene of a murder? Maybe. It wasn't of my doing in the least, though. After Yvonne asked, I couldn't have refused to help her.

"I've confirmed the lack of a pulse, sir," August said.

"Thank you, Jenkins," Lincoln said. "Secure the back door and then guard access to the remains."

"Yes, sir," August said.

"Mac, please step away and join us here," Lincoln added.

He said "please," but it was clearly an order. I stepped away. August must have already communicated that he thought Byrne's wasn't a natural death. If the guy had simply died back there, Lincoln wouldn't have asked me to remove myself. But what had made August think that?

"Ma'am, I'd like you tell me what you know." The detective addressed Yvonne.

"I'm Yvonne Flora." Yvonne raised her hand. "I found Mr. Byrne. I rushed outside and found Mac passing by on her way to work. I asked for her help."

I nodded my confirmation.

"Thank you, Ms. Flora," he said. "I'm Lincoln Haskins, a detective sergeant with the state police. I believe we met last March. Can you verify her account, Mac?"

"A hundred percent," I said. "She showed me where he was. Where he still is. And I called 911. That's all."

"You referred to him as Mr. Byrne." Lincoln shrugged out of his jacket. "Did either of you know him well?"

We both shook our heads. Yvonne pointed at me.

"I had him for freshman English at Westham High," I said. "But I haven't seen him since."

"Does this English teacher have a first name?" Lincoln gazed over the tops of his black-rimmed glasses.

"Bruce," Yvonne said. "Bruce Byrne."

"And how well did you know him, Ms. Flora?"

She cleared her throat. "Not too well." Her voice was low, tentative. She worried a thread on the cuff of her cotton sweater.

Lincoln tilted his head. "What is your role here?"

"I'm the chef and manager."

"Was Byrne a regular in the pub?"

My radar went up from the way Lincoln was looking at Yvonne. Did he already know the answer? Also, why did he ask her what she did here? He knew she was employed as a chef from the case in the spring. He must have intended to reconfirm her job.

"No," she murmured, not returning his gaze.

"What was that, ma'am?" he asked.

"No." She finally looked up. "He'd been in a few times lately, though."

"Thank you. I will have many more questions for both of you, but right now I need to take a look at our Mr. Byrne. Please sit with Ms. Flora, Mac. Do not communicate with the outside world, either of you, until I clear you to do so. I'd like each of you to lay your phones on the table."

He waited until we did so. I sat across from Yvonne.

"But I have to tell Carl," she protested.

"And Carl might be?" Lincoln asked.

"Carl O'Connor. He owns the pub."

That name rang a faint bell in the recesses of my brain, but I couldn't place it.

"He will certainly need to be notified," Lincoln agreed. "We will do that, however. Not you. Do I make myself clear?"

She gave a reluctant nod.

"Thank you," he said. "Mac, have you told anyone what you saw?"

"No, although I did text Orlean to tell her I'd be late. I didn't say why."

"Keep the news out of your book group for now, if you don't mind."

"I promise." Even if I did mind, I would follow orders. Nobody wanted to get in trouble with Lincoln Haskins.

"Good." He turned back toward the bar, then faced us again. "And no more talking with each other about what you found, if you don't mind."

That seemed extreme. But one doesn't argue with the police. The wail of more than one siren grew closer. My phone dinged and vibrated with an incoming text. I ignored it. Lincoln stretched a pair of gloves over his big hands. The gloves made the unmistakable snapping sound of nitrile.

I gazed at Yvonne. She looked terrible. Her already somewhat shopworn face was wan. Her ear-length dirty-blond hair, not yet tucked into her multicolored toque, appeared to have a new crop of white mixed in since the last time I'd seen her up close. I was about ten years younger than Yvonne, but this morning she appeared older than forty-seven.

"Are you okay?" I asked her in a soft voice.

"Not a bit. I've never seen a dead person before, Mac." She sniffed, bringing the back of her hand to her mouth, and added in a whisper, "Poor, poor Bruce."

Who was likely not only dead, but murdered, judging from how Lincoln was acting. The door opened again before I could ask Yvonne about being on a first-name basis with Mr. Byrne.

Another Westham PD officer hurried in, followed by Penelope Johnson, a detective sergeant with the department. I'd met the detective last winter for the first time. I later discovered she lived down the street from Tim's place. The Blacksmith Shop Road cottage was now also mine, ever since our wedding on New Year's Eve.

Lincoln stood from where he'd squatted at the entry point to the bar. Penelope paused near us, the patrol officer behind her, and raised a hand to Lincoln in greeting.

"Morning, Johnson."

Penelope nodded at him. "Sir."

"I'd like you"—Lincoln pointed at the officer—"to secure the front entrance and guard it."

"Yes, sir." The young woman headed outside.

"I've called the BCI, Haskins," Penelope said.

I'd learned in one of the last cases that the Bureau of Criminal Investigation assisted the Cape and the islands police, as well as the state officers, with forensic expertise.

"Excellent, thank you," he said.

"What would you like me to do?" Penelope asked.

Lincoln, who was with the state police, ranked above Penelope when it came to homicide. They'd worked together a couple of months ago when a man was found killed in the bookstore, and they hadn't seemed to get territorial with each other.

"I'll show you the scene, then we need to interview Ms. Flora and Mac. Separately, of course." He looked at Yvonne. "Where are the light switches for this room?"

"Next to the entrance to the kitchen." She started to rise.

"Please stay there, ma'am." Penelope pulled on gloves and switched on the lights, then joined Lincoln behind the bar. They both remained standing.

And we both stayed seated. I'd almost asked if I could be interviewed first so I could get to work. Except I knew from experience that the police did things in the order they needed to. All I could do was wait.

Chapter 4

Penelope and I perched on stainless-steel stools in the pub's kitchen twenty minutes later. The crime scene team had arrived. Lincoln had escorted Yvonne down the street to the police station to interview her there and get her fingerprints on file.

"I didn't kill him," she'd protested, her voice quavering, after he told her the plan.

He'd gently coaxed her out the front door saying that recording her prints was for elimination purposes only at this point, and that everyone had to clear the room where the body was found, anyway.

"Thank you for talking to me here," I now said to Penelope. "I really need to get to work at my bike shop."

All business, she tapped a few things on her tablet. "Do I have your permission to record this conversation?"

"Yes." I knew to say it aloud and not simply nod. I continued with the answer to what would surely be her next question. "My name is Mackenzie Almeida, and I live at 85 Blacksmith Shop Road in Westham, Massachusetts. Today is July fifteenth." I tacked on the year and folded my hands on the pristine stainless worktable between the detective and me. Even though I was a hundred percent innocent, being interviewed by the police invariably made me nervous, and I didn't want to fidget.

"Please tell me what transpired this morning," Penelope said.

"I was heading to my place of business, Mac's Bikes, a scant block beyond the Rusty Anchor pub on Main Street in Westham."

"You were on foot?" she asked.

"Yes." I went on to describe a distraught-looking Yvonne bursting through the door and her urgent request that I come inside and help her.

"Did she say why she needed assistance?"

"She couldn't seem to finish a sentence, but she mentioned a 'he.' I didn't know what she was referring to, so I followed her in."

"What happened then?"

"She showed me the body behind the bar." I thought of a mystery our Cozy Capers book group had read recently. It was part of a long-running series by Katherine Hall Page in which every title was something like, *The Body in the . . .* , followed by the location. I was pretty sure she'd never written *The Body Behind the Bar.* Maybe I'd shoot her an email. Or not.

"Did you recognize that person?"

"Yes." A lawyer had once cautioned me to answer

only the question that was asked. Seemed like good advice.

"Who was it?"

"Mr. Byrne, an English teacher at Westham High School."

"Do you know his first name?" she asked.

"I didn't, but Yvonne mentioned it later, calling him Bruce." Up to now, what I'd told Penelope was identical with my answers to Lincoln. I continued. "I had him for freshman English more than twenty years ago and hadn't seen him since."

"How well do you know Yvonne Flora?"

Her change of subject threw me for a second. "Not very well. We're acquainted, but we don't hang out at all."

"Did she happen to mention any conflicts she had with the deceased?"

"No . . ." My voice trailed off.

"Is there more?"

"I don't know. She said he'd been in a few times lately. Honestly, I felt like she wasn't saying everything she knew. I'm not sure whether she was holding back relating an emotion, an experience, or a piece of information."

"She's not the bartender, right?" Penelope asked.

"Not as far as I know. She's the main chef. You'll have to ask someone else about who tends bar here."

Raised voices filtered in from outside the back door. It pushed open, and Penelope jumped up, her right hand slipping inside the left front of her blazer.

"Sir, you can't—" August protested.

"I own this place." A man, fists on hips, filled the doorway as he blustered. "Who are you, kid, to tell me I can't go in? And why are two women who don't work here occupying my kitchen?" He glared down at me.

I pointed to Penelope and kept my mouth shut. I'd never seen the dude before, but if he owned the pub, he must be the Carl Yvonne had mentioned. Somewhere around fifty, he looked both fit and well-groomed. Under an open, knee-length raincoat he wore an ironed, pale-blue square-cut shirt over linen slacks and no socks in his boat shoes. The dark shade of his carefully tousled hair might have had an assist from a box of dye. He was one of the lucky middle-aged men who'd retained what must be his original hairline.

Penelope slipped her left hand into her pocket and flashed her badge at the man. "Detective Sergeant Brown of the Westham Police Department. What is your name, please?"

"Police?" He blinked blue eyes in a tanned face. "What are you doing here?"

"I'd like you to answer me, sir." Penelope's steely tone made it clear he had no choice.

"Yes, ma'am." He gave a little smirk. "My name is Carl O'Connor and always has been."

He looked good, but his voice didn't match. It had a reedy quality that grated on my nerves. A little bell again rang in my brain as if he was familiar, except hearing him didn't make the name or the face any clearer in my memory.

"I'm afraid your restaurant is currently an active crime scene," Penelope said.

"It's a what, now?" He headed for the swinging door into the pub proper.

"Sir, stop where you are." Penelope stepped in front of the door. "You can't go in there."

"Says who?"

She crossed her arms and spread her feet wider than shoulder width. "The Westham Police Department, along with the Barnstable County District Attorney and the Massachusetts State Police. That good enough for you?"

"I guess it's going to have to be."

Penelope made a rolling gesture with her hand.

"Ma'am," he added, narrowing his eyes as if thinking. "Forgive me if I spoke out of turn, ma'am." His tone had changed to heavy cream. Emphasis on the heavy, which matched the insincere smile he now wore. "It was the shock of hearing that my beloved pub has had a crime committed in it."

Had he also layered on a touch of a Southern accent? *Just . . . no.*

"Might I inquire as to what sort of crime, Detective?" he added.

"Not at this time." She gestured at the stool she'd vacated. "Mac, I think we're done. You're free to leave."

I stood. "Thank you. You know where to find me."

"Likewise," Penelope said.

I slid past O'Connor. He showed no interest in who I was. Instead, he'd whipped out a phone. I decided not to introduce myself. Maybe another time. We were fellow Westham business owners, although I'd never seen him at a Chamber of Commerce event. Or anyplace, for that matter, as far as I remembered. Maybe he seemed familiar because he reminded me of another person. Who, I couldn't say.

As I headed outside, I heard Penelope continuing to take charge of the situation.

"I need you to stop what you're doing and lay your phone on the table, sir. Yes, now."

She was doing her job. Lincoln was doing his. I was off to do mine.

Chapter 5

Rain still poured down in sheets and buckets as I hurried toward the shop at nearly ten thirty. Questions poured into my brain, too. Where did Carl live? If he was never around town, why had he shown up at the Rusty Anchor this morning, of all mornings? What was it about him I didn't trust?

Also, how had Yvonne known Bruce well enough to call him by his first name? What was she hiding?

Most important, how had the teacher died? How could August and Lincoln tell that Mr. Byrne's death was a likely homicide? And even more vital, who had killed him—and why?

A car driving too fast bumped through a canyon-sized pothole now roiling with water. Dirt-flecked rain splashed all the way up the legs of my jeans to the knees and added to the sodden nature of my sneakers. Beginning the day with wet pants and shoes was not my idea of a good time.

I pulled open the door to Mac's Bikes to find a dozen people milling around. A few calmly inspected new bikes. Several were holding up biking shirts and exclaiming. And three were modeling impatience in their expressions and their stances.

Orlean, from behind the checkout counter, tilted her head and gave me a look from under her Red Sox cap. "Retail. Rental. Repair." She ticked our three offerings off on her fingers. "Everybody wants all of them."

"I'm here now. Thank you, Orlean. I owe you. Now go do what you were hired for. I've got the rest." I knew how much she hated having to interact with the public. Her strength was being an expert in the intricate workings of bicycle mechanisms. It definitely wasn't interpersonal communications.

She turned without a word. I stripped off my raincoat and threw it over the back of the stool behind the cash register. I mustered my best small business owner's welcoming smile.

"Who's first?"

Over the next hour, I took money for a repaired derailleur. Sold three brightly colored wicking bike shirts that bore our Mac's Bikes of Westham logo. Accepted the return of a rental tandem and commiserated with the newlyweds about the weather not allowing them the biking honeymoon they'd been hoping for.

All the while, my texts were dinging off the hook, if that wasn't mixing too many metaphors. The Cozy Capers, my occasional partners in amateur crime solving, must have gotten wind of the Body Behind the Bar. I didn't have a single minute to read and respond.

And the customers kept coming. Every time I thought I was on top of the rush, another two or five or three bike enthusiasts would push through the door, undaunted by the storm.

By twelve thirty I was starving, but I told Orlean to take her lunch first. She grabbed her lunch bag and headed outside. Had the rain stopped? Now that I thought about it, customers in the last half hour hadn't come in drenched and dripping.

The numbers dwindled until only one person browsed the retail shelves. She selected a tool kit and added it to a basket full of small odds and ends like tire patches, socks, and a head lamp. She grabbed a neon-pink shirt off the shelves and brought it all to the checkout area.

"It looks like you're putting together a Christmas stocking in July." I began ringing up her purchases.

The woman laughed and ran a slender-fingered hand through her hair. It was about the same length as my inch-long dark curls, but her locks were blond turning white and straight. Her features and skin tone looked vaguely Mediterranean.

"It's my boyfriend's birthday Saturday," she said. "He's super into biking. Well, we both are, and I wanted to surprise him with a kind of care package."

"That's sweet. Do you have to send it far?"

"Only from my hand to his. I'm up here visiting for a while."

"Even better." I told her the total and waited while she inserted her card in the reader. "Where do you live?"

"North Carolina. But I'm a former Westhamite."

Her voice, plus a wistful smile, made me think she missed living here. I gave her another glance but didn't recognize her face. I thought she was probably over fifty, and I would have no real reason to have known her before. She was too old to have been a friend or classmate and too young to be a friend of my parents or a parent of my friends.

"I bet you got tired of the New England winters." I handed her the bag of her purchases.

"Um, not exactly." Now she sounded grim.

An interesting reaction, but none of my business. "My name's Mac Almeida, by the way." I smiled. "This is my shop."

"Nice to meet you, Mac. I'm Sita Spencer. You've got a nice place here."

"Thanks. I hope the weather improves so you can get some biking in with your guy before you leave."

"Things have already improved," she said. "Cheers."

The door opened to admit Florence Wolanski, otherwise known as Flo, Westham's head librarian and stalwart of the Cozy Capers gang. She did a double take when her gaze fell on Sita.

"If it isn't Sita Spencer in the flesh," Flo said. "What brings you back to town after all this time?"

Sita pressed her lips together, nostrils flaring. She pushed past Flo, muttering, "Excuse me," under her breath.

At least I thought that was what she'd said.

Chapter 6

Flo gazed at the door Sita left through and gave her head a couple of slow shakes. "Never thought I'd see her around Westham again."

"It sounds like you knew her when she lived here."

"Yes, Mac, I did." She held up a soft lunch box. "Do you have time to eat and talk? Seems quiet in here."

"It wasn't earlier, but I'd love to talk. Let me grab my sandwich." I washed up and fetched my own lunch bag out of the mini-fridge.

Flo had taken the other stool behind the counter and was mid-bite into what looked like a chicken salad wrap.

I unwrapped my ham and cheese but took a minute to check my phone. Which had about a dozen new texts.

"I set up a homicide thread with the group," Flo said. "You heard about the body in the bar?"

"I was the second person to see it this morning."

She gaped. "Seriously?"

"Yep," I said. "I was minding my own business and passing by the Rusty Anchor on my way here when Yvonne burst out looking kind of wild. She grabbed me and asked for my help."

"Is it true it was Bruce Byrne?"

I nodded, my mouth full of a bite of the same sandwich I had every weekday.

"And they think he was murdered," she said.

I nodded again, then swallowed. "He looked awful. I think he'd vomited, but I'm not sure beyond that why Lincoln thought it might have been a homicide."

"Bruce was a jerk, a bully, and a tyrant." Flo glanced around.

Orlean hadn't returned, and no new customers had come in. "Nobody's here," I said. "Although that could change in an instant."

"I shouldn't say this," she went on, "but I think it's a good thing he's dead."

"I hadn't seen him since high school, and he was certainly strict and unfair even back then."

"I'd seen him way more than I wanted to." Her lip curled as if she'd tasted a rotten piece of chicken.

"Because you're the town librarian-in-chief, and he was an English teacher."

"Exactly. The man made a lot of demands of the library, and me in particular, over the years."

"What kind of demands?" I took another bite of my favorite sandwich.

"You know. Things about books for his classes. Pushing me to take on the worst-behaving kid in the class as an intern. Challenging me on what we featured in the teen section. Bruce had a complete disdain for manga, for example. Well, graphic novels in general. I figure anything that gets a young person interested in reading is for the better."

"It absolutely is," I agreed.

"And don't even get me started on what he thought about science fiction and crime novels, including cozy mysteries."

"Did he want only 'literary fiction' on the library shelves?" I surrounded the term with air quotes. Our book group often talked about the snobs who looked down on genre fiction. We all agreed that the majority of cozies told good stories, gently included social issues in the background, and kept readers engaged with well-drawn series characters and settings. What more could you want from a book?

"Something like that." She drummed her fingers on the counter. "But then this other thing happened."

I waited. She kept drumming.

"What was that other thing?" I finally asked. Whatever it was seemed like a bad memory, or something she was reluctant to talk about, even though she'd brought it up. Maybe it was about Sita and how she knew her. We'd never gotten back to that topic.

Still staring at the counter, Flo had her mouth open to speak. She shut it when the door opened. I expected Orlean to come through, and she did. I didn't expect Lincoln to follow her in.

Orlean nodded at me and strode into her repair room. Flo blinked at the sight of Lincoln. He rolled his eyes, likely at two members of the book group putting their heads together mere hours after a murdered man was discovered.

"Come in, Lincoln." I smiled at him and popped in the last bite of my sandwich.

Flo did likewise, minus the smile. Under the counter, her knee set to jiggling. *Why?*

"Ladies," he said.

"Has the rain stopped?" I asked, more to fill the air and let Flo's reaction subside than because I needed to know.

"About an hour ago." He flipped open his palms, possibly to demonstrate that he stood there wearing no jacket over his signature Hawaiian shirt, which was dry, as was the thick dark hair grazing his shirt's collar. "At least for now."

Flo stuffed her wrapper into her lunch box and stood.

"Catch you later, Mac," she murmured.

"What can I help you with, Lincoln?" I asked.

"I was actually looking for Ms. Wolanski." He moved in the way of the door, fixing his gaze on Flo. "You weren't at the library, and I had a feeling I could find you here. Could we have a word in private, please?"

"I really need to get back to work." She lifted her chin.

"And I really need to speak with you. It can be here or down at the station."

Flo's shoulders slumped. "If I have to."

"You can use my office, if you want," I said. "You know where it is, Lincoln."

"Thank you, Mac. Ma'am?" He gestured for Flo to precede him toward the back of the shop.

She set her bag back on the counter. She also knew where the office was.

I watched them disappear into the tiny space that barely fit a desk and two chairs, plus a small safe. At least it had a door that closed. This interview could be about Flo's dealings with the exceedingly difficult Bruce Byrne—or something different.

Chapter 7

By one thirty, Lincoln and Flo had both left. She'd emerged from the office looking unhappy. She said only to read the text thread before she hurried off to the library down the street. Lincoln had thanked me and ambled away. What had transpired during their meeting was anybody's guess.

The afternoon so far in Mac's Bikes wasn't crazy busy with customers. My brother, Derrick, who usually worked here at least half of the day, was away until Thursday with his daughter, Cokey, and Nelinda Lavoie, his girlfriend of a few months. I'd sent them off with my blessing, saying I could bring in one of our occasional part-timers if I needed to. With four days of rain and counting, Orlean and I had so far been able to handle the business.

I'd opened Mac's Bikes three years ago after returning to my hometown. I had a Harvard degree and an MBA under my belt, plus five years working in Boston finance, a two-year stint in the Peace Corps in Thailand, and a couple of failed relationships. I'd missed my family and Westham, and my prudent money management had enabled me to buy and renovate the building and to equip my shop.

Bicycling had been a favorite pastime. Over the years I'd learned to repair and maintain cycles. A bad knee kept me from biking or running these days, but I'd retained my skills with the tools and parts needed to keep a bicycle in tip-top running condition. If Orlean ever had to be away, I knew how to do the mechanical side of the business. And I certainly was able to talk about it and navigate ordering parts and equipment.

The shop was popular with locals and tourists alike. The business's bottom line had been in great shape for most of the time I'd owned it, even in the offseasons like winter. I'd have thought the rain moving out would have brought in a flood of customers. So far, today wasn't at all normal.

I grabbed the opportunity to check the Cozy Capers text thread. It was mostly full of shock, question marks, and suggestions that we should meet soon. We should. I added a message.

We can meet at my house tonight. Seven?

I hit Send. And then cringed a little. I should have checked with Tim first. He was so easygoing, I doubted he would have a problem with the group taking over the living room. But I'd better ask him.

His text came back almost immediately.

The house is yours, sweetheart. Dinner at six?
Thank you. XXOO

He really was the best. I didn't cook at all. When it

was my night to put dinner on the table, the meal invariably involved takeout containers or pizza boxes. I always assembled my own cold breakfast and lunch. I could put together a couple of offerings to take to parties, such as avocado deviled eggs. Beyond that, I'd never learned to cook and didn't have the desire to. Nor the need, especially ever since Tim and I had joyfully joined our lives.

That man could bake bread and delicacies to make you drool, and he was also a talent in the dinner department. I had totally lucked out in love.

I peeked in at Orlean. She was tightening the brake cable on a women's Sora, a sweet alloy road bike.

Without glancing up, she said, "Heard about the death at the Rusty Anchor. You were there."

"I was." Westham was such a small town, the mouse at Town Hall had probably heard, too.

"You okay?"

"I am, thanks. I wish I knew more, but it's early for that."

"Yeah." She straightened. "Be careful. Byrne made a lot of enemies."

I wrinkled my nose. "You knew him?"

"After a fashion."

I waited. The taciturn mechanic didn't add anything.

"Where did you know him from?" I asked. "You don't live in Westham."

"I volunteer at the school. Tutor reading." She shook her head. "Think of it. High school kids who can barely read. Messes 'em up, big-time. I try to help."

"That's wonderful, Orlean." It was. And once

again she'd surprised me. She'd never breathed a word about her volunteer activities.

She lifted a shoulder and dropped it before turning back to her work. I was dying to ask more about Bruce, but she might have exhausted her conversational quota for the day.

"How's your sister doing, by the way?" Her sister, Sandy, had worked here for a little while in the spring. She'd had a few issues, and being employed by me hadn't turned out to be the best fit.

"She's real good. Thanks."

"I'm glad to hear it." The outside door opened. "I'll let you get on with that." I made my way toward the door and was surprised once again. Joseph Almeida—otherwise known as my father, as well as the minister of the Westham Unitarian Universalist Church—stood backlit in the doorway.

"Pa." I smiled and held out my arms. His tall, strong, gentle hugs were better than Tim's only in that I'd had several decades of them before I'd met my husband.

"How's my favorite daughter?" He stepped back.

"Your only daughter is okay." I tilted my head, gazing at him. Yes, he knew. I'd bet hearing that I'd reported the murder was why he'd stopped by. "Been better, been worse. You know."

"Yes, I do."

"Poor Mr. Byrne," I said. "Did you ever have dealings with him?"

"You mean other than when I had to go in and straighten him out on how he coached young students like yourself in the art of written self-expression?"

I'd forgotten about that. Pa had listened to my bitter complaints about undeserved low grades. He'd heard out my friends. He'd reviewed the writing in question. And he'd arranged a conference with Mr. Byrne. After that, the grades weren't quite as unfair, although, if anything, the teacher had grown even more unpleasant to be around, at least from my fourteen-year-old perspective.

"To answer your question," Pa continued, "Bruce and I interacted on several occasions. He was a member of our congregation, you know."

"He was?" I shut my mouth before the flies got in, as my grandmother often admonished.

"Indeed, *querida*. That was after you had declined to participate further in services. You even quit the youth group, as you might remember."

I gave a nod. I did remember becoming disenchanted with organized religion.

"You are always welcome back." He gave me a gentle smile. "Now I'd best continue on my rounds. Several of our elders at the old folks' home look forward to my Monday visits." He winked.

He knew very well it was the Westham Village assisted living and retirement community and not the old folks' home. Although, truthfully, it was where a collection of the town's old folks lived.

His expression sobered. "You'll be careful, sweetheart?

"I will."

We made our farewells. I knew how lucky I was in family as well as in love. But right now I wondered what other surprises lay ahead, what other secrets might surface.

Chapter 8

By six thirty, my plate was nearly as empty as Tim's. I sat catty-corner from him at the kitchen table, where we often ate for casual meals. Belle, my African gray parrot, perched on the back of the chair opposite me. Her bedtime was near, and she'd been unusually quiet during our meal.

"That chicken salad was so good," I popped a last piece of pecan into my mouth. The combination of shredded chicken, red grapes, toasted pecans, and crunchy celery atop a bed of baby lettuce had made a delicious dinner. A crusty baguette and a glass of chilled pinot gris rounded out the meal. "Simple and heavenly. What's your secret?"

"I'm glad you liked it." He sat back in his chair and sipped his wine. "I sneak curry powder and the smallest bit of Dijon mustard into the mayo, and scatter in capers for a bit of tang and bite."

"It was yummy. Thank you." I let out a breath. "And thanks for not asking about the murder while we ate." After I got home, we'd briefly talked about what had happened that morning, but I'd asked for a reprieve during the meal.

"Thanks for not asking about the murder," Belle muttered in an uncanny imitation of my voice. "Snacks, Mac?" She was suddenly wide awake.

Tim gave a low laugh. "Here are your grapes, Belle." He'd brought a small bowl of additional grapes to the table and now set it on the floor.

"Hi, handsome." She gave a wolf whistle, jumped down, and waddled over.

That bird, whom I'd had since high school, could always make me smile.

"That was sweet," I said to Tim.

He reached out and covered my hand. "It must have been awful for you to have to see your former teacher dead like that."

"It's never any fun to encounter a homicide victim." Which, unfortunately, I too often had in the last several years. "I couldn't stand him as a teacher, but I hadn't seen the man since I left Westham High. I felt bad for Yvonne, though."

"Any thoughts about who might have done it?"

"Everything's pretty murky so far. I'm worried about Lincoln coming to the shop today looking for Flo. He found her, and they had a private talk in my office. She didn't look pleased when she left."

"Our head librarian wouldn't have murdered anyone," he said. "Right?"

"Yes. She absolutely wouldn't have. On the other hand, I thought something was up with Yvonne about Byrne. And I don't know anything else."

"That's what your group is going to hash out."

"We're going to try." I checked the time. "Speaking of that, I should probably get this kitchen cleaned up—and myself, too." Leaving a mess made me itchy, especially in the kitchen. I wore my Neat Freak badge with pride, even though I knew certain others viewed me as the teensiest bit obsessed with my need for tidiness and order.

"What time are the book group members coming?" Tim asked.

"Seven." I stood and took his plate. I paused when I took another glance at him. The skin around his eyes was strained, and his shoulders sagged from his normal excellent posture. I set down the plate and sat. "What's going on, sweetheart?"

"It's nothing." He didn't meet my gaze.

I waited. His sister Jamie on the West Coast had ongoing addiction issues even while trying to take care of her three children as a single mom. He might be worried about her. Or it could be his continually dashed hopes that we would conceive a baby. Tim and I had abandoned birth control since before our wedding, but nothing had happened yet. He so much wanted to start and raise a family.

I also loved children, and family was everything to me. But I would turn thirty-eight in two months. I wasn't getting any younger. Neither were my eggs.

Or maybe my handsome husband had another matter going on I didn't know about. I didn't think he usually kept secrets from me. Except, one never really knows.

"You want to talk about it?" I finally asked.

"Not really. I'm pretty tired."

"Was it something I said?" I knew that wasn't the case. He didn't take offense lightly.

"No." He squared his shoulders and gave me a sweet smile. "I mean, I just don't want to talk right now. But I will."

"Are you sure?" I lowered my chin and peered into his face.

"Positive. Now, let me do the cleanup. You go get ready." He grabbed both our plates and rose.

"But you cooked."

"You've done so much for me, Mac, honey. Let me do this."

I reached up and pulled him in for a kiss. "Thank you."

In my opinion, he did so much more for me than the reverse. But I'd let him have his little fantasy. I totally was the winner in this relationship.

Chapter 9

I gazed around at most of the Cozy Capers book group. We'd settled with drinks on the chairs and the long, comfortable couch in the living room. My bestie, Gin Malloy, sipped white wine, but I went with seltzer. Zane King held a glass of pilsner. Tulia Peters sipped a Coke. Norland Gifford, the retired chief of police, had fully recovered from both breaking his leg and being attacked in the spring, and had chosen an IPA.

Mint and shortbread Girl Scout cookies that I'd dug out of the freezer were arranged on a plate. They'd have to do for snacks. Tim had disappeared upstairs, saying he had a software project to work on. I was a little worried about him, but trusted he would confide in me when he was ready.

"I was hoping to see Belle tonight," Norland said. "She's such a funny bird, and so cheery."

I shook my head. "She's asleep for the night. It's amazing how much sleep African grays need."

"Where's your main squeeze, Zane?" Tulia asked him.

Zane's husband, Stephen, had been a member of the group, but his attendance had gone way down.

The skinny, always dapper distiller scrunched up his nose. "He asked me to tell you all that he's leaving the group. He says he doesn't have time, with all his evening meetings. And ethically he can't be involved in the kinds of behind-the-scenes homicide investigations we've done in the past."

"Because he's the town clerk?" Gin asked.

"Exactly." Zane's cheeks turned pink. "Plus we have news I can finally tell you. Our friend is pregnant."

I beamed and clapped. The others joined me. He'd told us they'd found a local woman who had agreed to carry their baby if donor insemination worked. They'd worked out a legal contract and everything. I'd never learned if they'd used Zane's sperm or Stephen's. What I did know was that both men would cherish their child.

"That's so great, Zane," I said. "Do you know if it's a boy or a girl?"

"One of each. She's carrying twins." He rolled his eyes, but his delight was unmistakable. "And yes, we're going to have our hands full."

"So many congratulations, my friend," Tulia said. "Let us know when to start planning the double shower."

"Let's see," Zane began. "It's mid-July, and the babies are due in October."

"So, any time," Gin said. "Twins often come early. People, we need to get going on this."

"You and I can be Team Shower," Tulia chimed in.

"Sign me up, as well," Norland said. "I'm a good planner. And I'm retired."

I hoped Tim wouldn't be disappointed for us when he heard Zane's news. If he was, there wasn't anything I could do to fix his feelings.

"Sounds like a good planning committee," I said. "Listen, it's now seven twenty. Anybody know where Flo is?" She was usually both our notetaker and our assigner of action items.

"Did she reply to the text thread?" Norland asked. "I mean, after you suggested meeting at your place, Mac?"

"She did." Gin checked her phone. "And she said she'd be here."

"Maybe we should start without her," Zane said.

"We could . . ." I drew out the words.

Norland cleared his throat. "You have great news, Zane, but I agree that we need to get back to the reason we're here. I'm older than the rest of you, and I don't stay alert as late as I used to."

"Right," I said. "I only hope Flo isn't late because she's been called into the police station."

"Why would she be?" Gin asked.

I repeated what I'd told Tim about Lincoln taking Flo aside in my shop to interview her.

"And you don't know why," Tulia murmured.

"Not exactly. But before Lincoln arrived, Flo told me she'd had unpleasant dealings with Mr. Byrne over the years," I said. And she'd finished with that allusion to one more thing that had happened. I had to keep that up on my radar to ask her about. If not tonight, then soon.

"Didn't everyone?" Gin asked. "That guy was a nasty piece of work any way you look at it."

"How did you know him?" Norland tented his fingers.

"My daughter had him in school," Gin said. "And she was on the newspaper staff. The students staged quite the uprising to kick him out of the adviser role. They succeeded. But it meant Byrne had it in for my girl until she graduated. He never should have been allowed to be a teacher."

"It makes you wonder how people like that are allowed to remain in the system," Zane said.

A quick knock sounded at the front door. I was about to get up when it opened.

"Sorry I'm late." Breathless, Flo hurried in and lowered herself onto the last open seat.

"Are you okay?" I asked.

"Pretty much. Maybe." Her hand shook as she drew her signature yellow legal pad and a pen out of her bag.

"I think that means you're not really all right." Norland's voice was gentle.

Flo looked around the circle at each of us in turn. Her short white hair, usually spiked, lay limp on her head. Her black-rimmed glasses were smudged, and one sports-sandaled heel vibrated, making her knee jiggle at double time.

"You're right. I'm not really okay. Our pal Haskins asked me to go to the police station to be fingerprinted at the end of the day. While I was there, it turned out they wanted to interview me. With audio and video recordings."

"Did you consent to that?" Norland frowned.

"Did you call a lawyer?" I asked at the same time.

"Hang on, guys." Flo raised her palm. "I didn't kill the guy, okay? I don't have anything to hide. I answered their questions, and they let me go."

I sat back. She was super-intelligent. Highly educated. Well-read. Surely, she was aware that the innocent weren't exempt from being falsely accused—and sometimes convicted—of crimes they didn't commit.

Chapter 10

Flo insisted we move on to the case at hand, which was precisely what we needed to do if we were ever going to clear her name. I would try to circle back later in the evening to the part of my earlier conversation with her that had been cut short by Lincoln arriving at the bike shop. And maybe to what she knew about the mysterious Sita Spencer, too.

Now fortified with a few sips from a glass of white wine, Flo's vibrating leg quieted. She set down the glass and put pen to paper.

"What do we know?" she asked.

"Yvonne seemed evasive with Lincoln about Mr. Byrne this morning," I began. "She said he wasn't a regular at the pub but that he'd been in recently. I felt like she was keeping a secret, a piece of information unsaid."

"Yvonne Flora is noted," Flo said. "Do we have anything else on her?"

People either shook their heads or said they didn't.

"Who wants her as an action item?" Flo glanced around. When Norland raised his hand, she scribbled on her pad.

"Byrne taught English, right?" Tulia asked. She lived in nearby Mashpee, not in Westham, but she owned and operated the Lobstah Shack nearly next door to Mac's Bikes. She was pretty tied in with town affairs.

"Yes, and he was chair of the department for years," Gin said.

"He could have alienated fellow instructors as well as students and parents," Zane pointed out.

"Does anyone know any current or former Westham High English teachers?" Norland asked.

"The department had quite the turnover while Bruce was chair," Flo murmured. "I remember a Mr. O'Connor some years ago who made a big stink about not having his contract renewed."

I stared at her. "Carl O'Connor?"

"Yes, I think that was his first name." Flo cocked her head. "Do you remember that incident?"

"No, but a man by that name owns the Rusty Anchor," I said slowly. "When Yvonne told Lincoln she needed to notify Carl about the murder, the name rang a tiny, far-away bell in my brain, but I couldn't place it. Lincoln asked who Carl was and she told him. The dude himself marched into the pub's kitchen while Detective Johnson was interviewing me, and the bell rang again. I didn't remember his face, though."

"Well, he was laid off, or fired, or downsized, I don't know which. He didn't go happily," Flo said.

"When was that?" Norland asked.

"About twenty years ago," Flo said.

"I recall that the pub changed hands about then," Norland added. "Maybe that's when he bought it."

"I had Mr. Byrne for freshman English twenty years ago," I said, "but I wasn't ever in class with Mr. O'Connor. In fact, his name isn't familiar at all."

"If he taught a higher grade and left before you were in the upper classes, you wouldn't have known him," Gin pointed out.

"True, but I might have heard or seen his name and forgot because it wasn't important to teenage me," I said. "I can ask Derrick if he remembers. Although, he's five years older than me and might have been in college by then."

"What does this O'Connor look like?" Tulia asked. "If he owns the pub, he's probably a member of the Chamber of Commerce, right?"

"You'd think so," I agreed. "But I'm sure I've never seen him at meetings or events."

"The name doesn't ring a bell at all for me," Zane said.

"Nor for me," Gin, who owned the Salty Taffy's candy shop, chimed in. "He could be an absentee owner."

"His face is tanned," I said. "He could live anywhere warmer than New England."

"We need to research him. Who wants to take that action item?" Flo asked.

"I will," Gin said. "I'm curious about his story."

"We might want to shift to looking at opportunity,"

Norland said. "Who could have lured the victim inside after hours?"

"Like, who has a key to the pub, or access to a security code, you mean?" I gazed at Norland.

"Precisely."

"Yvonne is the manager, so she does, for sure," I said. "Uly Cabral does all the baking. I'll bet he has a key, too."

"Are there other managers?" Gin glanced around the room. "Head bartender?"

Tulia laughed. "Don't look at me. I don't even drink alcohol." She was a member of the Wampanoag tribe and had explained early on that she lacked the enzyme to digest alcohol. She'd said the few times she'd had a couple of drinks, it hadn't been pretty.

"I've seen Edwin Germain behind the bar a couple of times," I said. "He's Orlean's brother-in-law, or he had been before she divorced his brother." The multi-talented twenty-something was also Pa's accountant for the church and my occasional substitute bike mechanic. "He works for me once in a while."

"Do you think he killed Byrne?" Flo asked.

"What?" I gave my head a hard shake. "No. Definitely not. But he might know something."

"Edwin Germain is your action item, then, Mac" Flo said. "Who wants to check out Uly?"

Zane raised his hand. "I can."

"This is for Mac or Norland." Tulia leaned forward. "Do we know how Byrne died? That seems like it would be important in terms of who could do it. Right? I mean, for certain murder methods, the killer has to be taller than the victim, or strong, or whatever."

"I haven't heard a word," Norland said.

I grimaced. "And I don't know except by exclusion. I didn't see blood. Or a gunshot wound. Or evidence of choking. What I really don't know is why Lincoln seemed to think Mr. Byrne had died from a homicide and not a heart attack or stroke or any other kind of natural death."

"How old was he?" Zane asked.

"Mid- to late-sixties," Flo said. "He'd either recently retired or was going to next year."

"Health conditions?" Norland asked.

"I got nothing." Flo poised her pen on the pad. "But I can take him on as an action item. I'm friendly with the school academic admin. She'll tell me if he was ill at all."

I gazed at Flo. "That Sita woman you saw in my shop today. You seemed surprised to see her. I think you said something about her being *back* in town. Which happens to coincide with the murder. Would she have any connection with Mr. Byrne?"

Flo pulled her mouth to the side. "Maybe. She taught for a year or two and then left town."

"Did she teach English?"

"I don't know." Flo shrugged.

"I don't have an assignment yet," Tulia said. "I'll give her a stab."

"Her last name is Spencer, and she told me she lives in North Carolina," I offered. "But aren't you too busy with your business, Tulia? The Lobstah Shack is the most popular fast-food place in town. Wait, I don't mean fast food like a big chain, but . . ."

I didn't want her to think I was lumping her in with the ubiquitous burger-and-fries joints.

"No worries, Mac," Tulia said. "I knew what you meant. We offer takeout, and people love it. But you might have noticed the weather lately? Customers have been pretty scarce this past week, mid-July notwithstanding."

Our conversation turned to low sales and the weather. Flo, the only one present besides Norland who didn't own a Main Street establishment, drummed her fingers on the legal pad. It seemed she was keeping a past experience with Sita to herself. Did it matter? I had no idea.

Chapter 11

As the Cozy Capers mobilized to leave at around nine o'clock, I issued what was now our standard reminder.

"Remember to do your research online as much as you can. If you ask questions in person, come up with a cover story and be discreet. Lincoln's not going to like it if we're obvious in our investigating."

"He never likes it," Gin said.

"That's for a reason, Gin," Norland pointed out.

"But we've uncovered important information in the past," she went on. "I mean, Mac has, for the most part."

"And we don't want our Flo to be anywhere near the Persons of Interest list," Tulia added.

"I appreciate that," Flo said. "But don't worry. You're not hanging out with a murderer. Much as I disliked Bruce, the police have nothing on me."

Which was fine, except her gaze shifted away from our faces while she said that. That she appeared to be hiding information made me uneasy.

I locked the door after them and headed upstairs to see what Tim was doing. I found him cross-legged in the easy chair in the study, the open book on his lap long abandoned. His head rested on the back of the chair, his eyes were closed, and he snored softly.

Equally as softly, I laid my hand on his shoulder and kissed his forehead. "Go to bed, my love."

His big baby blues flew open. "Mmm, good idea." He pulled me in close for a long, luscious kiss. "I love you, Mac."

"Sweet dreams."

He got up at three in the morning every day to go bake bread. He needed his sleep and kept earlier hours than I did most evenings. We made it work.

He followed me downstairs, shutting the bedroom door behind him. I was about to pour a little of my favorite Scotch. I thought better of it and instead put water on for a cup of herbal tea as I cleaned up the glasses and napkins from the gathering. I popped the last minty chocolate cookie into my mouth and sank onto the couch with tablet and tea, putting my feet up on the coffee table.

Before I mounted a search into Edwin and his bartending, I sat with my thoughts for a moment. Zane and Stephen were going to be parents of twins. That would be a huge change in their lives. Having a baby was big for anyone, but two at once? Wow.

I wondered if Tim and I would need to go the adoption route. Was I unconsciously negatively influencing my fertility because I was afraid of the messy process of pregnancy and childbirth? I hoped not. I didn't even know if that kind of mental direction was possible.

I'd meant it when I told Tim I was all in on doing our best to conceive a child. I'd deal with the mess of it all when it happened. And no, I scolded myself. I wasn't going to use the "if" word.

After I sipped my drink, I set down the glass and brought the tablet to life. I opened a text file and tapped in what we knew. It was fine for Flo to use her yellow legal pad, but she took it with her when she left. This way, I'd have a reminder of what we'd learned—hardly anything—and what remained.

Sita Spencer had taught something at the high school for a few years and now lived in North Carolina. Carl O'Connor had had his teaching contract terminated and had been upset about it. Both Yvonne and Flo were hiding something. Uly likely had a key or the door code to the pub. And Edwin probably did, too.

We didn't know where Carl lived, but Gin was going to find out. We also didn't know how Byrne had died. Had anyone taken that as an action item? I didn't think so. I'd see what I could discover next time I spoke with Penelope or Lincoln, which I was sure would happen.

Was that all we had so far? Probably. I hadn't learned about Flo's "one more thing," but I hadn't asked, either.

I took a minute to check the weather forecast. "Ooh," I said aloud. The rain was moving out. Tomorrow was slated to be sunny with a high of eighty. Mac's Bikes was going to be busy.

Right now seemed like a perfect time to call Edwin Germain and see if he was free to sub in for Derrick.

But, because nobody made cold calls anymore, I texted him first.

Hey, Edwin, Mac here. Got a minute for a quick phone call?

He certainly wouldn't be bartending at the pub tonight. As a crime scene, it would be locked and barricaded until the team finished with it.

In reply to my message, the cell rang. We greeted each other.

"What's up?" he asked.

"My brother is away for another couple of days, and the rain's going away, too. I wondered if you could help me out with a few hours in the bike shop."

"Doing repair and maintenance?"

"Probably not. Orlean is working, unless she needs a break. But you also trained on the rental and retail side, right?"

"Yep."

"That's where you'd be the biggest help." I crossed my fingers he would agree. It got super hectic when we had only one person on the floor, whether it was me or someone else. My grandma helped out from time to time, but she had a busy schedule with all her activities, and I hated to ask her unless it was a bit of an emergency.

"Sure, I can do that. I'm part of the fabled gig economy, you know. I pick up all kinds of part-time work. Haven't started driving a ride share yet, but ya never know. Want me to come in tomorrow?"

Whew. "Yes. Fabulous. Let's see. Can you be there by ten?" With any luck, we'd have a minute to talk about the Rusty Anchor before the shop got busy.

"You got it. Hey, Mac?"

"Yes?"

"I got a call about what happened at the pub," he said. "Wicked terrible, isn't it?"

"I'll say."

"I'm not sure you know that I bartend at the Rusty Anchor. One of the many jobs I cobble together to make a living."

"I'd heard that, yes."

"Yvonne called me about not going to work there tonight, and why." He cleared his throat. "The thing is, that dude? The guy who was murdered? I might know something about him."

Chapter 12

"And then Edwin said he'd tell me today when he comes in to work," I said to Gin at seven thirty the next morning. We strode, swinging our arms and talking, along the rail trail on our usual morning power walk. We went every weekday unless it was pouring rain, which today it blessedly wasn't. The weather report had been correct. The rain was gone, at least for a day or two.

"That's kind of a bombshell," she said. "No clue what the dude thinks he knows?"

"Not a bit." When a gust nearly swept away my ball cap, I clapped a hand on the hat. The wind that had swept away the rain was still with us. The official temperature might get to eighty today, but it wouldn't feel that warm, not with such a strong breeze. "Hey, I know the murder took over last night's discussion, but have you made any progress with *A Very Woodsy Murder*, the actual book for the group?" It was the Cozy Capers' choice for this week.

"No, and I've never read anything by Ellen Byron so far. I'm looking forward to it, but we might have to postpone talking about the book for a week."

"Agreed."

"Exciting news about Zane and Stephen, isn't it?" Gin asked.

"I know. Two for the price of one."

She glanced at me. "How does hearing they're going to be parents make you feel?" She knew about our so-far fruitless efforts to conceive.

"I'm fine. I don't think Tim knows yet. We didn't get a chance to talk last night or this morning. He's the one who might be crushed."

"He's such a teddy bear, isn't he?"

I nodded. "With a big heart to match. We'll figure it out."

We strode in silence for a few minutes. I pumped my arms to get my heart rate up. Gin and I were near each other's height and could match our steps like we were sisters. I mused for a moment on what my childhood would have been like with a sister in the family along with a half brother. Would we girls have been closer than I was with Derrick? Or maybe we'd have fought more. It was a moot point, but interesting to imagine. I wasn't sure if I'd ever asked my mother why she and Pa hadn't had more children.

Today we headed north instead of south. This section of the trail ran through woods instead of over salt pools and marshes. With trees and undergrowth fully leafed out, I spied only quick glimpses of birds feeding and flitting about. Instead of salt air as the trail's cologne, here it was pine needles and leaf mold with a whiff of cut hay.

A few paces before the path opened up to a stretch of pasture, a loud hammering sounded. I glanced at the side of a big dead tree and grabbed Gin's arm to stop her.

"A pileated woodpecker," I whispered as I pointed.

A crow-sized black-and-white bird pistoned its red head and powerful pointed beak into the trunk, over and over, paused, and started up again.

"It looks like Woody Woodpecker." She suppressed a giggle.

"Almost, especially the crest. Isn't it gorgeous? I hardly ever see them."

The bird must have noticed us, because it flew off in a giant, silent swoop, revealing big white patches on the undersides of the wings.

I shivered. "I wouldn't want to be on the receiving end of that beak."

"No kidding."

"Let's get going." I was struck by a thought. "This might sound odd, but the point on the woodpecker's beak made me think of something. What if Mr. Byrne was injected with a kind of poison? I wouldn't have noticed a needle mark yesterday morning."

"And maybe Lincoln did?"

"Yes. Except he must have seen or smelled something else that made him think the guy didn't simply fall over dead."

"Speaking of the murder, I did a little digging into Carl O'Connor last night."

"Do tell." As I glanced at her, I caught my toe in a

strip of buckled pavement. I began careening forward, arms windmilling. Luckily, I caught myself and turned the near-fall into several jogging steps. "Close one."

"You all right?"

"Yes, thanks. So, what did you learn?"

"Carl seems to live in Raleigh, North Carolina."

"An absentee business owner, as we conjectured last night."

"Sure looks like it," she said.

"Is the Rusty Anchor his only source of income?"

"No. He's also listed as an employee at an arboretum down there."

"Like, landscaping?" I asked. "That's quite a departure from teaching English."

"So's owning a pub. I couldn't find out what he actually does at the arboretum. Maybe he writes promotional copy or does advertising for the place."

"Or he could have wanted a change of pace from working indoors in a classroom."

"True," she said.

"Were you able to learn why Mr. Byrne fired him from the Westham High English department? I suppose *fired* isn't the right word, but he was let go, right?"

"He was. And I wasn't successful in finding out why. I ran out of time, because I needed to go to bed. Some of us need our beauty sleep, Mac." She elbowed me.

"You are a lot older than me, after all." I elbowed her in return. My friend wasn't even ten years older than me.

"But get this." Gin held up her index finger. "Back

to North Carolina for a moment. The staff page of the arboretum's website also lists a Sita Spencer. How many people with that name could there be?"

I slowed. "She did say she lived in North Carolina. If they're a couple, they could have come up here together. She told me she was putting together a grab bag of bike stuff for her boyfriend's birthday."

Gin stopped and faced me. "And they both have a history with Bruce Byrne."

I gave a slow nod. "So they do."

A red-tailed hawk beat its wings as it flew over the pasture. It looked intent on spotting field mice or baby bunnies for lunch, or even an unlucky sparrow. Westham once again had a human predator prowling the streets, who might be seeking out another unlucky victim.

Chapter 13

I pointed the spray head of the watering can over one of the window boxes in front of Mac's Bikes. The pink, white, and red geraniums were healthy and blooming, and pale-green vinca trailed prettily over the edges of the red boxes, which themselves stood out against the blue paint on the walls. My Open flag flapped in the continuing strong breeze. I'd set up and locked together an array of display bikes next to the bike rack. Watering was the last item on my opening checklist, at least during the warmer months, a list I followed faithfully.

But it was now after nine o'clock. Where was Orlean? She was never late and rarely absent. I'd checked my texts. My mechanic hadn't written or called. At least I had Edwin coming in an hour or so. Between us, we could probably handle the business of the day. Still, I hoped Orlean was all right.

I watered the last box and headed inside, propping open the door, as I did on nice days like this one, and gave one more glance up and down Main Street for signs of my taciturn employee.

Instead of spotting her, I gazed at the backs of a couple who peered into the front windows of Cape King Liquor, Zane's store, which was situated nearly directly across the wide street from my shop. Even though I'd met Sita and Carl only once, and separately, I was pretty sure that was them over there. They stood arm in arm. She pointed to something. He faced her, laughing, and kissed the top of her head.

They appeared at ease and happy. If one or both had killed Mr. Byrne, it didn't seem to be disrupting their morning. Also, I had to stop calling him that, except it was hard to think of him as Bruce. I'd never even heard his first name while I was a student. What ninth-grader does?

I stepped all the way inside my shop. I didn't want the couple to turn and spot me at this moment. Maybe I should have called out to them, see if I could have engaged one or both in conversation. I might be able to learn something.

Nah. I wasn't prepared with questions and didn't feel like engaging in the investigation with people who might be killers. Instead, I straightened a few folded shirts. Checked the list of rentals due in by four that afternoon. Noticed the supply of helmets was running low and jotted down a note to order more.

I was about to wade into the sheaf of repair slips when a text dinged on my phone. I glanced at Orlean's name and groaned. This wasn't going to be good.

Srry. Wicked bad stmch flu or food poisning. CU tmrw.

The poor thing. Stomach upsets were the worst. I wrote back.

Don't worry about work. Focus on getting better.

Maybe I should dive into the first bike waiting for a tune-up or getting a flat tire fixed. I decided to leave that kind of work for Edwin. I knew he preferred it to retail, and once I got my hands greasy, I wouldn't be able to easily ring up sales or help our rental customers.

Two fit-looking women came in and approached me where I'd settled on a stool behind the counter.

"Our tandem is due back today," one began, her blue eyes brilliant in a tanned face.

"But we wondered if we could extend the rental through Sunday," the taller one said.

The first woman tucked her arm through the other's. "With the rain gone, we've splurged and extended our condo rental."

"I don't blame you." I smiled. "Let me check the rental book." I'd left it on the counter and now scanned the list. "That should be fine. We have one reserved for this afternoon, but we have several. What was the name?"

The petite one gave me a hyphenated last name. At the same time, she pointed at the book with her left hand, which bore an etched gold band. "That's us."

"Thank you," I said. "Enjoy the rest of your week."

The taller of the two glanced around and lowered

her voice. "What's up with the police tape blocking the door to the pub? We tried to go there for dinner last night."

I'd seen the yellow tape on my strolling commute to work an hour ago, a sad reminder of the tragedy I'd witnessed inside.

"Unfortunately, a man was found dead in the Rusty Anchor yesterday," I said. "I believe the police are still investigating."

"Do you know what happened?" the short one asked with eyes wide.

"No, but he was apparently in his late sixties." I didn't mind a little redirection if it would help Westham's reputation as a safe tourist destination. Which it was. Mostly.

"It's what happens when you get old." The tall one gave her head a slow shake. "That's why we try to stay active and healthy."

Thinking Bruce had had a heart attack or a stroke seemed to satisfy the couple. Upper sixties wasn't really that old these days, but I didn't push back. Active and healthy was always a good thing.

Chapter 14

At nine thirty and with no new customers in sight, I took a moment to order more helmets in several sizes and price points, along with a list of repair and maintenance supplies Orlean had given me at the end of last week. What else were we running short on? I perused the retail shelves.

In addition to the branded biking shirts, I also stocked several T-shirts with fun slogans. "Cyclists Do It While Touring," "Cyclopath and Proud," and "Bike Riders Do It on the Road," in addition to the more touristy, "Mom Biked Cape Cod and All I Got Was This Lousy T-Shirt." I noted which were running low, and checked the supply of wicking socks, which we sold in anklet and crew heights.

I was nearly done with the order when Lincoln appeared in the doorway. I held up my hand in greeting. He paused, then made his way in with a heavy step.

"Quiet in here this morning," he said.

"It is. Which is good, considering I'm alone so far. Orlean's home sick. Give me one second." I checked everything on the order. We used a tablet in a stand as cash register, order center, and more. I tapped the button to finish the order and glanced up. "What's up?"

"Unfortunately, not much."

"Want to sit?"

"I would, but I can't get too comfortable, so I won't." Today his Hawaiian shirt was in muted shades of green and brown. To match his mood, apparently. "But thank you."

I waited. He crossed his arms and gazed down at me over the top of his glasses. *Uh-oh.* That wasn't a friendly look. I might have misread his mood.

"Yes?" I finally asked. He was a lot better at out-waiting than I was.

"What aren't you telling me?"

"Nothing." I lifted my chin. I picked up a pen and rolled its smooth tube between my fingers to avoid any nervous picking I might do.

"I understand your group of amateur sleuths held an emergency meeting last night at your house."

Double uh-oh. Who told him?

He kept up the stern look, or maybe it was a glare. "Do I not explicitly mention every single time that none of you is to get involved?"

"Yes, Lincoln, you do." I swallowed. "All we did was talk about what we knew. I mean, it looks like you're starting to suspect Flo." I stood. "And that's ridiculous.

She's our friend. She's brilliant. Flo's a librarian, for Pete's sake. And she's not a murderer."

"All right." He held up both palms. "Don't get mad, okay? You should know by now I need to explore every avenue. Track down every clue. I doubt Ms. Wolanski murdered Byrne, but they'd had a number of public and heated arguments. I am obliged to investigate her, as I am with any person of interest."

"Yes, but—"

"Somebody killed Bruce Byrne, and I intend to find out who, as soon as possible."

At a noise from the open doorway, I turned my head.

"Mac, I . . ." Edwin's voice trailed off. His fingers unclasped the clip of his bike helmet under his chin. He let his hands drop, his expression as dark as his black T-shirt.

Lincoln stepped toward him. "Edwin Germain, I believe? I've been looking for you."

What? Why would Lincoln be looking for Edwin? This case was getting messier by the minute.

"Here I am." Edwin removed his helmet, revealing dark curly hair under a stretchy bandanna. He folded heavily tattooed arms across his chest, letting the helmet dangle from one hand. "I haven't received any communication from you, as far as I know."

"You work as an occasional bartender at the Rusty Anchor." Lincoln kept his tone mild. "You had an adversarial relationship with Bruce Byrne during your years at Westham High School. I'm sure you've heard of his recent death."

"I have," Edwin said in a quiet voice. "It's very sad."

"I'd like to speak with you about the victim." Lincoln added, "in private."

The detective's tone wasn't challenging, but he hadn't tacked on a "please" or an "if you don't mind."

"With all due respect, sir, I'm also an occasional employee of Mac's." Edwin's green eyes matched his head covering and were unwavering in their gaze. "And I'm here to begin my shift today. You can ask me your questions while I work, or you can ask them later."

"Thank you for arriving on time to help out, Edwin." I was about to tell Lincoln he could have a few minutes to speak with Edwin, but I changed my mind. Edwin had stuck up for himself, and rightly so.

Lincoln glanced at me over the top of his glasses, one of his favorite looks. It wasn't one of mine.

"I'm alone in the shop." I shrugged. "The sun's out, and I need him as my mechanic for the day."

To prove my point, two customers strolled in, then three more, followed by another.

"Welcome to Mac's Bikes," I told them. "We'll be right with you."

"Very well." Lincoln handed Edwin his card. "I'd like you to contact me at your earliest convenience, Mr. Germain. That is, today."

Edwin straightened his shoulders. "I will." He turned and headed for the repair area.

"Talk to you later, Mac," Lincoln murmured. "Please, no digging."

"Do you see a shovel?"

He shook his head and left. I winced a little. I wasn't usually snarky. What had gotten into me? I, too, gave my head a shake.

"How can I help you?" I asked the nearest customer.

Chapter 15

An hour later, I had rented five bikes in several sizes to a family. Sold our largest helmet and a pair of size-thirteen bike shoes to a man with a gentle smile who'd towered over me. And signed off on the sale of two hybrid bikes to a woman and a man who said they were newlyweds and wanted to start a habit of exercising together. My shop's bottom line was going to be firmly in the black if this kept up, not that it wasn't already.

After the last customer in the shop left, I thought I might ask Edwin if he had any idea why Lincoln wanted to talk with him. Had Byrne been rude to him in the pub? Lincoln had used the word *adversarial* when he spoke of Edwin's time at the high school. What was that about? I also wanted to know what Edwin meant last night on the phone, saying he knew something about the teacher.

Before I could inquire, my grandma bustled in. Diminutive physically but large in personality and heart, today Reba Almeida had forgone her hot pink tracksuit for red Capris and a rainbow-striped top that matched her signature slouchy beret. Cushiony sandals supported her arthritic feet, with scarlet-colored toenails peeking out. She toted a white paper bag that looked a lot like it held pastries from Tim's bakery.

"Abo Ree." I held out my arms. "I haven't seen you since, gosh, Sunday."

My grandma had been a lifelong Bostonian until she retired and moved to Westham, but her husband Alcindo, Pa's father, had been born in Cape Verde. Reba had embraced the culture and loved that I used the Kriolu word for "grandmother" as part of her name.

"Thought I'd better check up on my grandbaby, given what happened yesterday." She was nothing if not tuned in to the events of the town. "Are you all right?"

"I am." I assumed she already knew I'd been the person to call in the homicide. "It was a shock to see Mr. Byrne like that, but don't worry about me. How are you?"

"Never better."

I caught a whiff emanating from the bag she'd brought. Even though I'd eaten breakfast a mere two hours ago, my stomach grumbled, the bag smelled that good.

Reba laughed, a cascade of tiny bells. "Yes, I brought pastries. Baked by your handsome husband, naturally."

"You're the best."

"Is Orlean here?"

"No, she's home sick, but Edwin Germain came in as a substitute. You've met him, right?"

"Yes, your father introduced us once at the parsonage." Reba bustled over to the repair area. "I brought you a pastry, young man, when you have a minute."

I heard him thank her and say he'd be there in a second. I was midbite into a delectable cheese Danish when she returned and came in close.

"I have a tidbit to tell you, quick, while we're alone," she murmured.

"Please."

"I knew Bruce, may his soul rest in peace."

My eyebrows flew up. "You did? How?"

"I surely did. After I moved down here from Boston, I used to socialize with a group of retired and current English teachers."

"And he was in the group?" I asked.

"Yes." She glanced around before going on. "The poor man had suffered greatly, there's no doubt. But he never figured out how not to also inflict grief on others."

"How had he suffered?" The second part was absolutely correct, but I wondered what she meant by the first part.

"His wife and both children perished in an automobile accident. It was a great tragedy."

"Wow. How awful." I sat with that news for a moment. "Did he share that with the teachers' group?"

"Not at all. In fact, he only came to a couple of our gatherings. But I am able to persuade pretty much anyone to share confidences with me."

I smiled. "Yes, you are." Maybe it was because she was so tiny, or that people didn't feel threatened by her warm, open personality, despite her being a steel-spined force of nature when she wanted to be. What she'd said was true. I had shared worries and doubts with her when I was younger that I never would have told my own mom. Come to think of it, Reba's only son—my father—had much the same effect on people, including me.

"At any rate, I thought you should know," she went on. "It might have a bearing on the current investigation."

"It might." If I could find information about the incident, about the deaths. "Did this accident take place before you knew him, then?"

"Yes, by five years or so."

"His immediate family is gone, but do you know if he had any other relatives in the area?"

"I think maybe a sibling somewhere on the Cape." She popped her last bite of *pain au chocolat* into her mouth, then dusted off her hands and brushed crumbs off the front of her shirt. "Mmm, that tasted like Paris."

"You and I should take a jaunt to Quebec one of these days, Abo Ree. It's not Paris, but both Montreal and Quebec City have lots of fabulous bakeries. And those cities make you feel like you're in Europe."

"I like that idea." She slid off her stool. "Or we could stay right here in paradise and eat your husband's creations." She frowned.

"What's the matter?"

"When I was at the bakery counter waiting, Tim had brought out a tray of baguettes hot from the oven. He got a call on his cell phone. I couldn't hear, but he looked quite worried before he returned to the kitchen."

"Thanks for telling me," I murmured as the door opened to admit three young men with the thighs of serious cyclists under their shorts. "I'll give him a call."

We said goodbye, and my grandma left. I greeted the customers, swept the crumbs off the counter into the wastebasket, and set Edwin's pastry aside.

But mostly I was thinking about how Tim had been bothered by something last night. We hadn't had a chance to talk about it later, between the book group meeting and his early hours. We would tonight, for sure.

Chapter 16

Edwin waited until the bicycling-enthusiast guys had made their purchases and clomped out before he washed his hands and came for his pastry.

It was nearly eleven by now. I'd texted a quick message to Tim.

Love you

I didn't want to call him at work, especially not to ask about something emotional or difficult. I only hoped he would open up to me this evening about whatever was going on.

"You don't mind that I pushed back when the detective dude wanted to corner me earlier, do you?" Edwin bit into his pastry.

"Of course not. You would have known if I'd taken his side." I kept my gaze on the door in case more customers came in. "But you'll contact him after work, yes?"

"I keep my word, Mac. I told him I would, and I will." He savored another bite of Danish.

"May I ask, did you witness anything Bruce Byrne said or did that might bear on finding whoever killed him? At the bar or elsewhere?" I was positive Edwin had no idea he was my action item, and I intended to keep it that way. "Last night on the phone you said you might know something about him."

"I'm not sure." He popped in the last bite of pastry and kept quiet until he finished. "The thing is, it involved Yvonne. She's a super-nice lady. I'd hate to get her in trouble."

I wrinkled my nose. Yvonne was on our list, but only because she managed the pub and had discovered the body. Plus, I'd told the Cozy Capers I thought she'd been hiding something when she spoke with Lincoln.

"Had Byrne been rude to Yvonne at the pub or elsewhere?" I asked.

"Not so much rude, but he seemed to be threatening her one night. It was nearly closing time, and he'd apparently asked the waitperson to call Yvonne out from the kitchen."

"Did you hear what they said?"

"Unfortunately, no. I was down at the other end settling a check. Both of them were glaring at each other, and Byrne's neck was red."

"What night was that?"

"Saturday, I think." Edwin cocked his head, watching me. "Mac, I heard something from your dad. Joseph said you are sort of a PI."

I raised my palms, about to object.

"It's not a problem, truly," he went on. "If there's anything I can do to help, I will. Homicide is a horrible thing. Byrne wasn't a pleasant guy, but he didn't deserve to be murdered."

"Nobody does."

"Well, let me know." He glanced at his sports watch. "I'd better get back to it. A customer is coming at noon to pick up their street bike."

"Listen, Edwin, would you be able to work for me the rest of the week? Even if Orlean is back tomorrow, it's still July, and it's so much better to have three on the job."

"When does Derrick return?"

"Friday. He should be able to work on the weekend." I hoped.

Edwin gave a slow nod. "How about afternoons only? I have a few other gigs in the morning, and if the pub reopens, I'll be there until late."

"Sounds good. Noon to five?"

"You got it." He folded the bag neatly over his crumbs and crumpled it into a ball, then tossed it into the wastebasket. "We'll have to talk more later."

"Give me a shout when you want to break for lunch."

What I wanted to ask was whether he had personal experience with homicide. Maybe a person he was close to had been murdered. Except now was not the time. At least he'd committed to helping out this week. Knowing I'd have an extra pair of hands here was a big relief, especially at a time when I might want to foray out and do a bit of sleuthing here and there.

In the absence of customers, I took a quick break, then settled back on the stool behind the counter with my phone. I opened the group thread. Nothing new there. I wrote a message about seeing Sita and

Carl strolling arm in arm earlier this morning. I added a note about what Reba had told me.

My grandma was in English-teachers social club. Byrne told her he'd lost wife and kids in accident. Any other info on that?

What else did I have? Nothing, really. Lincoln's interest in interviewing Edwin was as yet nebulous, as was whatever Edwin knew. Should I drift back there and see if he'd talk while he was working on the bike at hand?

That question was answered for me with a half-dozen cyclists bustling in. They were on the senior-citizen end of my usual customers. These folks looked fit, were dressed for biking, and appeared eager to shop. It was all good.

I was in the middle of selling shirts and windbreakers to three of the seniors when my phone began text-dinging, repeatedly. I should have muted it. Too late now. Instead, I smiled at the customer and ignored the incoming messages.

"Is the Shining Sea Trail mostly out in the open from here?" a man asked. "The wind is quite strong today, and several of us have trouble with that."

"Going south it is," I said. "But if you head north, it's mostly in woods and should feel more protected."

He thanked me and accepted the bag I handed him. So the wind hadn't died down at all. I hadn't been outside since I came in from watering the window boxes. Now that I took a glance out the window, I could see the Open flag waving straight out. I smiled to myself when I imagined what Abo Reba would say. "That flag is flapping as fast as a lady in the middle of a hot flash." I was too young for menopause, fortunately, and the women cyclists currently browsing were surely well beyond that phase of a woman's life.

The customers finally finished and cleared out, and I had a chance to check my texts. *Ugh.*

Flo's was the first. She wrote that Penelope had been by to see her and wouldn't take "I'm too busy to talk with you" for an answer.

Next, Norland texted that he'd gleaned information about his action item, namely, Yvonne.

Byrne had apparently been threatening to reveal a secret she'd long held.

I wrote back, asking what the secret was, but he didn't respond. Gin texted that she had nothing to report about Carl. Zane echoed the same about Uly. Nothing came in from Tulia, who'd been assigned Sita. I added my own non-news.

Nothing of substance so far from Edwin. He's working here today. Will try later.

I sent it. A man and a woman with twin toddlers in tow came in next. I stashed my phone. Investigating murder around the edges of running a business was going to have to wait.

Chapter 17

After Edwin got a call at four thirty asking him to report to the pub to bartend at six, I sent him home.

"See you midday tomorrow, right?" I asked.

He snapped shut the clasp on his bike helmet. "I'll be here at noon."

I checked the rentals book. All the bikes due to be returned today had been. We'd had a busy but not frantic afternoon. Since the store was currently free of customers, I decided to close a little early and started in on my closing checklist.

The methodical straightening, stashing, and organizing helped my brain think, an activity I'd barely had time to do during the busy workday.

Edwin thought Byrne had been threatening Yvonne. Or had it been the reverse? Also, I was still unsure why Lincoln wanted to speak with Edwin. Maybe it wasn't only about what Edwin had witnessed while tending bar. He might have had his own run-ins with Byrne. For that matter, if the Germain family was from Westham, Edwin could have had Mr. Byrne in high school.

I headed out to unlock the display bikes and bring them in. Norland approached on the sidewalk and raised a hand in greeting. His gait was still uneven. He'd broken his leg in March while horsing around with his grandkids, and he'd said it was taking a long time to heal.

"Can I help?" he asked.

"Sure, thanks. Will you grab that flag for me?"

He lifted the Open flag's pole out of the holder and followed me and two bikes inside, furling the flag unasked.

"Let me get those last two bikes for you," he said. "I have a topic I want to pick your brain about."

After everything was done except locking the door after me, I said, "Do you want to sit in here or walk and talk?"

"You're probably eager to get home. I'll stroll along with you for a bit."

"Perfect." I shrugged into my backpack and slung on my EpiPen bag. With my body's extreme allergy to insect stings, I never went outside without the life-saving device. "What's up?" I asked once we were on the sidewalk.

"You might remember I volunteered to look into Yvonne Flora," he began.

"Yes."

"She seems to have had a connection with Byrne's wife. I'm still looking into it."

"Before the wife died in an accident. Interesting. You saw my text about that, right?"

"Yes."

"Edwin Germain is working for me this week," I went on. "He said Yvonne and Byrne were having it out at the bar on Saturday night. He thought Byrne was threatening Yvonne, but that she was super irate, too."

"He didn't hear the details?"

"No." I stepped around a dad bending over a stroller to speak with a toddler. "I wonder if Byrne had anything to do with the accident. Maybe he staged it." I shuddered and lowered my voice. "Which would mean he'd killed his own children."

"I hope that wasn't the case. Listen, I was thinking of going by the library, see if Flo is free," Norland said. "Want to come along?"

"I do. She should be able to talk. It's five o'clock." I slowed as we came to the Rusty Anchor. The yellow police tape was gone, and the lights were on inside. The smell of fried food wafted out. "Edwin said the pub was cleared to reopen."

"I heard that."

A shrub with pointy needles and small red berries that looked like little cups grew in a large wooden planter on one side of the door, with a matching one on the other side. Both plants appeared recently pruned, which they'd have to be so the branches didn't brush against passersby.

I went on. "It's hard to believe it was only yesterday that Yvonne grabbed me as I passed the pub to ask for my help."

He tapped his chin. "She must be in there cooking."

"Do you want to go talk to her?"

"No. But let's see if we can find Flo. Byrne himself was her action item."

"And with a librarian's search abilities being her superpower, she might have found something useful." I smiled. Flo was nothing if not a superhero at the computer.

"I like the way you think."

As we resumed walking, I took another glance at him. Ever since the death of his wife a few years ago, his shirts had grown increasingly faded, with bare edges on the collars. Today he wore a crisp navy-blue shirt with pale blue checks, and his jeans looked recently purchased, too.

"New shirt?" I asked.

"Yes." He rolled his eyes with a fond air. "My daughter insisted I freshen up my wardrobe, I think with help from my granddaughter, who turned thirteen last month. I don't want the kids to be embarrassed to be seen with their shabby old Poppa, although I'm sure the little guy doesn't even notice."

"Well, it looks nice."

Chapter 18

Two minutes later we stood at the door of Flo's second-floor office, after checking downstairs that she was still in. Our friend, whose array of three monitors sat perpendicular to the door, frowned at one of the displays, her fingers flying over the keyboard.

"Knock, knock," Norland said. "Got a minute?"

She held up an index finger without changing her gaze. "One second." She finished whatever it was she was doing and looked over at us. "Come in, you two. And shut the door, will you?"

"We saw your text." I closed the door and took the seat next to Norland's. "So, Penelope stopped by for a little visit?"

Flo scooted her rolling chair around the edge of the desk so she wasn't hidden behind her monitors.

"And then some." Her mouth pulled to the side.

"The police seem to know all about my dealings with Bruce."

"Didn't you tell them yesterday?" Norland asked. "That you'd argued with him?"

"Not in so many words," Flo said.

That surprised me. "Why didn't you come clean about your past with Byrne?"

"Probably because it would make me look guilty." She fiddled with a button on her lightweight blazer. "They appear to have discovered it on their own. Detective Johnson seemed to think I was some kind of homicidal maniac."

"But I see a big problem with that," I began. "How would you have gotten him into the pub, poisoned him, and locked the door on your way out?"

Flo swallowed. "Well, exactly."

"Have you been able to learn anything about Byrne you didn't already know?" Norland asked.

"After you wrote about the accident, Mac, I tried to dig up the facts," Flo said. "But it was quite a few years ago."

"I might be able to talk to a retired investigator," Norland said.

I gazed around Flo's book-filled office. At the framed letter of commendation for service from the governor that hung on the wall. At the photos taken at library association meetings, also framed, of Flo with two of her favorite authors. In one, she smiled at the camera next to the great Sue Grafton. In the other, Flo stood with the late cozy mystery author, Sheila Connolly. The sound of the name *Sheila* made me think of Sita.

"Flo, what was up with you and Sita Spencer yesterday morning? She seemed unhappy to see you, and you and I never got back around to talking about her. Last evening you said you didn't think she needed looking into. But if she worked with Byrne, maybe she does."

Flo took a moment to respond. "She definitely had ties with Bruce. I think she thought she was his favorite or something. If so, why did she leave teaching?"

She looked out the window as she spoke and not at us. Last night I'd felt she was keeping information back. It still seemed that way.

"How did you know Sita?" I pressed.

"She and my son dated for a short period of time, and it didn't go well. That Sita Spencer is a piece of work."

Son? I had no idea Flo had more than one child. The book group had gathered at her house several times. I'd met her daughter before she moved away from Westham. I now realized I'd never seen family photographs in Flo's home.

"I wasn't aware you have a son," Norland murmured.

Flo lifted her chin. "Unfortunately, we're estranged."

A son who had dated Sita was probably in his forties, and I wouldn't have known him in school. Flo's daughter was considerably younger, thirty at most. Did she have a different father, like Derrick and I did? I didn't know. Maybe one day over a glass of wine I could ask Flo. Right now in her office wasn't the time. She didn't elaborate on the estrangement, and neither Norland nor I asked for more information.

"Flo," I began, "Yesterday afternoon when you and I were talking about Byrne being killed, you mentioned something else that had happened. With him?"

She glanced at the corner of the room. She let out a noisy breath. "Yes, but I don't want to talk about it right now, if you don't mind."

"Okay." I drew out the word. "But soon, at least if you think it pertains to the case."

She bobbed her head but didn't meet my gaze.

Norland and I sat without speaking for a moment.

"We'll have to wait for Tulia to report in about Sita," Norland finally said. "We have so many loose ends."

"We do," I said. "Right now, I need to get home." Despite wanting to get to the bottom of it with Flo, I was eager to sit down with Tim and find out what had been troubling him last night.

Flo's desk phone rang. "And I'm late for a meeting. Stay in touch, both of you."

"We will," Norland said.

All the ends were loose, and we had a lot of them.

Chapter 19

Out for a run, back by six thirty with dinner. Tim's note sat on our kitchen table.

I should volunteer to make dinner tomorrow. Surely, I could come up with a meal other than take-out. I bet I could pull off a simple pad Thai. I'd learned to make it in the Peace Corps in Thailand. How hard could it be to remember how, a half-dozen years later?

After I chatted with Belle for a few minutes and fed her, I poured a glass of seltzer and took it out back to my tiny house. Its cedar shingles were silvering nicely. The window boxes were planted with flowers in yellow and orange. A flagstone path led to the little abode from the cottage, and another from the tiny house to the gate in the fence leading to the street.

I'd had the house built to my specifications after I came back to Westham. Belle and I had happily lived in it on the land I owned behind my shop. All tiny houses are built on trailers, and before our wedding, Tim and I had moved the tiny house here and hooked it up to electricity and water. It had always had a super-clean composting toilet. I kept the shower and sinks stocked with organic and eco-friendly soap and detergent, and the wastewater from the shower and sink went into a tank for watering the garden. These days the house was rarely slept in, though, unless we had guests from out of town. That was about to change.

The wind was now blowing in dark rain clouds, so I hurried to unlock the door and step inside. Tiny houses are like boats. Space is at a premium, and this one had all kinds of built-in storage nooks and drawers, which was perfect for a slightly obsessed neat freak like myself. As Abo Reba liked to say, a place for everything and everything in its place. The house also had a sleeping loft with a wide clerestory window and a fully equipped, if miniature kitchen. I'd even included a small, attached porch with two blue Adirondack chairs.

Tim and I had decided to make a bit of money off the house and rent it out as vacation housing through Labor Day. High-season market rates on Cape Cod were, well, high. We would easily make enough to pay a service to come in and clean between guests, plus a lot more. We'd taken out a small equity loan last winter to help fund the downstairs renovations in the cottage and hoped to pay it off with the tiny house rents.

At four hundred square feet, the little residence was cozy, but it would be fine for a couple or a single guest, as long as they could handle the slanted ladder to the loft. Tourists mostly didn't spend much time in the place they stayed, anyway, with all the Cape had to offer. And guests could come and go through the side gate, although they'd have to park on the street.

The house was booked as of Saturday. I knew the bed in the loft was made up and everything was mostly ready to go. I'd come in later in the week to give it a final dusting and make sure all was perfect. Right now I wanted a little time in here to think.

I sank onto the small sofa in the nook tucked under the loft. I'd met Tim after I'd moved into this house. We'd shared conversations right here on the sofa and meals at the small table, along with a few disagreements and lots of growing love. My commute to work had been one minute long. Belle and I had had a few adventures in here, too. I'd witnessed an attack on the shop one night, and once a bad guy had tried to pick the lock during a hurricane—unsuccessfully, thank goodness. Another time, a killer had pounced on me as I opened the house, grabbed me, and pushed me inside.

Smiling, I remembered how Belle had come to the rescue that time, using her adoration for Alexa to summon help. I hoped being attacked here—or anywhere—never happened again.

But it might. My smile slid away. I'd been inquiring about another homicide in our town. Including asking questions of Edwin, who was apparently a person of interest, or at least someone with information Lincoln wanted, and with whom I'd been alone in the shop. Edwin's older brother had served time in prison, although not for murder. Corwin was now a responsible member of society and held a steady job.

No, I'd never seen anything to make me mistrust Edwin. He was Pa's accountant, after all, entrusted with the funds of the church. I was pretty sure I didn't need to worry about Edwin Germain. Yvonne I wasn't so sure about, nor Uly. And Carl and Sita were nearly complete unknowns, except for whatever Flo hadn't wanted to explain about her son and Sita.

How sad to have an adult child with whom you weren't close. I wondered what had happened to cause that separation.

I'd left the door open to the fresh air. Outside I heard the crunch of tires on gravel. I smiled at the sound of my husband arriving with dinner, and earlier than he'd promised. It was only six o'clock. I grabbed my glass and headed out.

Chapter 20

Except that was not an older-model Volvo wagon parked behind Miss M, my red sports car. It wasn't Tim's car. Whom did it belong to?

My heart thudding, I quickly locked the tiny house door behind me. I wouldn't let anybody trap me inside ever again.

I stared at the sleek black sedan. Had I ever seen it before? I didn't think so. It didn't belong to a friend or even an acquaintance. Should I make a break for the back door to the cottage and lock myself in? I gave my head a shake. I was a competent adult woman in my own yard. It was daylight, albeit a bit dim from the storm clouds overhead. My phone was in my pocket. Wasn't it? I felt for it in all the pockets.

Uh-oh. I'd come out here without that emergency lifeline. But the other matters stood. I swallowed and wiped sweaty palms on my pants.

Rain spattered on my head, and I shivered. I still wore the light windbreaker I'd walked home in over my white tee and skinny jeans, but the temperature had dropped. Bare feet inside my plastic garden clogs didn't help. Neither did a touch of fear. *No.* I willed myself not to be afraid.

I strode toward the gate, head up, shoulders back. The driver's-side door opened.

"Hey, Mac," Penelope said. "Got a minute?"

I didn't quite skid to a stop, but it felt like it as I stared at her. Not a threat at all. I rubbed my forehead.

"Um, you okay?" she asked.

The breath I let out was a noisy one. "Yes."

"If this isn't a good time, we can talk later."

Tim wasn't home yet. I could spare a few minutes. "It's fine, until my dinner arrives. Want to come in?"

"Okay, thanks."

"Could you please move your car to the street first? You're in the spot where Tim parks."

"Of course," she said.

"Come in the front door. I'll open it for you."

I went through the back door to shed my wet clogs and jacket. I slipped on a house sweater and slippers in time to greet Penelope at the front door. Belle, eager for attention, followed me. I sat on the sofa, with Belle on the arm. The detective perched in an armchair.

"What's up?" I asked.

For once, Belle didn't mimic me. I stroked her smooth, feathered head to keep her calm.

"I understand you know Uly Cabral," Penelope began.

"I don't, really."

She waited in silence.

"I mean," I continued, "I've met him a couple of times, but that's it."

"Did you ever see him interact with Bruce Byrne?"

I thought back. "No, I don't believe so."

"And you didn't overlap with Cabral at Westham High School."

"Not at all." I peered at her. "Penelope, he's at least ten years younger than me."

"Right."

"Do you have a reason to suspect Uly in the homicide?"

"I understand Edwin Germain is working for you."

"Yes." If she wasn't going to answer my questions, she was going to have to work for my answers.

"Has he mentioned anything about Byrne?"

"No." Except he had confided in me about Yvonne's and Bruce's clash at the bar. But Edwin should have already spoken to Lincoln. Why was she asking me? When she showed up, I'd thought she and my favorite Statie were tag-teaming. Maybe they were in competition instead. Not sharing information. That didn't make any sense at all. More likely, they were practicing a divide-and-conquer approach, with Penelope questioning me to see if she could learn anything I hadn't told him.

"Has Germain mentioned Cabral?" She continued with her inquiries.

"Uly? Why would he?" I gave that a moment of thought. "Oh, because they're about the same age. And they both work at the pub." *Interesting.*

She neither confirmed nor denied.

They both might have had bad experiences with Byrne at the high school. But so did every other stu-

dent who'd ever had him. The two guys could have
been friends. Now I wished she'd leave so I could
check the group thread. Maybe Zane had reported
what he'd learned about Uly. I could ask Edwin tomorrow if he and Uly were buddies or had at least
overlapped. I didn't know exactly how old either was,
but I thought they were in their mid-twenties or
thereabouts.

As if she'd read my thoughts, Penelope asked, "Has
your book group uncovered anything of interest?"

"Not that I know of. I always report back to Lincoln,
you know, if any of us happens to learn something." I
held up a palm. "And please, no more cautions. We're
not doing anything." I mentally crossed my fingers.
We weren't doing anything *in person*. Nothing dangerous. We did have our action items, and Detective Sergeant Penelope Johnson didn't need to know about
that.

The door swung open. Tim, cheeks flushed from
his run, moseyed in, holding two fragrant paper bags.

"Sorry, am I interrupting?" He glanced from
Penelope to me.

"Hey, handsome," Belle said in my voice, then
gave her wolf whistle and switched to Tim's. "Am I interrupting?"

Penelope snorted.

"It's fine." I stood. "We were finishing up." I was all
done talking with her on a one-way street, with me of-
fering information and her returning none. I didn't
really care if she was finished with me.

"Hello, Detective," he said. "I'll put these in the
kitchen, Mac." He disappeared through the door.

Penelope rose. "Thank you for your time, Mac.
We'll be in touch."

Chapter 21

Between bites of Westham's Yoshinoya sushi, the best on Cape Cod, I glanced at Tim. He'd grabbed a quick shower and wore a long-sleeved Greta's Grains tee and soft, loose drawstring pants. His shoulder-length dark-blond hair, now damp, was tied back at the nape of his neck. As always, but especially when he was showered and relaxed like this, my mind went straight to thoughts of getting those clothes off him and working on baby-making.

But he wasn't talking much and was smiling even less. Right now wasn't the time to close the bedroom door behind us. At least Belle was quiet. I'd put her to bed while Tim was in the shower.

"This is delicious," I said. "Thank you."

"I know you like sushi, hon."

"I do." I lifted my wineglass and took a sip. "I'm going to cook dinner tomorrow."

That got a smile out of him, finally. "Seriously?"

"Yes." I only hoped the meal would be edible. "You shouldn't have to be responsible for all the home-cooked dinners."

"You know I don't mind doing it, but I look forward to savoring your creation. Should I ask what it will be?"

"No." If the pad Thai didn't turn out, I might have to resort to an omelet and frozen tater tots. Or a tater-tot hot dish, a casserole I'd heard was popular in parts of the Midwest. Tater tots were delicious and indestructible, in my book. I savored my last piece of soft, perfectly fresh tuna on tangy rice, backlit by a smear of sinus-clearing wasabi. Sushi was the perfect food, in my book. I wished I knew how make a dinner like this one.

"Don't forget to save room for dessert." He gestured toward the kitchen counter.

"What is it?" I'd seen the upside-down aluminum roasting pan but hadn't had a chance to check out why it was there.

"Go see."

I lifted off the pan to reveal a work of art. A flat, rectangular pastry bigger than a sheet of printer paper was covered with concentric rows of summer fruits on a whitish base. Blueberries marched around the outside, with a circle of sliced peaches next to them. The center was made up of red raspberries. A tinted glaze covered it all.

"I call it the Ode to Summer Fruit Tart." Tim smiled.

"It's a work of art," I said. "And you went ahead and whipped it up this afternoon?"

"It's easy. You bake a big, flat shortbread cookie,

cover it with softened cream cheese, and top with fresh fruit covered with melted currant jelly."

"Easy for you, maybe. You wouldn't even want to see what a mash I would have made of it."

"You could learn if you wanted to, hon, but I'm happy to be the baker in the family." Tim sipped his beer as his expression turned somber. He lifted the last bite of seaweed salad with his chopsticks.

"What's up, love?" I asked in my gentlest voice. "Something was bothering you last evening, but we didn't get a chance to talk about it. You still seem to be chewing over a concern, a worry."

He popped in a piece of cucumber roll and finished it. He tucked a strand of hair behind his ear and rubbed his neck. He didn't meet my gaze.

"Tim?" I tried to lean into his line of vision. "If you don't want to talk about it, that's okay. But I wish you would."

His breath out was a noisy one. "Remember earlier in the year, when the father of Jamie's two oldest kids wanted to take over primary custody of them?"

I nodded.

"He succeeded. They're going to live with him as of Friday. My poor sister is beside herself."

"That's so sad," I said. "Is he a decent guy?"

"He seems to be. I've met him. And Jamie has visitation rights. She can have the kids every other weekend. But they've always lived with her. They're upset, too, as you can imagine." His big blue eyes filled.

"As they rightly should be. I'm so sorry." I covered his hand with mine.

"I wish we could have adopted them or become their foster parents."

I sat back. Take on the care of two children in elementary school? That was one way to get a family going, but not one I'd expected.

"I realize it wouldn't solve anything," he said. "They'd still be apart from their mommy. I've asked her to move out here and have a fresh start away from her usual bad influences, but she won't. She says she's lived in Seattle a long time and expects to die there."

That gave me a chill. Jamie had tried to end her life last year. I hoped she didn't have plans to attempt it again.

"At least she still has the little one," I said. "Ella." Her full name was Daniella, but Jamie had always shortened it to Ella. I hadn't met any of the children, or Jamie herself, for that matter.

"Yes." His face went darker still.

Did he have more bad news from the West Coast? My heart broke for him, mostly because I knew his was breaking even worse.

My phone vibrated with a call. I checked the ID. It was Gin. She might be canceling on power walking with me tomorrow. But I didn't have to answer now. She'd text me if that was the case. I glanced up.

"Go ahead and get that," Tim said.

"I don't need to. It's Gin. I can talk to her later."

"Go ahead. See what she wants. I'm going to make an early night of it." He stood and picked up his plate. "I didn't get my beauty sleep this afternoon. Between my run, the Ode, and thinking about Jamie and her kids, I'm beat."

"I'm not surprised. I'll clean up." I blew my sad man a kiss and connected the call. "Hey."

"Have you checked the thread?" Gin asked, breathless.

"No, I haven't had a chance." I usually turned down the sound on my phone during work hours, but I hadn't noticed any texts coming in lately. "You sound like something has happened."

"I'll say. Norland used his police contacts to find out that there were suspicious circumstances surrounding Byrne's wife's accident."

My eyebrows flew up. "What kind of 'circumstances'?"

"He doesn't know yet."

"Is the implication that Byrne was responsible for their deaths?"

"That would be horrible," she said. "Murdering a spouse is bad enough, and it happens all too often."

"True. But also killing your own children? That's a nightmare."

"Wait. They were his stepkids. You didn't know?"

"I sure didn't." I blinked. "Does it matter? They were still children. So, is Norland following up on this?"

"He said he would."

"Good." I yawned. My day hadn't been as long as Tim's, but I was tired, too. "Anything else urgent I need to know? I promise I'll look at the thread when we're done talking."

"I guess they believe Byrne was killed with a poison, but Norland couldn't find out what. I think maybe the police don't know yet."

"Interesting. I'd wondered that after I saw his body."

"Listen," Gin began. "I know it's raining now, but it's supposed to stop around midnight. Walking tomorrow?"

"I'm in. We can hash through more details then."

"See you in the morning."

We disconnected. I cleaned up the kitchen, then went into the bedroom to see if Tim was still awake. He wasn't, so I gave his slumbering cheek a gentle kiss and closed the door softly behind me.

I made a cup of tea and made sure all the doors to the outside were locked. I'd formerly felt safe in Westham. Now, not so much. Especially with an unsolved homicide looming.

Chapter 22

Feet up on the coffee table, I left my tablet cold and inactive on my lap for the moment. I sipped the single-malt and thought about families.

Tim was healthy, responsible, and a productive member of society, not to mention a caring, gentle, talented man. His parents, while divorced, were interesting people and led similarly healthy and productive lives. His only sibling hardly seemed related, except physically. She had the same big blue eyes as Tim, the same full lips and dark blond hair, and stood five foot ten, tall for a woman. There was no question they were birth siblings.

But at thirty-one, she'd only ever worked retail or in fast-food restaurants, and she had been fired from all of those jobs. She drank and used drugs, didn't exercise, and had a bad habit of hooking up with men without using contraception, partners who had no intention of staying with her. She got by, barely, with a housing subsidy, welfare, food banks, and the occasional gig job. Tim had said he was grateful that at least she didn't smoke cigarettes, which would be terrible for the health of the children, even though the drugs were much worse.

Tim and their mom and dad had each tried to help her find her way to a healthier life, without noticeable success.

Back in my Boston finance days, I'd had a friend whom Tim reminded me of. He was tall, good-looking, sweet, and smart, with the difference being that he was gay. A mutual woman friend, who was single, asked him if he had any brothers. He looked at her and asked if she wanted the brother in prison or the one with schizophrenia. Families could be funny that way.

In mine, Derrick and I were half siblings. Mom had been married before, but Derrick's father had died when he was only a year old. After she married Pa, he'd adopted Derr and raised him like his own. Derrick was great, and we had a good relationship. I knew we both had lucked out in the parent department. But I was sure Tim's parents had also given both him and Jamie a good upbringing.

A framed picture of Jamie and her children from last year sat on the bookshelf across the room. The two older kids, a boy and a girl about nine and seven, were as pale-skinned and light-haired as their mom. Little two-year-old Ella was mixed race and beautiful, with soft dark curls and big brown eyes. I wondered what explained Jamie's issues. Did she have a genetic predisposition to dysfunction or mental illness? So far her children hadn't shown any evidence of serious problems.

I shook my head. I doubted I'd ever know about any of it. It was time to shift gears.

After I tapped the tablet into life, I scrolled through the group's messages. I read Norland's description of his discovery and added a reply.

When or how do you think they'll find out what poison it was?

I added another message.

Penelope came by asking questions re Edwin and Uly. Were they friends in HS? Are they now? Also, Edwin reported conflict btwn Yvonne and Byrne.

I sent that and waited. Gin reported in, saying that her daughter had gone to school with both Uly and Edwin. Gin would ask her about them. Tulia wrote that Sita seemed to be staying in an Airbnb in Falmouth. She was driving a rented gray SUV.

A new message dinged in from Flo.

Can't find anything susp re Byrne's accident from my end.

Byrne was librarian Flo's action item, but she didn't have access to the police databases that Norland apparently still did. Either that, or he was hitting up friends in the force for information.

Tulia added a note.

Don't worry, I didn't tail Sita. She and Carl came into Lobstah Shack. We chatted. I spied SUV they got into with their takeout.

I tapped out a response.

Glad you're staying safe, Tulia. If Carl and Sita are a couple, they must be staying there together, yes?

Interesting that Zane hadn't reported anything about Uly. Maybe he was busy, or maybe he hadn't been able to dig up information relating to the murder or to Uly's past encounters with everyone's least-favorite English teacher.

Except somebody must have loved him. I wondered who grieved for Bruce Byrne this week. Maybe he had siblings in the area. He might have cousins here or elsewhere, nieces and nephews. Family would be the ones to hold a funeral. Reba had said she thought he had a sibling in the area. Pa might know.

Even though Byrne was Flo's item, I ran an internet search on the last name, which wasn't a common one. Nothing about Bruce Byrne popped up in the first dozen results. I was about to set down the tablet when the name Hal Byrne caught my attention.

I clicked the link. Hal was a watercolor artist. His paintings were soft and evocative of the dunes and the sea. One showed a wooden boat resting on its side amid dune grass. Another depicted colored dories clustered around a dock.

I found a photograph that showed a gray-haired man with half glasses. Something about his expression spoke of kindness. Ooh, and he had a show at a gallery in Falmouth beginning this week. A little jaunt to look at some fine art might be in my immediate future. If he was Bruce's brother, I could offer my sympathy at the very least, and possibly learn about the victim's past.

I yawned. With nothing more coming in from the group, I switched off the device and picked up *A Very Woodsy Murder*, the Ellen Byron book. It was the first in her new Golden Motel Mysteries series, not that we would get to discussing it until after this case was buttoned up and a murderer was behind bars. Right now? There was nothing like a good cozy mystery to take my mind off a real-life killer.

Chapter 23

The rain had barely cleared the next morning, but at least it was reduced to a fine mist. In a quick call at six fifty, Gin and I had agreed that striding in the fog was better than not walking.

"It's only water, right?" I'd asked.

"Right. And it's not cold. Let's do it."

Now we strode along on our return trip amid poison-ivy leaves dripping moisture beyond the verge of the paved path. Whoever pruned back or mowed the greenery at the edges of the trail did a good job. They didn't seem to apply pesticides or a blowtorch, which was good, although I wouldn't want to come in contact with the water on those poison-ivy leaves or the toxic leaves themselves.

So far we'd hashed through everything we knew about the homicide case and the persons of interest in it. Nothing had changed from last night's group-text thread.

"I can't believe we don't know more by now," I lamented.

"We are amateurs, you know."

"I'll say." I swiped moisture off my forehead, glad I'd put in my contacts before I'd set out. "I gather you didn't hear back from your daughter?"

"I did hear from her." Gin slowed and smacked her forehead. "I forgot to tell you. And Lucy reminded me that her yearbooks are still in her room. She has them from all four years she was at Westham High."

"So, did she go to school with Uly or Edwin?"

"She sure did. They all graduated the same year."

"Seriously?"

"Yes." Her brows came together, making her look worried.

I waited for her to say more as we approached a gradual curve in the path. Around the bend, a tandem came toward us on the other side of the yellow line in the middle, with two women pushing hard on the pedals and riding fast. This was not a casual morning ride. I took a second look and raised my hand in a wave. If I wasn't mistaken, that was Yvonne in the front riding with her partner behind.

Gin grabbed my elbow. "Is that Yvonne?" she whispered.

"Yes." I kept my voice to a murmur. "Which means they haven't detained her for anything."

The extra-long bike slowed and braked. Yvonne put her right foot down. The woman on the back frowned but also set her foot on the pavement. Neither wore a helmet, and the short blond hair of the one in back was windblown.

"Morning, you guys," Yvonne said to us.

"Have you recovered from your shock of Monday morning, Yvonne?" I asked. "That was pretty bad."

"It was." Yvonne said. "What's worse is the police thinking I was involved with the murder."

"They do?" Gin asked.

Yvonne gave her a suspicious look. "Who are you?"

"Gin Malloy. I own Salty Taffy's. I think we've met before."

"Oh, yeah. Sorry. This business has me all off-kilter."

"How's the Rusty Anchor owner taking it?" I asked.

"Carl?" Yvonne gave a snort. "He's all pumped up, as usual. Says any press is good press, which is ridiculous. Who wants to eat in a restaurant where a dead body was left behind the bar?"

No kidding. "Has business been slow?" I asked.

"I'll say."

Her partner tapped Yvonne on the shoulder. Yvonne twisted in her seat. The woman spoke in sign language. Yvonne signed back.

To us, Yvonne said, "Sorry. We have to get a move on."

Both women put feet on pedals and began to move.

"Take care," I called after them.

"Looks like her partner is deaf," Gin said after they were underway.

"It does. I hadn't known." I kept gazing down the path the way they'd gone. "I think American Sign

Language is fascinating. A friend had a deaf sister, and I've always wanted to learn ASL."

"We could take a class together. It's probably good for anyone to know, especially in retail."

"Good point," I said. "Let's do it. So, what else did Lucy say about Uly and Edwin?"

"She actually was friends with Uly."

"Didn't you know about that at the time?"

"I suppose I did. My girl hung out with a group of boys and girls, and the cast of characters was a little bit fluid. I might not have been aware that Uly had rotated into it."

"Did she have good memories of him?" I asked. "Or bad?"

"Mostly good, I think. But she did mention that the year they had Mr. Byrne, he and Uly were forever getting into it."

"Like into fights with each other?"

"Well, disagreements," Gin said. "Not between the two of them, but with their teacher. Uly's smart, and he challenged Mr. Byrne constantly. Uly got detention more than once for his lip."

"I guess it's ever thus. What about Edwin? Did Lucy know him well?"

"She was about to tell me when something came up, and she had to get off the call. I'll try to get back to her soon."

"Maybe you and I could sit down and have a look at the yearbooks before too long," I suggested.

"Good idea."

We moved on, both literally and figuratively. I confided Tim's concerns about Jamie to Gin. She'd always been a good sounding board and a compassionate listener. As my wedding attendant, she'd heard all about Jamie reversing her decision to bring the kids to the ceremony. Their absence had crushed Tim and his big, soft heart.

We didn't solve anything, but unburdening always felt good. And by the time we were finished, the mist had lifted, and the sun was trying to peek out.

Chapter 24

"Hey, Mom." I smiled at Astra MacKenzie, otherwise known as my mother, when she breezed into my currently empty shop at around ten. She'd never taken Pa's last name, or her first husband's for that matter, and she'd given me my first name with a small change in capitalization. A professional astrologer, Mom was both keenly intelligent and little bit woo-woo. I loved her for all of it.

"Good morning, sweetheart." She hurried toward me with her usual flyaway gray-blond curls, multi-colored scarf, and airy affect. "I sensed you needed me to check in with you this morning."

I came around the counter and kissed her cheek. "You did?" I gazed into her light-green eyes, identical to mine. She smelled of fresh air and the herbal shampoo she used.

"Yes." She glanced around and lowered her voice.

"I'm not surprised there was another murder this week. With Saturn so prominent in its transit through Sagittarius, death is common."

I nodded and ignored her astrological analysis, as I always did.

"Your father and I," she went on, "we never liked that Bruce as a teacher, may he rest in peace."

"Pa told me Byrne was a UU."

"He was," she said. "He chaired the building and grounds committee for a number of years. I thought he did a good job of stewardship."

"Too bad he wasn't a good steward of teenagers' education."

"I would have to agree. Say, do you know? I saw a woman around town I used to know. She and I were in the Garden Club together."

"That's nice."

"She has an unusual name. Sita. Doesn't that conjure images of South Asia?"

"Sita Spencer?" My senses went on high alert.

"That's her. She moved away, I don't know where, and I hadn't laid eyes on her until yesterday."

"Did you speak with her?"

"I didn't get a chance," Mom said. "She and a man were climbing into a car in front of the Lobstah Shack."

After Sita and Carl had bought takeout lunch from Tulia.

I gazed at my mother. We still didn't have any customers in the store. "Mom, can I ask you a question?"

"Always, darling."

"Why didn't you and Pa have any more children after me? I realized recently I've never asked you."

A shadow passed over her face. "I *should* say we

were so happy with you we didn't want any more babies."

"But?"

"But we had planned on a bigger family. I will say, this might be hard for you to hear."

"I can handle it," I murmured.

"Well, it never happened. We mostly didn't conceive, but the few times we did, the pregnancy ended in a miscarriage."

"I don't remember that at all."

"You were a toddler. You wouldn't have. And they were all in the first trimester." She shrugged. "That's life, right?"

Yes, it was. In my case, I hadn't even reached the conception stage.

"Don't get me wrong," Mom went on. "We were deliriously happy to have you, and we were grateful you and Derrick bonded so well. But I'm sorry to share that story, now that you're going through your own journey."

I reached out and hugged her. "It's fine. And important for me to know." Although I thought I might not tell Tim right away. Hearing about my parents' infertility could dishearten him about our own baby-making prospects.

"Now then, are you alright?" Mom shook off her feelings and focused on me, as she did. "I mean, after finding poor Bruce."

"I am," I said. "Thanks for thinking about me."

"I always think about you, darling." She peered at me. "But what else is bothering my girl? I can tell something is."

I tilted my head. "It's Tim." I filled her in on the

situation with Jamie's older kids. "I think there's more, but he hasn't let me know what it is."

"He's a good man. But Jamie has to lead her own life, wherever it lands her."

"Absolutely."

Her expression brightened. "I wondered what I came in here for, besides to see how you were, but I just remembered. Your father and I are having a party."

"That's great. When?"

"Why, Saturday, of course. It's our fortieth anniversary."

"This Saturday?" My voice rose. A big anniversary party with three days' notice?

"Why not? It'll be a fun thing in the backyard. You know, a cookout, with potluck sides, and dancing after dark under fairy lights." Her smile lit up her face. "I do love dancing."

I took a deep breath. "Fabulous. You let me know what Tim and I can do." No mention of what happened if it rained. Or of the famous Cape Cod mosquitoes, whose favorite time to feast on humans was after dark. Or of notifying people who lived far away and might have wanted to fête the couple. "Tim and I will handle the cake, at the very least."

"Lovely, hon. You make sure Lincoln Haskins is invited, will you, please?"

"Mom, it's your party. Shouldn't you do the inviting?"

She laughed. "Sweetie, you know I'm not a stickler for all that conventional business. I expect you'll see the fine detective before I will."

"I'm sure I will."

"He's the dreamiest dancer I ever had the pleasure of cutting a rug with. And you know Joseph isn't really the dancing type."

"Got it." I did know. I also knew my father didn't mind in the least when his wife sought out other men to dance with.

Mom caught sight of Orlean in the repair area. "Yoo-hoo, Orlean." She hurried over there and invited my now-healthy mechanic to the festivities, then waved goodbye to me and blew out the door.

Instead of "Astra MacKenzie, Professional Astrologer," Mom's shingle should read, "Astra MacKenzie, Force of Nature."

I wished I could call Derrick and talk about this party fiasco, that is, plan. But I didn't want to gripe to him on his getaway vacation. He'd be home Friday. Had Mom even informed him about the event? I did need to give Tim a heads-up that I'd volunteered him for an anniversary cake for Saturday.

Saturday. I scrunched up my nose. I'd been counting on Derrick to work here that day. And what about Orlean? I might need to close the shop at around noon, after the morning rentals had been picked up. We could check the book and call anybody with a pickup or return on Saturday and make other arrangements.

Family should be more important than commerce, always, at least for an event like this.

But now the pressure was on to figure out the case and get it closed, especially if Mom wanted Lincoln there. Nobody wanted to be called out from a party to confront a homicidal criminal. Even worse if the criminal decided to crash the festivities.

Chapter 25

Edwin showed up on time. Orlean and I had each taken our lunch breaks, and the store was pretty quiet by one o'clock.

"I'm going across the street on a couple of errands," I said to Edwin.

"Sure. I got it." He waved me on.

Equipped with EpiPen bag and a credit card in my phone case, I headed out into the now-sunny afternoon. I wanted to grab a bottle of wine that would pair well with pad Thai, and Cape King Liquor was the place. If I could pick Zane's brain a little about Uly or anything else, so much the better.

In the store, Zane was behind the counter frowning at his phone. He glanced up and flashed me a wan smile.

"Is everything okay?" I asked.

"What? Why wouldn't it be?"

Something didn't ring true about his words.

He came around the counter, sliding his phone into the back pocket of his stylish jeans. I'd never seen him without his signature bow tie, which today featured pink seashells on an azure background. His crisp Oxford shirt, the cuffs neatly folded up on his forearms, matched the seashells. "What can I help you with, Mac?"

Whatever was bothering him, he didn't want to talk about it.

"I'm making chicken pad Thai tonight, and—"

"You're what? Did I hear Mac Almeida say she was going to be preparing an actual dinner?"

"As a matter of fact, yes." Or I'd try, anyway. "So I wanted to get a nice bottle of wine to go with it."

"Hmm," he said. "Thailand isn't renowned for their vintages. But you're going to want to drink a light and cool wine, I think. Have you ever tried Vinho Verde? It's Portuguese."

"I'm not sure. If you recommend it, I'll give it a try."

"I think you'll like it." He selected a bottle and rang it up.

I glanced around to be sure no one else was keeping us company in here. "Any progress on your action item?" I left out Uly's name in case an inquisitive customer might be lurking in the beer aisle.

"Uh, no. Not really."

"Did you try talking with him or asking around?"

"I haven't had a chance." He looked relieved when the door opened to admit what appeared to be a couple of tourists.

"Let me know when you do, okay?" I picked up my paper bag of wine and slipped out. I'd never seen

Zane so evasive, and I didn't have a clue why he'd answered the way he did.

I probably still had a few minutes before I needed to get back. I'd love to talk with Yvonne again. Except after the way she'd reacted to Gin this morning, I thought I shouldn't. The Cozy Capers were all about staying out of danger. Bugging one of the persons of interest with questions about the body she'd discovered wasn't a safe choice.

From where I stood, I could see the Rusty Anchor across the street and down a few storefronts. An actual rusty anchor swung from a rod that extended out from above the door. Carl emerged onto the sidewalk in front. If that wasn't serendipity, I didn't know what was. I waited a moment. If he moved in my direction, I would head that way. If he turned away, I'd return to my shop.

Fate smiled on me when Carl pointed himself to the right—that is, toward me. I crossed over and moseyed along the sidewalk. When he approached at a fast clip, I slowed and smiled at him.

"Carl, right?"

"That would be me."

He looked me up and down in a way that made me want to go take a shower without delay. Or slap him. Or both.

"I'm Mac Almeida, a fellow business owner here on Main Street." I extended my hand, even though I'd rather have kept it to myself.

"What's your business?" He shook my hand a bit too vigorously. "You look kind of familiar."

I detached my hand. His was callused in a way that seemed to clash with his slick demeanor.

"I own Mac's Bikes. Rental, repair, and retail. I

haven't seen you at any Chamber of Commerce events here in town. Are you a new owner of the pub?"

He peered at me. "How did you know I own the Anchor?"

"I was in the pub right after the body was found."

"You were, were you?"

I nodded. "In fact, I was in the kitchen speaking with Detective Johnson when you came in."

"That's where I've seen you. So, you found the victim. How did that happen?" He folded his arms on his chest. "The pub wasn't even open yet."

"I didn't find Mr. Byrne, but I was passing by, and Yvonne called to me to help her. She actually discovered the body, not me." He must already know that. Yvonne was his employee, after all. Perhaps he was testing me.

"You were acquainted with the man, I gather?" he asked.

"Like almost everybody who has attended Westham High in recent decades, I had him for English one year."

His lip curled for a brief second before he rearranged his features into a bland expression.

"Did you know him?" I asked.

"A long time ago." He cleared his throat. "I'll let you get on with your day, Mac."

"I hope we'll see you at the next Chamber event."

"I seriously doubt you will." He sauntered away.

He'd gone in the direction where I should be heading, that is, back to my shop. I couldn't follow him, at least not until he was out of sight, since I'd been pointed in the opposite direction when I'd waylaid him. I sank down on a bench to people watch for a couple of minutes instead. And to think.

Carl had been as vague as possible about how and when he had known Byrne. He also hadn't explained why he wasn't active in the Chamber. Who could blame him for not wanting to talk with me? I was a complete stranger. But I hadn't missed that flash of scorn when I'd mentioned Byrne's association with the English department at Westham High School.

A text came into my phone. Edwin wrote,

Getting busy here.

That was my cue to stop woolgathering and get serious.

BRB

But first I picked up a paper bag of lunch detritus from the ground next to the bench and tossed it in the town trash barrel. Litterers offended my sensibilities, big-time.

Chapter 26

Edwin was with a gaggle of rental customers when I hurried in. A man in a Panama hat waited at the retail counter. I had my mouth open to say I'd be right with him when he turned.

"Norland," I said. "I didn't realize that was you. Nice hat."

"Do you like it? It's new."

"It looks great." I gazed at the counter, where a pink-and-black windbreaker lay. "Expanding your color palette? That looks kind of small for you."

He laughed. "No, it's grand-girl number two's eighth birthday, and she loves riding her bike. I thought I'd get her some real gear."

I lifted the nylon jacket. "Got it. Child's medium. Anything else today?"

"No, that'll be it for her." He leaned closer and

lowered his voice. "Any news on your end?" He tilted his head toward Edwin.

I busied myself with the purchase as I murmured, "Not yet, but I hope to get a chance to dig a little before we close today. You?"

"Nothing more than what I mentioned about the link between Yvonne and Byrne's wife."

"Where did you hear about that?"

"From an acquaintance in the WPD," he said.

"But they didn't say what kind of link it was."

"No. I kind of wonder if it was a relationship, though."

"A romantic relationship?" I asked.

"Yes."

Other customers approached. Norland lifted his bag and thanked me. I busied myself with the customers, but part of my mind stayed glued to this supposed link Norland mentioned. In the spring, Yvonne had made no secret about being gay. Maybe Byrne was as abrasive a husband as he'd been a teacher. His wife could have tired of him and turned to Yvonne for love. He might have discovered their affair and tampered with his wife's car so the brakes or steering failed.

That was all still speculation, though. Norland hadn't texted his idea about the romantic relationship to the group. Had Gin texted yet what her daughter had said about Edwin and Uly? I didn't think so. Flo hadn't shared any progress, either. Was our little band of amateur sleuths splintering? Each of us brought important and different skills and contacts and insights to a case. We'd be much less effective at crime-solving if we didn't work as a group.

Perhaps it was inevitable that people would drift off. We'd contributed—I, unfortunately, more than the rest of them—to solving five cases in a year's time, and this was the sixth.

I shoved those thoughts into a drawer when I realized a cyclist had asked me a question, and I hadn't answered it.

It wasn't until four o'clock that the place emptied out enough for me to take a minute to talk with Edwin. I moseyed over to where he was lifting bike tools and supplies out of boxes and restocking the shelves where we sold them.

"Yesterday you mentioned wanting to help our be-hind-the-scenes homicide investigation," I began.

He gave a slow nod.

"You probably went to Westham High, right?" I asked.

"I did. And before you ask, I had Mr. Byrne for freshman English. I realize he's dead, but the truth is, he was a jerk."

"Don't worry. I had the same experience with him when I was a student there. Were you and Uly Cabral at Westham High at the same time?"

"Yesss." He drew out the word. "Why?"

"I was curious. You seem to be about the same age."

"We are. But we didn't hang out then, and we don't hang out now." He gazed at me, rolling a valve stem between his fingers. "Let me guess. It's because he works at the Anchor, and he might have a key?"

"As my grandma says, there's no flies on you. That's what I was thinking, yes." I tilted my head. "In what ways was Byrne a jerk toward you in particular?"

"You know Corwin." Edwin glanced toward Orlean over in the repair area.

"I do." Edwin's older brother plowed the snow off my parking lot in the winter. Corwin was also Orlean's ex-husband.

"Mr. Byrne used to give me a really hard time about Corwin being incarcerated. Said that kind of bad blood ran in families. I hated what he thought he was getting at, even though our mom had done time, too, and we never really knew our dad. Anyway, I pushed back, hard." He gave a low laugh. "I spent a lot of time in the vice principal's office that year."

"Did he say those things in front of the other students?" The teacher had been worse than I'd thought.

"He implied them, and he sure said them to my face after class let out. He'd call me up to his desk under the pretense of talking about work I'd done. There was nothing he liked better than to hint about the secrets people held. How he could let the wrong people know."

"So, your classmates didn't know about Corwin?"

"Mac, I didn't give a flying fluffernutter if they knew. I didn't keep it a secret."

"What did Byrne say he wanted in exchange for his silence?" I asked.

"I have no idea. I never stuck around long enough to hear." He pressed his lips together. "Corwin got out and turned his life around. Byrne is dead. End of story, as far as I'm concerned." He focused on the shelves in front of him.

"Thanks. I'm sorry to bring up a hard time in your life."

He gave his head a shake. "It's okay. I really don't care." But he didn't meet my gaze.

Orlean called me over to consult with her on an expensive repair. Customers appeared and wanted help. Rental returns poured in. The noise level rose. Time for talking about murder was over. For now.

Chapter 27

I cruised Falmouth's main drag until I spied the art gallery. A curb parking spot was available, but I hated to leave Miss M on the street. I found a spot at the edge of the municipal lot around the corner instead.

I'd been able to get out of Mac's Bikes before five, glad I could squeeze in a potential spot of investigation before swinging through the large supermarket here to pick up my supplies for dinner.

A sandwich board on the sidewalk in front of LeGuin Fine Art advertised the Byrne watercolor exhibit with an opening reception tonight at seven. I paused. Maybe I should skip this drop-in visit and come back tonight after dinner.

No. The artist would be busy schmoozing with attendees during the event. And I often didn't want to go out again in the evening after I was comfortable at home with my sweetie. I stepped through the open doorway.

They weren't kidding about fine art. The white walls were lined with tastefully framed paintings of all kinds, from abstract to seascapes to portraits. The entire right half, though, featured watercolors all labeled to be by Hal Byrne, with the display stretching into a room beyond.

I moved along the wall, gazing at each piece of art. From what I'd seen last night on the internet, my impression of evocative paintings was magnified in person. The man had a gift for capturing the atmosphere of Cape Cod, but it was more than that. The waving dune grasses, the dark clouds shading the ocean, the skiff stranded on a desolate stretch of sand—all were imbued with emotion.

Stepping into the room at the back where the art continued, I came across a man separating a stack of plastic wineglasses and setting them on a table. He peered through his half glasses, concentrating on the task. I shuffled my feet so I didn't startle him.

He straightened and turned. "Pardon me, ma'am. I didn't see you." The soft-looking skin of his face was wrinkled and ruddy. Smile lines crinkled around blue-green eyes that reflected the color of the ocean on a cloudless day. His work pants were dotted with spots of paint, and his T-shirt was a faded pink.

"Not a problem. I was just looking at the paintings. They're lovely."

He inclined his head.

"I'm afraid I don't know the language to talk about art, but these make me feel things." I shrugged. "In a good way."

"I'm glad to hear it." He ran a hand through thinning white hair in an absent-minded gesture.

"You must be the artist."

"I am." He extended his hand. "Hal Byrne."

"Mac Almeida. I'm honored to meet you." I swallowed, suddenly less eager to turn the conversation with this seemingly gentle man to a darker topic. But that was what I was here for. "I had a high school teacher at Westham High School named Mr. Byrne. Are you related?"

The light went out of his expression. "Bruce. My brother. He was murdered this week."

"Yes, I heard. I am so sorry for your loss, Hal."

"Thank you, Mac." He squared his shoulders. "We were about as different as two brothers can be."

I nodded but didn't speak, hoping he'd go on.

"I try to live without regrets, but I hadn't seen Bruce in three years. I deeply regret that now."

"Please accept my sympathy."

He gazed at me over the top of his glasses and gave a wistful smile. "We had a tough upbringing. I chose moving on and joy. He chose wallowing and bitterness. It was hard for us to find a middle ground. And now we never will."

"Harold, time's getting short." A tall woman in flowing purple pants and a long linen top hurried in from an interior door. The gray knot of hair on top of her head made her look like Katharine Hepburn. "Pardon me. Didn't mean to interrupt."

"That's all right, darling," Hal said. "Mac, this is Malvina LeGuin, owner of this fine gallery and my sainted wife. Mal, meet Mac Almeida. She knew Bruce."

Malvina blinked behind half glasses that matched her husband's.

"Happy to meet you, ma'am," I said. "And you, too, Hal. I need to run. I'm sure you have a lot to do to get ready for your reception."

"Like someone changing his clothes, for example?" Malvina pointed at the paint-spattered pants.

He gave her a sheepish smile.

"I'll be back, with a closer eye to buying a painting," I added.

"Thank you," Hal said. "I appreciate that."

I moved to go but turned back. "May I ask, are you planning a service of any kind for Bruce?"

Hal shook his head and flipped his palms open. "Who would come? All he had left were enemies."

Chapter 28

Five forty-five found me racing through the over-air-conditioned aisles at the supermarket. This large grocery store was the only place I could pick up rice noodles, fish sauce, bean sprouts, and the other ingredients I needed to put together my planned Thai dinner. The little Westham market didn't make a practice of stocking what they considered "exotic" foods.

While I was in town, I had also wanted to cruise by where Sita was staying. That thought was now out the window, since I'd used up any extra time at the gallery. As things were, I'd be lucky to get dinner on the table before seven. Before I left the shop, I'd shot a quick text to Tim, saying I was running late but would be home before long, ready to cook.

Murphy's Law being what it is, I naturally landed the slowest cashier in the longest line, the one with

Trainee on his name badge. Every piece of produce, every item he couldn't find the price on, slowed him more and more. He was taking forever laboriously scanning the endless array of groceries of the person in front of me, whose carriage had towered with everything from cabbage to chips, Hamburger Helper to hummus, pork chops to Popsicles. I finally had room to unload my purchases onto the moving belt behind one of the divider sticks.

I stared at my items and cursed under my breath. I'd forgotten the rotisserie chicken. I couldn't exactly make chicken pad Thai without chicken, and no way was I bringing home a piece of raw meat. Even the thought of all that bacteria made me shudder.

I turned. Three carts and their people had lined up behind me.

"Excuse me." I squeezed past the cart directly behind me. "Sorry. I'll be right back."

"Better hurry," the shopper warned in a dire tone. "The kid is almost done."

With any luck, the beginner would also fumble with the card transaction or cash payment. I hurried, speed-walking, toward the deli, sliding past slow-strolling customers and dodging heavy carriages coming straight at me.

I reached the freestanding, stainless-steel contraption where the rotisserie chickens always were. But instead of holding fat, glistening-tan, spit-roasted chickens smelling so good you wanted to rip off the plastic film and bite into a drumstick on the spot, the shelf under the orange warming lights was empty.

No! How could they be out of chickens? It was dinnertime. Was I going to have to substitute tofu in my dish? I liked the bland soy protein, which was only a vehicle for other flavors, but Tim had confessed he didn't care for it. And anyway, on the rare occasions when I cooked, I needed to follow a recipe. My brain simply worked that way. No kitchen improv for me. In this case, the recipe was in my head, but it called for shredded, cooked chicken.

"Be right with you, hon." A hair-netted woman who spoke from an aisle away wore the green jacket of all employees. She pushed a cart holding a couple dozen chickens toward me.

I wanted to race over there and grab one. In a minute the impatient customer in the line behind where I'd left my stuff might throw it all overboard. But I waited until the deli woman arrived, then I selected a package containing one juicy and fragrant bird.

"Careful, they're pretty hot," Hairnet cautioned.

This one sure was. I used both hands to hold the roasted chicken package by its edges.

"Mac, right?" a woman's voice asked from next to me.

I whipped my head around. And blinked. It was Sita Spencer herself.

"Yes, hi," I mumbled. *Great.* Exactly the person I wanted to talk with, but no time to talk. "You're Sita, aren't you?"

"That's me."

"Did Carl like his birthday gift?"

Her smile vanished in a poof of smoke. "How do you know what his name is?"

"What? Somebody told me." I lifted a shoulder in what I hoped looked like a casual move. I wasn't about to let on that I'd first seen Carl in the restaurant kitchen shortly after Yvonne dragged me inside to see the body behind the bar. I took a step away. "I'm not sure who."

"Uh-huh." Her eyes narrowed. "As it happens, that is his name. But like I told you, his birthday is Saturday. He hasn't seen what I bought yet."

"Right, right. Well, gotta run. Left my items on the belt." I rushed back to my line. Were her eyes burning holes in my back? I hoped not, but it felt like it.

I wanted to kick myself for using Carl's name. I could have used the word *boyfriend* and come out of the conversation without her suspecting me of anything. Too late now. Her reaction had broadcast suspicion. Or maybe Carl had told her about my conversation with him, which would be even worse.

Miracle of miracles, all my items were still on the belt. Sure enough, the newbie cashier was still ringing up the previous customer—or trying to. He switched on the flashing light that signaled Need Help and gazed desperately toward the manager's station.

I excused myself again to the woman behind me in line and slipped into my slot, letting the aromatic, dinner-saving chicken join the other ingredients.

Chapter 29

The kitchen clock read six fifteen by the time I got home and inside with my bags. But the house felt empty.

"Tim?"

No answer. He hadn't left a note on the table. He was always either home by six or had left me a message.

"Tim?" Belle echoed. "Hey, handsome."

"Ssh, Belle, be quiet, okay?"

"Okay. Okay. Treats?"

I made my way into the living room, but the door to our room was open and the bed was made and empty. I ran upstairs to check. No Tim. I trudged back down.

Where was he? *Oh.* I pulled out my phone. Sure enough, he'd left a text. I hadn't glanced at the phone since before I'd left my shop, and it was on vibrate.

Sorry, rain check on dinner. OT baking tnight for big event tmrrw. Isaac out sick. Be home late. Love you. XXOO

I studied the message. *OT* must be *overtime*, even though he was the owner. Too bad his assistant baker, Isaac, was ill. Should I go over and offer to help? No, I should not. I was Ms. Fumbles in a kitchen, and I'd never baked even a potato in my life. Baking fine breads wasn't my thing. I tapped out a message.

Did you eat?

Yes.

OK. See you when you get here. Love you oodles.

That news changed my evening entirely. I'd cook tomorrow instead. Not spending the evening with Tim meant one more day of not fully knowing what was bothering him, which was disappointing. Tomorrow, I'd coax it out of him if I could.

Selfishly relieved not to have to prepare dinner and face all that could go wrong with such a plan, I stashed all the cold groceries in the fridge, swapping out an open and mostly full bottle of chardonnay. I left the chicken on the counter. A thigh and a drumstick with a thick slab of Tim's bread sounded like a perfectly good solo dinner, and it would still leave plenty of meat for tomorrow's meal.

Hands washed, I gave Belle her dinner and poured myself a generous glass of chilled white. I sank onto a chair at the table and sipped. And thought.

So much had happened today, including hearing about my own parents' experience with infertility, an ordeal I'd never heard a word about from anyone.

Right now I decided to organize my thoughts about the murder.

Did I have a handle on all of it—or even any of it? I sorted through the people I'd spoken to. Nothing really had gone on between Sita and me, except that I might have made her suspicious of me at the market. I certainly hadn't learned anything from her. For that matter, I hadn't learned much from Carl, either. On the contrary. He hadn't clarified how he'd known Byrne nor why he wouldn't be at the next Chamber event.

Thinking of Carl reminded me of Zane's slightly odd behavior when I'd asked him about checking into Uly. I'd never known Zane to be evasive. But he'd certainly acted that way in his store this afternoon.

And then there was what Norland had mentioned about Byrne's wife possibly having an affair—and possibly with Yvonne. The wife was dead, as was Byrne. Did it matter after all this time if he'd tampered with his wife's car and caused the crash? It did if Yvonne had been waiting for her chance to exact her revenge. But I couldn't question Yvonne. That wasn't destined to go well.

I thought back to what Edwin had told me about pushing back against Byrne. My eyes widened. Gin had said nearly the same thing about Uly, that he'd challenged the teacher and spent plenty of time in detention. Edwin had gotten in trouble for a different matter and had repeatedly landed in the vice principal's office, but the behavior was the same.

Yet Gin's daughter had been friends with Uly but apparently not with both of them. Were the two guys buds or not? No, Edwin had said they hadn't hung out. And he'd made a point of saying they didn't hang out now, either.

"What do you think, Belle?" I stroked the head of the oddly quiet parrot perched on the back of the chair next to mine. "Is that significant?"

She perked up. "Alexa, is that significant? What do you think? Belle's a good girl."

I laughed. "Belle's a very good girl. I'll get your dinner, and then it's nighty-night for my favorite bird." Once again I was glad we kept the smart speaker switched off when we left the house. Belle had a bad habit of asking Alexa to start a shopping list, and once she'd even succeeded in placing an order. I arrived home to find a box on my stoop containing grapes, peanuts, and anything labeled Snack. I now called the device the "spy speaker."

"Nighty-night, Mac. Belle's a very good girl. Snacks?"

After she'd eaten and was on her perch in a covered cage, I dwelt for a moment on my chat with Hal Byrne. Our investigation might be helped by an interview like that with a sibling or old friend of the various persons of interest. Maybe we could dig up a relative of Carl's or a classmate of Yvonne's. A person's difficult background didn't excuse criminal behavior, but knowing about it could shed light on the why behind their actions. And sometimes the acquaintance or loved one had information about the person in the present.

Asking in-person questions of a dead man's brother, however, was entirely different from inquiring about a potential murderer. The Cozy Capers had a pact not to put ourselves in physical danger, and I planned to abide by that.

For now, I put away my thoughts and enjoyed my

simple dinner, contemplating nothing more than diving into *A Very Woodsy Murder* as soon as I was finished eating. I would have started right here at the table, but eating was too messy to mix with the pages of a book, no matter how good that book was.

My phone jangled me out of my reverie.

"Okay if I bring those yearbooks over?" Gin asked without preamble.

Chapter 30

Gin sat in an easy chair at right angles to the couch, where I had my feet curled up, each of us with one of the four yearbooks she'd brought. She'd accepted a glass of wine.

"Where's your main man?" she asked.

"Baking for a big event tomorrow, and his assistant is sick."

She nodded and gestured at the yearbooks on the coffee table. "Tonight, this seems to make less sense than it did earlier," she said. "What do you think we should look for?"

"We already know both Uly and Edwin went to Westham High, and both had conflicts with Mr. Byrne. I don't know, maybe scan for pictures of one or both with him? Or maybe a candid showing anger or another strong emotion." I scrunched up my nose.

"You might be right. Yearbooks won't have snapshots of fistfights or a teacher sneering at a student."

"It's worth a shot. Which year do you have?"

I held it up.

"That's their freshman year," Gin said. "I'll begin with Lucy's senior year, and we can meet in the middle."

"And then swap. I'm sure we'll each see different things."

"Sounds like a plan."

I started paging through. The book, which smelled of paper and ink, began with the usual portraits of the administration, the staff, and the faculty. I paused at the photo of Mr. Byrne and examined it. The picture was less than ten years old, and he didn't look that different than he had when I'd seen him—except for being dead. The teacher held a pointer in one hand and a dry-erase marker in the other. He looked as if he'd just turned toward the camera from the whiteboard, on which was written an underlined *Homework*. The photographer must have told him to smile, and he had, but it was lackluster, bordering on a frown. Exactly like twenty years ago.

The senior class came next, with senior pictures taken the summer before and those stupid popularity awards like Most Likely to Succeed and Best Dancer.

I examined every page. Byrne was in only a few candid shots. When I came to the freshman class individual photos, I first saw Uly Cabral. Nobody looks great in ninth grade, particularly not skinny boys with braces. Edwin Germain's face was on the same page. His hair was shaggy and half obscured his eyes, his cheeks were smooth and still boyish, and he didn't smile for the camera. Gin's daughter, Lucy, on the other hand, had wavy hair on her shoulders, a V-necked top, makeup, and a big smile.

"Whoa," Gin said. "You're going to want to see this." She extended the open senior-year book toward me and pointed. The photograph showed the Rainbow Club. A group of boys and girls posed in front of and atop a stone wall. Two girls were kissing, and two boys held hands. Mr. Byrne stood in the periphery as if he'd been passing by and glared at the students.

"This looks like what we used to call the Gay-Straight Alliance," I said.

"Right, except now it's called the Rainbow Club. But it was Lucy's senior year, when everybody signs each other's yearbook at the end of the year. Check out that comment in the margin."

Someone had used purple ink to write "Gay-phobe" in a circle with an arrow pointing to Byrne.

"Wow," I said. One of the kids caught my attention. I peered at a skinny guy with one pierced ear, hair shaved up the sides but long on top in a classic fade, and a big braces-free grin. "That looks like Uly. I wonder if he's gay."

"It does look like him. If this is the current incarnation of the Gay-Straight Alliance, anybody can join."

"True. Can you ask Lucy about Uly's preferences?"

Gin tilted her head. "Does it matter?"

"It might." I filled her in on what Norland had said about a link between Byrne's wife and Yvonne, and his thought that it might have been a romantic relationship. "If it was and Byrne found out, he could have been furious. I mean, he might have already had homophobic tendencies, but that would have notched it up a level."

"And we all know how gentle Byrne was to students who were different." She gave a snort. "Not."

We both went back to our paging through the smooth, shiny paper of the books. After the four years of class photos came the clubs and the sports teams. I flipped past the Garden and Landscape Club, then turned back. Mr. Byrne apparently was the faculty adviser for the group. While I was a student, I wouldn't have been aware of the club's adviser. I'd never had the slightest urge to put my hands in the dirt. The students each held a shovel or a trowel, and Byrne beamed at them.

"Did you ever once see Mr. Byrne smile?" I asked Gin.

"Never."

"Take a look at this." I showed her the page.

"Amazing. He must have liked growing things."

"I guess. My mom said he was the chair of the UU building and grounds committee, so that fits. The kids in that club might have been the only ones in the history of the school who saw his good side."

"I think that kid standing apart is Edwin Germain." Gin pointed. "Isn't it?"

"You're right. I hadn't spotted him. Same shaggy hair, baby-faced cheeks as in his class picture. He doesn't look happy to be there, though." If he didn't like being in the club, why had he shown up for the picture?

I finished paging through the freshman yearbook and sat back.

Uly's resentment against Byrne might have been festering for years. He could have seized an opportunity to get back at the teacher in the most final of ways. Except if the method of death was poison, that wasn't a spontaneous crime. Spur-of-the-moment murders involved beating over the head, strangling, stabbing, pushing the victim over a cliff. A restaurant kitchen shouldn't have a lot of toxins lying around, except for cleaning supplies.

"Gin, do you feel like the group isn't communicating as well about this homicide?"

"Now that you mention it, yes. On the other hand, it's high season for all of us. Everybody's super busy."

"True." I took a sip of my wine. "Today I asked Zane if he'd learned anything about Uly, and he got weird."

"Weird how?" Gin asked.

"I don't know, kind of evasive. He wouldn't meet my gaze. But then, he had customers and couldn't talk any more. Also, Flo is usually on top of her action items. I haven't heard a word from her about Byrne."

"Interesting. She's, like, the only one who isn't flooded with summer business, too."

"Exactly. Plus Norland. He, at least, told me about the thing with Byrne's wife, but I didn't get a chance to ask if he'd turned up anything on Yvonne."

Gin raised a hand. "I'm supposed to be digging into Carl, but so far, I've come up emptier than the calories in a bag of sugar. And it's mostly because I haven't dedicated the time."

"I hear you. Listen, after I saw Zane today, I happened to run into Carl on the sidewalk."

Gin grinned. "Sure, you did."

"It's true. He had a reaction when I mentioned Byrne's name, and I tried to find out how they knew each other. All he would say is that they went way back. And then I mentioned the next Chamber gathering. He basically said he wouldn't be there."

"So noted. You should group-text that stuff."

"I will," I said. "Can you add what we saw in the yearbooks?"

"Sure."

"Speaking of the yearbooks, maybe we should get back to them." I couldn't help yawning.

"Or not." Gin closed hers. "We've picked up a few bits about Bruce. I'm tired, too." She drained her glass and stood. "But maybe we should have a group meeting tomorrow night."

I groaned out loud.

"What's that for?" she asked.

"I can't. I was supposed to make dinner for Tim tonight—"

"Whoa, whoa, whoa. What happened to Never-Cooks Mackenzie Almeida?"

I laughed. "I can try, right? But anyway, I postponed my gourmet gala meal until tomorrow, because Tim was already gone when I arrived."

"The Cozy Capers should meet soon and catch up with each other's info in person."

"I know, but for me it'll have to be Friday. Happy hour somewhere?"

"As long as it's not in the Rusty Anchor." She raised her eyebrows. "Plus, you know they can't call it Happy Hour, right?"

"I know. It's illegal, and we have to call it Not Happy Hour. Same difference."

I hoped Tim would be home soon. What I really wanted to do was have a happy few minutes curled up in his arms. He would tell me all his worries, and I could forget about murder for an evening.

Chapter 31

I woke up the next morning at six with my knee bothering me, as it occasionally did, and texted Gin to cancel our exercise together. Last night she'd left at eight thirty, with neither of us having discovered anything else in the yearbooks.

Tim had arrived home at nine, thoroughly exhausted. He'd kissed me.

"I'm going to bed, sweetheart."

I stood. "I'll come with you."

We'd cuddled and spooned, his soft snoring beginning almost immediately. I wasn't tired enough yet, so I switched on the little reading light that clipped onto my book and sank into the mystery until ten.

He'd given me a goodbye kiss early this morning, as usual, and headed out to work. I'd become an expert at falling back asleep.

Now I stretched in the bed. Would Lincoln and Penelope have a breakthrough in the case today? I hoped so. That way the Cozy Capers could go back to being a book group. On the other hand, we might not have been as diligent lately about passing along information to the detectives in charge. I could use my newly found hour this morning to fix that.

After Belle was up and fed, and I'd ground beans and set the coffee to drip, I settled in at the kitchen with my tablet. First, I checked the weather and groaned. No wonder my knee ached. Another massive storm system was circling our way. Way to ruin more of the tourist business, Mama Nature.

In the mornings when I had time, I often popped into a social media group of African gray parrot owners. Today a member had posted a video of two parrots having a video chat with each other. They appeared to be truly interacting and enjoying it.

Huh. Belle might like that. I clicked open the article, which described the social benefits to parrots of chatting with their friends while they were home alone. Belle was by herself for hours every weekday. But I had my doubts about leaving the tablet powered up and online while my bird was alone with it. Having seen what she could do with her buddy Alexa, I wasn't sure I wanted to risk it.

But maybe she'd enjoy the stimulation while I was here and otherwise occupied. As I was about to be.

I poured a mug of heavenly dark roast, then figured out how to connect to the parrot meet-up site. I selected a bird who was online and not already chatting. I propped the tablet up against a stack of books before I called Belle over.

"Belle, your friend Malik wants to say hi."

She perched on the back of the chair nearest the device and tilted her big head. "Belle wants to say hi."

The parrot on the screen said, "Hey, gorgeous." He gave a wolf whistle exactly like the one Belle emitted when she saw Tim. "Malik's a good boy."

"Malik's a good boy," she muttered. "Belle's a good girl. Am I interrupting something?"

"Not at all," Malik said in a low voice. "Love me some grits."

His owner had to be a man.

"Love me some grits," Belle said. "Snacks, Malik?"

And they were off, imitating and muttering and schmoozing away.

Me, I picked up my phone to dictate a few texts. I carried my mug into the living room. It was only prudent. I didn't want the two parrots to overhear me discussing homicide. Malik's human wouldn't be happy about that.

I sipped the coffee, and a little sigh of contentment slipped out. Such a perfect drink, rich and fragrant and delicious.

I considered where to begin. Yesterday had been busy and full. How much of it did I need to pass along? I considered the yearbook photograph of the Rainbow Club and Byrne's glare at Uly. Maybe that would be better conveyed with a photo of the photo, which we hadn't thought to snap last night.

I shot off a quick text to Gin, asking her to do that and to send it to both the group and to Lincoln. I thought of one more thing.

And send one of Edwin in the garden club, too, ok?

She sent back a thumbs-up icon.

I tapped out another text to Norland.

Did you tell Lincoln re Byrne wife link w/Yvonne?

Now that I thought about it, I didn't feel like we had much news at all to share with the detective. Everything was still speculative. But I did have one thing to tell Lincoln, something blessedly unconnected to murder.

My parents are having an anniversary party in their backyard Sat PM. Astra specifically requested you. Time TBA. PS - Prepare for dancing.

Next I wrote to the group. I took a minute to consider a good alternative place for our next meeting. Jimmy's Harborside was a big, conventional seafood restaurant here in town with a bar area that was both large and nice. And it wasn't the Rusty Anchor.

Meet tomorrow (Fri) not-happy-hour Jimmy's Harborside bar? Flo, nothing more on Yvonne? Zane, what about Uly? Norland, news on Yvonne?

I sent the text. A millisecond later, my phone dinged with my own message.

Gin wrote right back.

Am in for NHH at 5:30 at Jimmy's. Drinks'll be full price, but apps are half off till 6.

For bars or restaurants to offer discounted drinks at the end of the day was against the law in the Commonwealth. The legislation had been an attempt to reduce drunk driving, but the law was passed well before ride-sharing became a thing. Lawmakers sponsored regular attempts to change the law. So far, a revision had never made it all the way through the legislature and across the governor's desk.

I thought about my own action item, Edwin. I realized I did have one more thing to tell the group, but I didn't really want to communicate it to Lincoln.

Edwin said Byrne used to give him a hard time about

Corwin's incarceration. Threatened to tell the "wrong people." Edwin didn't care and pushed back. I asked what Byrne wanted in exchange for silence. Edwin said he didn't know.

If I also sent that to Lincoln, he might think it was a motive for murder. A flimsy one from way in the past, but still. Edwin did not strike me as a murderer. I'd been fooled before, though.

I added one more text.

Might not be important, but I met Byrne's artist brother Hal in Falmouth yesterday. Said he hadn't seen Bruce for several years. I asked re service. He said nobody would come. Prbly true.

Sipping coffee, I waited a few minutes, but nobody wrote back. Zane and his evasiveness about Uly bugged me. Even if Uly was gay, I couldn't imagine why that would have impeded Zane from asking questions or researching him online. Finding out would have to wait for a time when Zane and I were both free and had a chance to really talk.

In the other room, the birds were talking up a storm. Good for them. I'd have to cut Belle off when it was time for me to go to work. I doubted she'd be happy about that.

"Son of a b****—" Belle said, copying Malik's male voice. "I'd like to shove that mayor's policy up where the sun don't shine."

"Belle," I yelled and hurried into the kitchen. "None of that now."

"I wanted to throttle him," Malik muttered. "Flaming socialist, just like the rest of 'em."

I reached for the tablet. "Goodbye, Malik."

Belle barely had time to say goodbye before I

switched off the app. I was going to have to screen the owner's use of language next time. If there was a next time. Maybe the site included a place to leave reviews of various birds. I'm sure Malik was a very nice African gray, although I wasn't sure about his human. I was even more sure I didn't want Belle picking up bad language or attitudes.

Chapter 32

By nine o'clock, the Open flag in front of Mac's Bikes was flying, or, rather, hanging limply. My spirits were doing the same.

The Cozy Capers seemed to be withholding information. Either that, or nobody was trying particularly hard to gather it. I still hadn't had a sit-down with Tim to find out what was bothering him. My right contact lens was uncomfortable, as if I hadn't cleaned it well. Maybe a speck of dust was in my eye or under the contact. I'd brought my glasses with me in case the irritation didn't resolve itself.

Rumbling thunder and sharp cracks of lightning accompanied by sheets of rain didn't help one bit. I couldn't expect many customers to cross the threshold here today. I stared out the window, trying to blink away the dust or whatever it was. And blinked again at two figures, one medium-tall and one tiny, hurrying in rain jackets and rubber boots through the deluge. They kept right on coming up my walkway until the vision resolved itself into my mom and grandma.

"Good morning." I held the door open for them. "But what are you two doing out in this weather?"

"Mackenzie, it's only water." Mom, dishing my own words back to me, pushed back her slicker hood.

A sharp report sounded outside. Deep, rolling thunder followed.

"Water and lightning," I pointed out. "It's not safe to be outdoors in an active thunderstorm." I stooped to kiss Abo Reba. "It's not safe for either of you, but especially for you, Abo."

"I'll be fine, *querida*." She beamed and shrugged out of her child-sized raincoat in rainbow stripes that matched her slouchy beret. "I've made it through eight decades of New England weather—so far. I'm not scared of it. Now, be a dear and hang this up for me, will you, please?"

I took her jacket and Mom's and hung them on the set of hooks by the door.

"Coffee?" I offered, having brewed a pot as part of my opening checklist.

"Yes, please," Astra said.

Reba nodded as she drew a pad of paper and a pen out of her extremely large bag. I set two full and fragrant mugs on the counter for them and slid onto the stool next to my grandmother. Mom wheeled over our adult tricycle display model and climbed into the seat.

"Mac, honey," Mom began. "I might have information about Bruce that maybe you can use while you're wearing your lady PI hat."

"I'm all ears." Which had perked up nicely with that teaser, along with my mood.

"You see, one day I was looking for a tool or something in the basement of the church. Not the nice part of the basement, where we hold the free dinners and have the free food market, but the real cellar, where the furnace and plumbing and fuse box and that kind of thing are."

She meant the circuit-breaker box, but I didn't correct her. I waited for more.

"Anyway, Bruce was down there moving boxes around. Good heavens, the man looked awful. Sweating and pale and panting. I told him to stop what he was doing right that second."

"Did he have the flu or something?" Reba asked.

"Worse, but not contagious. He and I had a little chat, and it turned out he had a heart condition. He wasn't supposed to be exerting himself physically at all, and here he was chair of the building and grounds committee. I told him quite firmly he would have to stop doing strenuous chores. We would find a younger and healthier churchgoer to head up the effort."

"Excellent advice," Reba said. "I'm surprised Joseph didn't take measures earlier."

"I don't think he knew about Bruce's health," Mom said. "You know how most men don't like to talk about such things with each other."

"How did Byrne take that?" I asked. "Being asked to step back from his volunteer commitment is a big deal for certain people. He'd been in charge, right?" He might not have liked being challenged like that, and by a woman.

"Yes, but actually, he seemed glad to be relieved of the responsibility," Mom replied. "He stayed on in an advisory role for a period of time but stepped down from the committee last winter."

"When did you discover this about his health?" I folded my hands on the counter.

"I think that business happened about two years before," Mom said.

"Now then." Reba cleared her throat. "We're really here for party planning. Astra seems to have forgotten." The words might have sounded harsh, but her tone was kind.

The party. I wanted to sink my head into my hands, but I didn't. I also didn't remind my mom that Derrick and I would have been happy to have organized an anniversary gala for them, given a little more notice. We probably should have jumped on that and let them know, but we hadn't. The actual anniversary wasn't until August third, anyway.

"Okay," I said. "But Mom, why are you having the celebration now and not in a couple of weeks?"

A blush came to her cheeks. "Your father and I are going away for a private celebration, just the two of us, on the actual date."

I was not going to think about what that blush meant. No child wants to think about their parents' intimate lives, not at any age, although I was more than glad mine were still happy enough together— and healthy enough—to have that kind of intimacy in their sixties. Plus, I'd expected her to elaborate on the astrology of this Saturday. She usually mentioned what was influencing what and why it was the best date. I didn't mind the omission.

Reba tapped the pad of paper. "Let's get to it, shall we? You know, before your shop gets busy."

Which was unlikely to happen on a day like today. Fifteen minutes later, we'd hashed through most of the details, except one big one.

"What are you going to do if it's pouring rain like this?" I gestured toward the window.

"It won't be," Mom proclaimed.

I waited for her to say the stars predicted good weather for Saturday. I couldn't imagine how that would be possible, but she frequently ascribed the behaviors of people and larger institutions to the movements of the stars and planets. Not this time, apparently.

"And if it does rain," Mom continued, "we can always set up in the church fellowship hall. It won't be as much fun as outdoors, though."

"By the way, I invited Lincoln for you," I said.

"Excellent, thank you, honey." She stood and bustled off to wash Reba's and her coffee mugs.

A minute later, as if he'd heard us talking about him, Lincoln pushed through the door, sliding his raincoat hood back off his head.

Chapter 33

"Why, if it isn't the man himself." Reba beamed. Lincoln glanced behind him, then at us. "Who, me?" His eyes smiled behind his glasses. "Looks like I'm interrupting a family meeting."

Reba hopped down from the stool. "We're all done. You're coming to the party Saturday?"

Mom returned from the sink, drying her hands on a paper towel. "I hope you say yes, Lincoln."

"I shall do my best, Astra." His smile disappeared. "As you know, though, it depends on my work."

"I understand," my mom said.

He turned to me. "Speaking of that, Mac, do you have a minute?"

"We were about to leave," Reba said.

"Sure." I stayed on my stool.

Reba and Astra said their goodbyes as they re-donned rain jackets and headed out.

"Looks like it's still pouring out there," I murmured as I blinked a few times. My eye had cleared up while I was distracted with talk of the party logistics, a welcome relief.

"It is."

"Do you want to take your jacket off, Lincoln?"

"I suppose I will, if you have time. Could I trouble you for a cup of coffee, please?" He hung his jacket on a hook.

"Sure. I should have offered."

He declined the offer of a stool but seemed grateful for the coffee.

"Before you ask, our group truly doesn't have much to offer," I said.

"I appreciate the initiative you and Gin took to peruse the school's yearbooks. She sent me several photographs this morning."

"Good."

"Is Edwin Germain here?" Lincoln asked.

"No. Not until around noon."

"Good. I will say, he was remarkably tight-lipped with me when I spoke with him." Lincoln took a sip of coffee. "Have you acquired any information about dealings he might have had with the victim?"

"A bit." I was going to have to tell him, after all. I repeated nearly verbatim what I'd texted the group. "Edwin told me that when he was a student, Byrne used to harass him about Corwin's incarceration and threatened to tell the 'wrong people.' "

"Who did Byrne mean by that?"

"Edwin told me he didn't know who these 'wrong people' were," I said. "He said he didn't care who knew and refused to cooperate with Mr. Byrne, but he repeatedly got in trouble for it. I asked him what Byrne wanted in exchange for silence. Edwin said he didn't know that, either. I don't know any more than what he told me."

"Did he say if he and Byrne had had any contact in recent years?"

"He didn't." I gazed at Lincoln. "But they must have. Edwin said he tends bar occasionally at the Rusty Anchor, and apparently Byrne was an evening regular in there."

"Okay."

"And I told you about him seeing Yvonne and Byrne having a heated disagreement Saturday night. I thought I asked him to tell you."

Lincoln didn't react.

"Didn't I?"

"I don't believe so, no," he said.

"And he didn't, either." I swore softly. "I'm really sorry. I meant to pass that along." I smoothed an imaginary speck of dust off the counter.

"Germain told you he witnessed that?"

"Yes, although it was at the other end of the bar, and he didn't hear what it was about. He told me Tuesday, I think, or it might have been yesterday," I said. "Speaking of the pub, have you learned how Carl O'Connor knew Byrne?"

"Did they know each other?"

"I'm not sure. Carl asked me—when I happened to run into him on the street, Lincoln, calm down—how I knew Mr. Byrne. I said I'd had him for freshman English. His expression slipped and he sneered for a second, but then composed himself. So I flipped the question around. He would only say it was a long time ago."

"Interesting," Lincoln said. "Thank you. Now, here's a morsel for you, but please don't say where you got it. Byrne died of cardiac arrest, but it seems to have been brought on by a botanical toxin."

Ooh. "What was the poison?"

"It's called taxine."

"I've never heard of that. But get this. My mom told me minutes before you walked in that Byrne had a heart condition. He had been in charge of the UU building. A couple of years ago, she found him lifting boxes and looking awful. He told her about the condition."

Lincoln bobbed his head. "We're aware of his heart issues, thank you."

I should have known they were on top of Byrne's health. The autopsy would have revealed it. "Where does this taxine come from?" I was pressing my luck, but he could always refuse to tell me. And if he didn't, that was what an internet search was for.

Orlean bustled in, lunch bag in hand. Her hat looked damp, but it wasn't dripping. A half-dozen customers followed her in, bringing the smell of salt air. None of them had a hood up.

"Good morning, Ms. Brown," he said to Orlean.

"Haskins, Mac." She kept on going into the repair area.

"I'd best be off. Talk to you soon, Mac." In a murmur he added, "Look it up."

He swept out of there faster than a wave receding into the ocean.

My fingers itched to look up the toxin. I practiced patience and smiled at my customers instead.

"Welcome to Mac's Bikes," I said. "It looks like the rain might have stopped."

"Yes, ma'am," one man said. "And just in time."

I didn't care if it was for the day or for an hour. If the precipitation going away made a paying cyclist happy, that was all I needed.

Chapter 34

That earlier pause in the rain turned out to be temporary. By ten o'clock, the deluge had returned with a vengeance. But once again, a cool, rainy July day turned out to be surprisingly good for business. I guess people wanted to be ready to get out and bike whenever the sun shone again.

Orlean and I kept busy until eleven thirty, when the shop emptied and stayed empty for so long I stopped keeping track. I perched on a stool and texted the group.

Lincoln says poison is taxine. Mom told me Byrne had heart condition.

Flo sent a message to me privately not more than two minutes later.

You free? Am on my way over.

I told her to come on ahead. Maybe she'd quickly dug up information about the toxin. One could only hope. Or she could have unearthed information about Byrne. Or both.

I headed over to the doorway to the repair area. "How's it going?" I asked Orlean.

She glanced up from the workbench. "Good." She focused on the brake assembly in front of her.

I considered whether to ask her about Edwin and his conflict with Byrne but decided against it. If Corwin had already been in prison, Orlean wouldn't have had much contact with his little brother. And she didn't like being interrupted while she worked.

"Take your lunch any time you want," I said.

A single nod was her reply. I expected no more.

A few minutes later I got a lot more out of Flo. As with the first customers this morning, her hood was back, and her hair was dry.

"Did the rain stop again?" I asked.

"It did, and this time it's forecast to stay away. A pretty stiff offshore breeze is blowing the clouds right out to sea." She perched on the stool next to mine.

"So what do you have?" I reached for a pad of paper and a pen.

"As you know, Bruce was my action item. I dug up a mention of his cardiac condition, but I hadn't gotten around to letting the group know yet."

No, Flo, you hadn't told us. She hadn't told Lincoln, either. I kept my mouth shut.

"The minute you wrote about taxine," she went on, "it didn't take long to learn that ingesting the toxin can affect a person with heart issues a lot faster and a lot worse than someone with a healthy ticker."

"Ooh. That's interesting. So, one question is whether the killer knew about Byrne's condition."

"We won't know until the authorities lock up the bad guy, and maybe not even then," Flo said. "More's the pity."

"My next question is, where is taxine found?" I asked.

"According to what I read, it comes from the American yew plant, or tree, or shrub, whatever the heck it is."

"I'm not sure I know what that looks like."

"It has spiky needles, but it isn't a conifer. All parts are super poisonous except the red covering around the seed, which is called an aril. They kind of look like berries but, again, aren't."

She dragged and tapped her finger on her phone, then laid it on the counter in front of me. "This is a yew."

I peered down at a common-looking shrub. "But that plant is everywhere. Like in front of people's houses and stuff. I think I've seen whole hedges of it."

"Exactly."

"Do you have to, I don't know, process it or anything to get the bad stuff? Boil it down or grind it up?"

"I haven't gotten that far yet," she said.

"Relay all that to the group, okay? And let Lincoln know, too." I rethought that. "No, wait. He's the one who told me about that, uh, substance, and he already knows about the heart stuff." I didn't want to say the name of a murderous toxin out loud with all these people around. "I'm sure he knows where it comes from. And he'll know we're digging, which won't make him happy."

"Gotcha."

"Flo, has Lincoln or Penelope questioned you any more about your conflict with Byrne?"

Her expression darkened. "Detective Johnson came by my house last night. She kept pressing me about where I was that night. I mean, I live alone. What am I supposed to do?"

"Plus, you don't have a key to the pub."

Flo glanced away and swallowed. She rubbed a fold of her sleeve between her fingers in a fast move that broadcast *Nervous*.

"Do you?" I pressed. "Have a key?"

Her shoulders slumped. "While my daughter still lived in town and managed the bookstore, she dated Carl for a while. He gave her a key."

"Uh-oh." A key to the pub right there in Flo's house was bad. Having the key could be the reason she'd seemed evasive and nervous earlier in the week. Who wouldn't be worried in a situation like that? She had both a contentious history with the victim and access to the place his body was found.

"Ya think?" Her mouth twisted as if she'd tasted a bad clam. "It was still hanging on the key rack by the back door to my house. Right where Suzanne left it. I'd forgotten about it until all this business blew in."

Flo's daughter had managed the bookstore in town and lived with her mother. Suzanne had moved away a year or two ago. Maybe that was when Carl left town, too.

"When Detective Johnson came by to question me," Flo continued, "we were in my kitchen. The minute she asked about a key, my eyes went straight to that rack. I couldn't help it."

"That shows that you're not a criminal. Anybody with something to hide would have kept their gaze away from the key as they lied. And you're innocent, so you didn't."

"From her reaction, I'm not sure Johnson agrees with you." She raised a finger. "And before you ask, yes, it is strange that my children had prior connections with both Carl and Sita. But they were in the past. What's done is done." She pressed her lips into a line.

I had my mouth open to ask her about that "other thing" with Byrne when a flurry of customers swept in through the door, bringing salt-scented fresh air with them. Edwin followed, unclipping his bike helmet as he walked.

"I guess my free moment is over," I said.

"I have to get back to the library, anyway."

"Thanks for digging up that info so fast, Flo."

"All in a day's work for the research-loving librarian."

Our group was lucky to have her.

"And don't worry," I added. "Key or no key, you didn't do it."

"But will they believe me?" She trudged out the door.

That was the question, for sure.

Chapter 35

Once Edwin was settled, I excused myself to go out for my own lunch. I'd brought my usual sandwich, but I felt like changing up my routine. The ham and cheese would keep in our mini-fridge until tomorrow.

I pointed myself two doors down the street to the Lobstah Shack. Tulia and I hadn't chatted in a while. Plus, one could never go wrong with her fish chowder and a side of slaw.

As I went, I slowed my pace. Flo with a key to the pub on her home key rack worried me more than I'd let on to her. Obviously, she hadn't killed Byrne. But having access to the Rusty Anchor felt like a game-changer, that and her conflict-ridden past with the victim. Conflict that had been quite public. Which gave us all the more reason to find the real killer, and soon.

Inside the Lobstah Shack, I took my place at the back of the line of hungry diners eager to place their takeout orders. Tulia hadn't adopted online ordering. She'd said if people wanted lunch, they could come in and wait for it. She didn't seem to be hurting for business at all as a consequence.

A young person behind the counter took the orders and money, and bagged the food, but Tulia herself did the sandwich assembly. She ladled out chowder and coleslaw and plated up tuna melts, lobster rolls, and crabcake wraps. All those fabulous smells made me hungrier and hungrier.

By the time I reached the order counter, I was still the last person in line. I smiled at the employee and waved a hello to Tulia, who was putting together an order in the kitchen area at the back.

"Mac, come on back." Tulia called to me and gestured. "I'll make you whatever you want."

"Thanks." I folded up the hinged end of the counter and slid through, closing it after me.

"Give me one second, and I'll be done with this one." She checked the order slip, slipped a pickle spear into a wax paper bag, and added it to a cardboard takeout box. She fastened the box closed and slid it down to the end of the work counter. "Here you go," she said to the helper, then smiled at me. "What can I fix you, Mac?"

"I'd love a chowder sandwich." It was a funny name, because it wasn't soup. But imagine fish chowder with all its flavor and creaminess reduced down to a thick spread like tuna salad, except better, and that was a chowder sandwich. Tulia had invented it, and she'd said it was one of her most popular menu items.

"It's yours." She threw it together in no time, adding a little container of slaw, a bag of Cape Cod potato chips—because, of course—and a pickle to the red-and-white paper boat she used for in-store eating. "Want to sit out back for a minute?"

I glanced at the wall clock. "Sure." Edwin or Orlean would let me know if things got crazy in the shop.

"I'm taking a quick break," Tulia told her employee, then pushed through the back door and held it for me and my box.

"So, what news?" she asked after we'd both sat on the bench in the alley.

It wasn't scenic back here, with the view being the backs of other buildings, and the bench was hard, but it was private.

"For starters," I said, "Byrne was killed with a toxin from the yew shrub, and it was made worse by a heart condition he had."

"Taxine," she murmured, her brow furrowed. "That stuff's wicked bad."

"Apparently." I took a big bite out of my sandwich, which she'd piled into a toasted sub roll. The flavors were, well, to die for. No, they were like heaven invading my mouth. "Sounds like you already knew of taxine."

"My people use it in a particular ceremony, but only a trace."

Her people were the Mashpee Wampanoag tribe, the original—and continuing—residents of this part of Cape Cod.

"So, Lincoln must know about it, too." The state police detective was half Wampanoag.

"I'm sure he does. What else?"

I swallowed my current bite. "Flo came by to see me a little while ago. She doesn't have an alibi, living by herself, but get this. Her daughter used to date Carl. He gave Suzanne a key to the pub, and it's still in Flo's house. She'd forgotten all about it."

"That's no good. She has that history of arguing with Byrne, right?"

"She does." I popped in a bite of the tangiest, sourest, perfectest pickle I'd ever eaten. "What have you learned about Sita?"

Tulia wrinkled her nose. "Unfortunately, not much. She hasn't come in for food again. I did find her on social media, though."

"Good idea." I nodded my approval. "What does she post?"

"She loves putting up pictures, like lots of the kids do, not that she's a kid. Her food photos are actually pretty good."

"How did you think to look online like that?"

"She posted a picture of her Lobstah Shack lunch and tagged my place," Tulia said. "I try to keep up with that stuff. I checked her profile and started liking her posts on a couple of sites. I think she automatically cross-posts."

"You didn't friend her, did you?"

"Not at all, Mac. I never post anything personal except to my family's private group. Normally I only put stuff up on the Shack's business pages. I don't want anybody snooping around in my personal business."

"Especially not a person of interest in a homicide case, right?"

She laughed. "Especially that."

"Does Sita seem to be acting guilty in any way?" I

took another big bite of sandwich, sad that I was almost finished with it.

"I don't know what that would even look like online. She has mentioned feeling nervous because of the murder when she comes to Westham." She gave me a wry look. "But maybe that's because she's afraid she'll be caught."

I had my mouth full, so I gave her a thumb's up instead of exposing a half-chewed bite. Nobody needs to see that.

Chapter 36

On my way back to Mac's Bikes, I crossed the road to Cape King Liquor. Maybe I could find out why Zane had been evasive with me. But the person working the cash register said he was out for the day.

Interesting. His absence could be related to the pending twins. He was usually here, either in the retail section or out back in the distillery. Alternatively, he could have caught a summer cold or be having a bad allergy day.

I moved on. I'd seen Tim so little this week, I wanted to stop by his workplace and give him a hug. The rush in his bakery would be over by now. I passed my store on the other side. No cars graced the parking lot. We did get walk-up and bike-up traffic, but it looked quiet to me. I kept going, crossing at the next side street.

An alley didn't run behind my shop, but it did in the adjacent blocks, and that was the only access to the bakery's back door. I cut through a passageway between buildings. It was narrow and shielded from the sun, so it was cool—and creepy. I shivered, hurrying for the alley itself.

Bad things could happen in alleys. Access to stores and businesses was hidden from the general public. People with bad intentions broke into places to rob them and at times harm the owners. The person who murdered the victim Tulia found in her walk-in cooler last year had come in through the alley, and maybe whoever left Bruce Byrne behind the Rusty Anchor bar did, too. An alley was never a good place to linger, even in full daylight.

I made my way down the alley and pulled open the screen door to the Greta's Great Grains Bakery. Tim had named it for his mom, who had been the first person to teach him to bake bread.

Sure enough, my man was wiping down a counter. His tired face lit up to see me. I said nothing as I wrapped my arms around him and pressed my face into his chest. We stood there for a long moment until Isaac pushed open the swinging door from the front.

"We're clean out of baguettes, correct?" the heavily tattooed dude asked, staying in the doorway. "Oh, sorry, guys." The veteran was Tim's assistant baker but also helped out with sales in the front.

"No worries, man." Tim stepped apart but kept hold of my hand. "Yes, no more baguettes or boules back here."

"Thanks. Hey, Mac." The door *fwapped* shut behind Isaac.

"To what do I owe this immense pleasure?" Tim lifted my hand and kissed the palm with lips more tender than a baby's cheek.

"I was out, and I missed you. Dinner tonight, right? On me."

"I miss you, too, hon, but I wouldn't miss dinner for anything. I shall be your sous chef if you want one."

I smiled up at him. "I might take you up on that." I remembered the party. "Listen to this. Mom stopped by and said she and Pa are having a fortieth-anniversary party day after tomorrow."

"Kind of short notice, no?" he asked.

"Definitely. It's nuts. But do you think you might be able to make their cake?" I hunched my shoulders, hoping I hadn't way overstepped by promising his baking expertise.

"I'd love to. That's not a problem, Mac. Were you worried I would say I couldn't?"

"Kind of. I mean, yes."

He laughed. "It's totally fine, and it'll be my honor. Let me know by tomorrow noontime about how many people will be there. Is there a color theme to the decorations, or should I just make something pretty?"

Whew. "I have no idea about colors or decorations. I'd ask Mom, but she'd probably rope me into a job I'd rather avoid. Just make it pretty. You know, flowers and squiggly lines or whatever."

He laughed at my notion of a pretty cake.

"You know what I mean," I protested. "All that really matters is that it tastes good. Which it will."

"Consider it done."

"Thank you. I'd better leave you to your cleanup and get back to my shop so I can clear out again and make that dinner I promised you."

He blew me a kiss as I let myself out.

Chapter 37

In the alley, I was about to turn left to make my way back toward the bike shop when I spied Yvonne pacing behind the pub. The Rusty Anchor wasn't far from the bakery. I still hadn't heard from Orlean or Edwin about being frantically busy, so I pointed myself in Yvonne's direction.

Almost as soon as I did, she stopped pacing. She stood, arms folded across her chest, facing away from me. I was a few yards away when she spoke.

"Uh-huh. Yeah, well, that's not happening."

She must have a Bluetooth device in her ear, or earbuds I couldn't see. She fell silent, as if listening.

"No! I told you, I don't want to be involved in that."

I didn't like the sound of this conversation. She wasn't using any endearments, so she probably wasn't speaking with her partner at home. I was dying to hear more. Except, at any moment she could turn and see that I was eavesdropping. I backed up a few steps, then scuffed a foot as I headed toward her again.

She whirled, her eyes dark with alarm. White wires trailed from her ears to a phone in her hand.

I smiled and held up a hand in greeting.

Yvonne quickly said, "I'll call you back." She jabbed her finger at the phone. And yanked out the earbuds.

"I was down at the bakery and saw you out here." I thought it was best to jump in quickly with my story. "Thought I'd say hi."

She barked out a laugh. "For a second there, I suspected you were spying on me."

"Not in the least," I lied. "How are you?" I'd love to figure out an excuse to ask her what the call had been about, but I didn't hold out high hopes for her telling me.

"How do you think?" She wrapped her arms around herself. "The police are around here—and my house—at all hours. Carl is getting harder and harder to deal with. And all I can see is that poor dead man's face behind the bar." She didn't look the best I'd ever seen her. Her hair was messy under her toque, and she hadn't applied any makeup. A bare face wasn't unusual for me, but it was for her.

"That's really tough," I murmured. "How is Carl being difficult?"

Yvonne stared at the back wall of the pub for a moment. "He's not usually around. Now that he is, he's trying to micromanage everything. Me, primarily. As if it's my fault we had a body behind the bar."

"That's crazy. It isn't your fault." Unless she'd

been the one to kill Byrne and fake her reaction that morning. "Do you know when he's going back to wherever he lives?"

"North Carolina. No, he hasn't said when he's leaving town. Yesterday wouldn't be too soon, as far as I'm concerned."

"I hear you," I said, although I imagined the police would rather he stuck around until the murderer was identified and apprehended. "Why are the authorities harassing you? You wouldn't have any reason to kill Byrne, right?"

She regarded me. "No, but they might think so."

I waited, not quite holding my breath but hoping she'd continue without me pressing her.

She glanced away, then back at me. "Quite a long time ago, I had a, uh, romantic entanglement with his wife. While they were married. We didn't take the moral high ground, but it happened."

"I imagine our victim wasn't happy about that."

"Bruce was furious at the time, and he's blamed me for her death ever since."

The screen door to the pub swung open, and Uly stuck his head out.

"I had no idea where you'd gone," he said. "It's getting nutso in here."

My presence seemed to register. Was that alarm on his face?

"Hi, Uly," I said.

"Mac, what are you—" he began.

"I'm coming," Yvonne stepped toward the door. "Catch you later, Mac." She almost pushed Uly back inside. The door clicked shut behind her.

Byrne blaming Yvonne for his wife's death was certainly motive for her to get rid of him. For a high school English teacher, he'd become enmeshed in so many people's lives. He'd apparently incited simmering resentment in many of them. But only one had taken it a step further—to homicide.

I turned back toward my shop, trudging with my head down as I considered Byrne's impact on people. I hadn't cared for him as a teacher, but I truly hadn't thought about him in many years. On the other hand, I'd been a teenager, not an adult with a livelihood to lose.

"Oof." I walked into something solid but not rigid and started losing my balance.

"Watch it now," a man growled.

I glanced up to see that I'd collided with Carl O'Connor at the junction of the alley and the walkway between buildings that led to the street. The dark, narrow passage loomed like a menace.

Carl grabbed my wrist. "Are you all right?"

I stepped back, regaining my equilibrium. I pulled my wrist away from him, but he didn't relinquish it.

"Listen, Mac," he began.

Pointing to my wrist, I cleared my throat.

He glanced at my arm as if unaware he was holding on to me. "Sorry." He let go.

"You have a good day, Carl." I took a step around him in the direction of my shop but staying in the alley. I wasn't going down that dark, foreboding tunnel.

"Wait."

When he reached for my wrist again, I folded my arms on my chest and turned to face him, feet slightly apart.

"What?" I asked.

He opened his mouth. And shut it. He glanced down the alley toward the pub's back door. And back at me.

"Never mind. Have a nice day." He headed toward the Rusty Anchor.

Fine with me. Carl was pretty much the last person I wanted to have a cozy alley chat with. Now or ever.

Chapter 38

I made it home by five thirty, to find a note from Tim that he was out on a run. There went his offer to be my sous chef, but that was okay. I wanted to see if I could pull off an entire dinner without help.

Well, except for Belle's. As usual when I arrived home, she set to chattering nonstop, asking for snacks, saying what a good girl she was, all her usual phrases.

I set down her dinner of pelleted parrot food, plus a handful of cut-up vegetables, and stroked her for a while.

"Flaming socialist," she muttered in the man's voice I'd heard coming from Malik. "I'd like to shove it where the sun don't shine."

"Belle," I scolded before she turned to even worse language. "None of that now."

"None of that, Mac. None of that."

All I could do was shake my head and hope if she

didn't keep hearing that kind of language, she'd forget about the brief online visit with her buddy Malik—and what he'd learned from his human.

Now the rice noodles were soaking in boiling water. I sipped from the beer I'd poured and peered at the recipe. I had to make the sauce next. I began pulling open drawers. Where the heck did we keep measuring spoons? And whisks?

Measuring spoons surfaced in the last drawer I tried. I grabbed a couple and began measuring tamarind paste, fish sauce, and chili-garlic sauce. And brown sugar. I'd thought having the pad Thai recipe displayed on my tablet would be a great idea. But once my hands had sauce on them, swiping was messy. I should have printed the directions.

I stirred what I'd assembled with a spoon. It smelled great, but it was too thick. I checked the recipe again. *Aha.* Plus hot water. I was supposed to use a whisk but had not come across a single one, so I added the water and kept stirring with the soup spoon.

Busy hands freed up my brain to consider what I'd learned today. So Byrne had known about Yvonne's affair with his wife. Had the group known that? Had I? My hands now slippery with sauce-y things, I couldn't grab my phone to check the text thread.

Uly hadn't looked happy to see me in the alley with Yvonne. I wasn't sure why, unless he thought I suspected him of killing Byrne. Did I? Maybe. Either way, Yvonne had brought that encounter to a quick close.

One thing I hadn't learned was whom she'd been talking to when I approached her from behind. I also hadn't found out what she'd been discussing. It probably wasn't her partner, unless her phone turned voice into text. Which was possible, but often resulted in super error-ridden messages.

And then I'd had the weird encounter with Carl.

I gave my head a shake. I wasn't going to get this dinner made by woolgathering instead of cooking. What was the next step? I had to shred two cups of cooked chicken. And scramble four eggs. And do something to the scallions.

Man. Cooking was complicated. No wonder I rarely attempted it. When I'd watched a friend's mother prepare pad Thai in Thailand, it had looked simple. Her hands had flown, chopping and assembling and frying. My hands were not flying, and my brain was stymied.

Now I apparently needed a cutting board and a sharp knife, which I eventually located. I managed to cut the ends off the scallions and slice them thinly without adding any bits of fingertip. I was supposed to separate the white parts from the green parts. Okay, that was easy enough. I made two little piles and rewarded myself with another swig of beer.

I pulled the skin off pieces of the rotisserie chicken from last night and shredded the meat onto a plate. A few shreds found their way into my mouth, which was fine, and it wasn't really unhygienic, because the pile would get rewarmed soon. Plus, we had plenty of chicken. When only the last drumstick and wing remained on the carcass, I unearthed a two-cup measuring cup. *Whoa.* I'd shredded, like, twice that much. I guess I could throw it all in. Extra protein, right?

I cracked four eggs into a bowl and mostly succeeded, with only a couple of tiny bits of shell among the eggs. I wished Lincoln could crack the case as easily. The slimy whites made it impossible to fish out the shell fragments. In they stayed. Exactly like all the possible homicide suspects kept staying active in the investigation, because the facts were too slippery. As far as I knew, nobody had ruled out Yvonne, Uly, Carl, Edwin, or Sita. I wouldn't even consider Flo in the mix. I refused to believe she'd killed Byrne.

When my eye itched, I swiped at it with my finger. And cried out as it burned. What had I done? I must have touched the hot sriracha or a drop had splashed onto my hand. I ran to the sink and closed my eye, splashing running water onto it over and over. Straightening, I dabbed the eye with a paper towel.

It still burned, but not as badly. Still, I scrubbed my hands with soap, then hurried into the bathroom off our bedroom to remove my contact lenses. It couldn't be good for a lens to have contact with hot pepper of any kind. This one was going in the trash despite today being only a week into the month the disposable lenses were good for.

Back in the kitchen, bespectacled me tried to re-member where I was. *Aha.* The eggs. I'd broken them into a bowl but hadn't beaten them. Still whisk-less, I used a fork to stir them around and mix them as best I could.

Was all my prep done? Recipe checked once more, I realized I needed to chop the peanuts. I thought we might have a jar of roasted peanuts in the pantry. I found it, shoved aside my piles of scallions on the cutting board, and poured out a handful of peanuts.

Popping a few into my mouth, I leaned against the

counter. And chewed. My brain would not stop chewing on this mess of a case. Would Uly or Edwin really have held on to such a strong hurt from their high school years that either of them would murder the perpetrator years later?

My eyes widened. What if Byrne was not only a strict and unfair teacher but also an abuser of young people, boys in particular? The thought was horrible, but it certainly happened. Had the teacher been in a position to be alone with kids? Maybe he'd taught Sunday school at the church. Or he'd abused the students he'd arranged to intern with Flo. She hadn't been happy with that arrangement. Was there more to the story?

So many questions, and no way to answer them right now. Instead, I retrieved the knife and applied it to the peanuts. Which resulted in peanut bits flying all over the kitchen, plus my swearing out loud. *Oops.* I glanced at Belle, but she seemed to be snoozing on her roost. How was a person supposed to chop peanuts without making a mess?

Gently, perhaps. I swept the ones on the floor into a heap out of the way, then tidied the pile on the board. I thought I'd seen Tim chopping vegetables once with his left fingers carefully holding the flat of the knife's tip end while levering the handle up and down. That worked, mostly. I scooped the chopped nuts into a measuring cup. Not quite enough. I added more, ate more, carefully chopped more. And, as with the chicken, I now had too much. Who doesn't like a few extra peanuts?

I glanced down at a pecking sound. Belle was helping herself to the pile of spilled peanuts on the floor. I let her. We kept the kitchen floor clean enough.

Tim still hadn't returned, so I didn't think I should start cooking yet or it would all be cold. I stuck the chicken carcass back under its foil and stashed it in the fridge, then cleaned up what I could.

I'd settled in with clean hands and phone at the kitchen table when a noise came at the back door. For a brief moment, my heart thudded. Someone could be breaking in. I was positive I'd locked it.

Then the lock clicked. The handle turned. And Tim hobbled in, looking distraught and in pain.

Chapter 39

My caring, talented, beautiful, athletic husband had stepped in a pothole.

"It was dumb, I know," he said. "I wrenched my ankle, but I was able to limp home."

"It wasn't dumb." I got him settled at the table with his foot on a chair and an ice pack wrapped around his ankle. "The town is always behind on repairing the streets, and we both know how roads sprout new potholes after every winter. Also, you could have called me. I would have picked you up anywhere."

"I know, sweetheart." He gave me a wan smile. "I was almost home. It really was stupid of me. I wasn't watching where I was running."

I kissed his forehead. "Do you want water, beer, or a stiffer drink? Brandy?"

"A big glass of water would be great, thanks, and a few ibuprofen. And then maybe a beer."

"You got it." I delivered the water and the bottle of pills that should reduce both the pain and the inflammation. I stroked his hair, which was sweaty. "Would you like a dry shirt?"

"You read my mind, Mac."

I came back with a long-sleeved, cotton T-shirt from the seven-mile Falmouth Road Race he'd run last summer.

He grimaced when he saw the shirt. "I hope I didn't do real damage to my ankle."

"When is this year's race?"

"In a month. I should be fine by then."

He might have to miss the race, but I didn't remind him of that possibility. Instead, I hugged him.

"Yikes, and what about work?" He cast his gaze around as if for a solution. "I can't bake if I can't put weight on this foot."

"Tim." I set my fists on my waist and kept my tone gentle. "Let's assess in a couple of hours. If you have to close the bakery tomorrow or scale back what you offer for a day, worse things have happened, right? Plus, you have employees, and Isaac, your assistant baker. All of them are well-trained in running your business."

"You're right. Of course." He drained the water.

"Ready for that beer?"

"Yes. And is that a jar of peanuts on the counter?"

"Want some?" I poured nuts into a small bowl and also delivered a cool beer carefully decanted into a pint glass.

"Please," he said. "So, it looks like you got your prep done without my help."

"I seem to have. Should I get going on assembling dinner?"

Tim extended his hand. "Come here first." He pulled me onto his lap and wrapped his arms around me.

"I'll hurt your ankle," I protested, despite how good it felt to be in his embrace.

"Am I wincing? Stay here. You're good."

We sat like that without speaking for what seemed like forever.

"Son of a b—" Belle again mimed Malik's male voice.

A rumbling laugh burbled up in Tim. I sat back.

"Where did she get that?" he asked when he caught his breath.

I told him about the parrot-buddies app. "Next time, if there is one, I'll screen who the human is, or see if the birds have references. I can only hope Belle forgets what she picked up if she stops hearing it."

"Good idea."

"Do you know what a group of parrots is called?" I asked.

He shook his head.

"It's a prattle. A prattle of parrots."

"Which is perfect." Tim munched on a few more peanuts as his expression grew more serious. "Mac, honey, there's more about Jamie I need to tell you."

I fetched my own half-consumed beer from the counter and sat again, my hand on his.

He took in a breath, as if girding himself. "Jamie told me she's pregnant again."

Wow. I gave a slow nod as I took in the news. "Is the father in the picture?"

Tim's grim look was my answer.

"When is she due?" I asked.

"Soon, apparently. It's been months, Mac, and she didn't say a word to me, nor to our parents. My feelings swing back and forth between being heartbroken for her and furious she let it happen. Again."

"I can understand that."

"Has she never heard of the pill? I mean . . ." He flipped open his palms in a *what gives?* gesture.

"Her fourth child," I murmured. When we hadn't conceived even one so far.

"Exactly." He gazed at me. "I'm sorry I didn't tell you earlier. It was a lot to get my head—and heart—around."

"Please don't apologize. I knew you'd tell me whatever you were worried about when you were ready."

His stomach growled in response. I laughed as I stood.

"Dinner assembly shall commence." I headed back to the counter and tapped my tablet back to life. "Uh-oh. I was supposed to have drained and rinsed the noodles after ten minutes. Which was a long time ago. Do we have a strainer?"

"A colander, perhaps?" Tim smiled sweetly at my incompetence and pointed to a bowl-shaped thingy full of holes hanging from a hook above my head.

I thanked him. I set the colander in the sink and poured the bowl of noodles and water into it. And stared.

"They're all, like, stuck together. Wait, I'm supposed to rinse them." I ran water over the translucent strands. I jabbed them with a fork. Still glued together. I faced Tim. "What do I do now?"

"Bring me the tablet." He extended his hand. "Rest the colander over the bowl and bring those over, too. And two forks."

I did as he asked.

Belle came to from her postprandial nap. "Hey, handsome. Bring me the tablet. Snacks, Tim?" She finished with a wolf whistle.

"Hey, Belle," he said. "Good girl, but I think it's bedtime for Bonzo."

"What does that mean?" I asked.

He laughed. "It's a reference to a super-old pop-culture film that Ronald Reagan acted in. Bonzo was a chimpanzee they tried to teach human morals to, using nineteen-fifties childrearing practices."

"Got it. Belle, Tim's right," I told her. "And you're my favorite Bonzo."

While Tim investigated how to rescue our dinner, I got Belle in her cage. I drew down her cover even as she muttered, "Bedtime for Bonzo" into her slumber.

Twenty minutes later, we sat down to a delicious pad Thai dinner—served over linguine. After working to separate them, Tim declared the glued-together rice noodles a lost cause. I'd used the entire package, so we pivoted to one of the boxes of pasta we always stocked in the pantry. I pretty much redeemed my reputation with the sauce, and the combo wasn't bad at all.

"I'd say this was a success, Mac," Tim said. "I mean, other than the noodles."

"Cooking is so complicated," I said. "All that stuff to prepare, like, all at once. I don't know how you do it."

He smiled. "There are tricks, sweetheart. And as

with anything, experience is a big help. But I'm proud of you."

"Thank you. No night's a good one to twist your ankle, but if you had to do it, tonight was a perfect time. I actually got dinner on the table, and you didn't have to."

"I appreciate it. Listen, I overhead a conversation this morning. You might be interested to know that Reba and a woman named Sita were chatting in the bakery today, maybe near noon." Tim took another bite.

"Seriously?"

He nodded.

"You and I haven't talked about the case at all, which is fine," I said. "But Sita Spencer is one of the persons of interest in the homicide, at least that's what the Cozy Capers think. Did you hear what she and Abo Reba were talking about?"

"Not all of it. It seemed they had being teachers in common. Maybe Sita had taught at Westham High? I'm not sure."

"Hmm. Thanks. I'll quiz my grandma tomorrow." I forked in one more piece of chicken. "As we both know, she can make friends with anyone in about two minutes flat."

"Every time. It's an art."

"How's the ankle feeling?" I asked. "Let me swap out the ice pack." We always had at least two professional-grade ice packs in the freezer.

He swung his leg down and set his heel on the floor, gingerly rotating his foot. "Still hurts, but it doesn't feel as critical as it did before. You can take this ice pack, but I think I'll hop to the bathroom and get ready for bed. You can bring me a fresh one once I'm ensconced, okay?"

"It's a deal." I removed the pack and bestowed a kiss. "Thanks for rescuing my dinner, *querido.*"

"We're the mutual rescue society."

Chapter 40

After Tim was settled on the bed in PJ pants with a fresh ice pack and his phone, ibuprofen at the ready on the nightstand, I cleaned up the kitchen. I felt stupidly proud of my dinner accomplishment, but I didn't have any plans to keep up the practice. That was what takeout was for.

I fixed an herbal tea, peppermint tonight, and settled myself on the couch with the mystery du jour. Except instead of opening the book, I stared at my thoughts.

Jamie was pregnant again. She was pretty far along, was what Tim had said. I shook my head. Some people got all the fertility mojo. But how in the world was she going to support another child? And was she staying clear of drugs and alcohol until after the birth? Judging from how Tim had described his sister, there was no guarantee of that.

As he'd expressed, one couldn't help but be torn between heartbreak for her and the child and deep anger at her choices and lack of responsibility. Still, Tim and I didn't have any other option. Jamie wasn't my blood relative, but she was Tim's only sibling. She was family. We would stick by her in whatever form that took.

For starters, maybe I'd write her a note. I'd offer my congratulations on the baby and ask what we could do to help. No, better to ask what she needed for the baby—open-ended offers could steamroll in the wrong direction. Either way, it couldn't hurt to pretend everything was fine, at least for now.

I'd heard Tim murmuring on the phone in the bedroom earlier, but all was quiet now. His assistant had been sick yesterday, but Isaac had seemed fine this afternoon. He could cover for Tim tomorrow, if necessary. Tim could drive to work and perch on a stool to shape loaves if he couldn't stand on the ankle. He was in such great physical shape, and I couldn't imagine him not bouncing back with ease from turning his ankle in a pothole.

What I could imagine was getting this homicide case resolved and done with. The worry that a murderer was out there blithely going about their business nagged at me. It had been almost five days since Byrne was killed, and still no one was behind bars for that horrible crime. Whoever did it had to be feeling pretty smug right about now, safe from arrest. But who was it?

I reached for the coffee table and swapped out the book for my tablet. The group thread didn't have anything new. That didn't mean I couldn't sit here and do my own research.

Edwin was my action item, but I thought I'd dug up everything about him that I could. The fact that Pa trusted him meant a lot, too.

Sita was one of the persons of interest I hardly knew anything about her other than her apparent romance with Carl and the fact that she worked at an arboretum in North Carolina. Tulia had probably already run an internet search on Sita. I figured it couldn't hurt to see what I could learn on my end, especially since the name *Sita Spencer* shouldn't have too many duplicates, if any.

I clicked through to the arboretum's website. Where had Gin said it was located? Raleigh, I thought. Sure enough, I found a ten-acre arboretum and botanical garden attached to a university. Sita Spencer was listed as one of the tour staff.

Maybe a travel review site would have more interesting information. I poked around, combining search terms in different ways until I found reviews of the arboretum's tours. Sita had quite a few four- and five-star comments left by visitors who praised her depth of knowledge of the trees and flowering shrubs.

My eyes widened when I clicked on several entries awarding only one or two stars. The first I read said Sita had been rude and condescending to the children in their group. Another wrote that she'd made fun of the North Carolina accent. And the one-star review mentioned her scary fascination with poisonous plants.

I sat back. It was scary, indeed, especially if she'd used that knowledge to murder Bruce Byrne.

Gin had said Carl also worked at the arboretum. I focused on the tablet again but came up empty-handed, at least in connection to the arboretum. Either his job didn't bring him into contact with the visiting public or nobody had anything to say about him—good or bad.

It was a Barnstable County notice that grabbed my attention. Carl O'Connor was listed, among many other property owners, as owing back taxes on the pub. A lot of taxes. Did Yvonne know that?

Chapter 41

After I clicked around further and didn't uncover anything else unusual about either Sita or Carl, I set down the tablet.

Then I remembered that bit of conversation Tim mentioned overhearing between Reba and Sita. Had Reba already been acquainted with her, or had they struck up a conversation in the bakery for the first time?

I knew one good way to answer that question. I tapped Reba's number. It was barely eight thirty, and she usually stayed up until at least nine.

"Mackenzie, darling. I was hoping you'd call."

"And I did. How are you?"

"Well, the planning is going apace."

"'Planning'?"

"Mac." Reba put on her sternest tone. "Saturday?

Astra and Joseph's anniversary celebration? Don't tell me you've already forgotten."

Oops. "Of course not, Abo Ree. I've had other things on my mind, is all." I had a lot of things on my mind. The party was the least of them.

"Your parents and I have much of it under control," she said. "And Derrick sent a message that he and Neli would be happy to take on whatever roles we assign them."

Was I supposed to now chime in about all the tasks I would do but didn't want? I attempted what I hoped would be a deft change of topic.

"So," I began, "Tim told me you and Sita Spencer were having a heart-to-heart at the bakery today. Did you already know her?"

Reba made a *tsk*ing noise. "I know you're changing the subject, my dear. Fear not, I'll circle back. But to answer your question, Sita Spencer's name came up in that teachers' group I mentioned to you the other day."

"Tell me more."

"Let me see. I'm not certain exactly who mentioned her, but they said she'd taught at the high school quite a few years back and hadn't had her contract renewed."

"Did they say why?" I asked.

"No one seemed to know the entire story. Between you and me and the hedgehog, I wondered if it didn't concern that poor man who met his maker earlier this week."

"I'm wondering that, too." Maybe the hedgehog also wondered. "How did you know she was Sita when you saw her today?"

"Honey love, have you ever ordered a coffee to go?"

"Yes, many times," I said.

"Did you have to give your name, and then it was called out when your order was ready?"

I snorted. "Silly me. Got it, and hers is a unique name. What did the two of you talk about, after Sita picked up her order?"

"You know. A little of this, a half dozen of that."

My grandmother, queen of the mixed aphorism. Again, I waited.

"I did have it in mind to telephone you, to be honest," she said. "But what with all this gala planning, it flew right out the top of my head and continued straight on down to Ptown."

I groaned silently. So, the party was a gala now. *Great.*

"Did you learn anything from Sita about why she left the high school?" I asked.

"Only a whiff."

"What does a 'whiff' mean?"

"It appears she had received excellent peer reviews and student evaluations, but the chair of her department—according to Sita—manufactured a reason not to renew her contract."

"Let me guess," I said. "The department chair was Bruce Byrne."

"Yes, indeed. Naturally I brought up the recent homicide."

"As one naturally does." I loved my grandma with a passion, but especially at moments like these. Her casual sleuthing wouldn't rouse anyone's suspicions. "And?"

"And Ms. Spencer did not appear to be a bit heartbroken by the man's death. I do believe I detected a bit of a grimace when his name came up, as if the cream in her coffee had gone off. Or perhaps it was a sneer."

"Was she with a man? A tanned, fit-looking dude?"

"It didn't appear so," Reba said. "Why?"

"She's apparently in a relationship with Carl O'Connor, who owns the Rusty Anchor pub. He had a history with Mr. Byrne I haven't been able to find out about. Yet."

"Leave it to me, Mackenzie."

I could almost hear her rubbing her hands together, eager to get going. And that could be a major problem, despite what I'd thought a minute ago about her presenting an innocent front.

"Abo Ree, don't you dare start poking into this case. There's a real live murderer out there. If anything happened to you, I would curl up and die."

"Hey, you, we'll have none of that, now. Don't worry, I'll be careful. Nobody thinks a tiny old lady is up to anything, much less providing her favorite PI with important intel."

"You might have a point," I admitted. "But please, please, be careful. Promise?"

"Girl Scout's honor."

"By the way, I met Bruce's brother, Hal, a couple of days ago. He paints stunning watercolors. He's having a show this week in the—"

"LeGuin Fine Art Gallery in Falmouth."

"You already knew that?" I asked.

"Sure as shooting. Did a little research of my own. That Malvina's a fine woman, don't you know?"

"She was impressive. Unfortunately, Hal wasn't any help about the homicide except to confirm that they'd had a difficult childhood and that adult Bruce was a man who could alienate almost anyone he met." Which I'd already known.

"I found middle ground with him, but I can make a friend out of almost everyone I meet. Anyway, Mackenzie, we'll talk tomorrow," she said. "Go give a kiss to that fellow of yours."

"I will."

Said fellow was sound asleep with the light on, a lukewarm ice pack on the bedside table. At least he'd gotten himself under the covers before heading into snoozeland. I kissed his cheek, grabbed the ice pack, and switched off the lamp.

I only wished I could switch off my thoughts as easily.

Chapter 42

As we usually did, Gin and I accomplished our pre-walk stretching in front of Salty Taffy's the next morning at about seven o'clock. Her candy store was a popular destination for tourists and locals alike, and it also provided her and her partner, Eli, with an apartment upstairs. You can't beat a thirty-second commute to work. Especially when your workplace is filled with artisanal fudge, every flavor of saltwater taffy, chocolate truffles, and giant spiral lollipops, among other treats.

"The group thread has been so quiet this time around," she said.

"I was thinking the same thing."

"What you added last night about Sita Spencer having taught at the high school has been the only new piece of information. Although it's an interesting one."

"Agreed. You haven't been able to dig up anything about Carl?" I asked.

"No. But didn't you say you'd asked him how he knew Mr. Byrne?"

"I tried. He basically refused to say how, only that he'd known him in the past."

"Have you spoken with Zane at all lately?" I glanced at Gin. "He seems to have gone quiet."

"No. With any luck, he'll be at non–happy hour later."

"Right." I did one last side-to-side stretch. "Shall we?"

"Sure."

We began our brisk pace down Main Street toward the access path that led to the trail. It was one of those perfect summer mornings of cool air full of birdsong and early sunshine. The cloudless sky meant it would be hot later, but that only brought thoughts of a salad with local tomatoes and cucumbers, sweet corn on the cob, grilled chicken, and a frosty gin and tonic.

"Did you see what I wrote about taxine yesterday?" I asked.

"I must have missed that."

"Lincoln said it was the poison in Byrne's system, and Flo found out it comes from the yew plant."

Gin's eyes widened. She grabbed my elbow and made me turn around. We hurried the other way down Westham's main drag.

"Where are you taking me?" I asked.

"One minute. You'll see."

We passed the town hall and library complex on the other side of the street. The two buildings were relatively new but had been constructed in a classic older style, with white trim framing the brick. Wide, grassy areas surrounded the complex on three sides, with trees and paths, so it also served as a town park.

All was quiet at this hour, and the only vehicles moving along bore Massachusetts or Rhode Island license plates. Tourists who drove to town weren't usually up and about this early. If they were, they headed straight for a stroll on the beach or to a birding excursion at the wildlife refuge.

Tim hadn't been next to me when I'd awakened this morning. He'd left me a note that his ankle was mostly all right, and he was driving to work. I'd slept straight through his rising and departure. His bakery was a little farther down the street. If we went by it on wherever Gin's mission took us, I would insist on going in to see how he was doing. If not, I'd stop by on my way to work in a couple of hours.

Gin came to a halt in front of the darkened windows of the Rusty Anchor.

"You know they're closed, right?" I asked.

She pointed at the planters holding the plants that had been recently pruned. "Those are yews."

"Ooh. I get it." I gazed at the branches, which had been lopped off to keep them away from the building and from sprawling onto the sidewalk. "You're thinking the taxine came from right here on the property."

"That's exactly what I'm thinking, Mac."

"All right. So, it could have been a person associated with the pub. But anyone passing by could also have snipped off a few branches."

"On Main Street?" Her voice rose.

"Okay. In the wee hours of darkness. The thing is, Gin, yews grow all over the place. The taxine didn't have to come from these particular plants."

She scrunched up her nose. "You're right. It did seem too easy."

"Thanks for showing me, but I'd like to get back to our walk. Can we do that?"

"Let's go."

We reversed course and soon enough strode along the wide, paved trail frequented by bicyclists and pedestrians in both directions. I thought about the days when this path was the bed of a busy rail line carrying visitors and workers up and down this part of the Cape from Bourne to Woods Hole. I pictured women in long skirts and straw boaters traveling to a cannery job or a position in a hat factory. Men in Irish caps and sackcloth jackets bringing handdug clams to a restaurant in Falmouth or coming home from a long day at a boat-building shop.

I shook myself. That was then, this was now. I thought of hashing over Tim's news about Jamie with Gin but decided to keep that to myself for the time being. I did have one more thing to talk about.

"Gin, I forgot to tell you that my parents are having an anniversary party tomorrow late afternoon and evening. I was supposed to invite you and Eli."

"That sounds like a big deal."

"You'd think so, right? Sorry about the last-minute invite, but get this. I heard about the party exactly yesterday."

"That's hilarious," she said. "Knowing them, it'll be casual. They want to have friends together to have a good time. Am I right?"

"Yes to all of that. Plus dancing. Can you guys make it?"

"I'll check with him, but I'm pretty sure we can."

"Great," I said. "I know how much they like both of you."

We strode along, swinging our arms, getting our heart rates up in air that smelled of salt softened by the sweet fragrance of deep-pink rosa rugosa. Before we got to the cutoff leading to the bluff, usually our halfway point, I suggested reversing direction.

"We're running late today," I added.

"That's fine."

We pivoted and pointed ourselves back toward town.

"I think I have one more lead to check about Carl," Gin said. "This thing is stretching out way too long. I want to stop thinking about murder already."

"You and me both, unless it's in the pages of a book."

Chapter 43

After I arrived home, I zipped through a high-speed shower and got myself ready for the day without dallying.

While I was eating breakfast, I stayed away from another screen playdate for Belle, who blessedly seemed to have forgotten all about both Malik and his bad language. I felt bad about denying her that social outlet, two-dimensional though it was. But it seemed to include too much potential for problems, especially if I left her alone with a device connected to the outside world. We'd already been down that road.

She pottered around the kitchen humming while I took a minute to see if anything new had come in on our group text. Tulia had written.

Sita Spencer has sister who lives locally. Am trying to track down name, address, etc.

Talking to Sita's sister could be useful, as long as they weren't co-murderers.

I also wrote to the group.

Yvonne mentioned her relationship with Byrne's wife when I ran into her in alley behind pub. She'd been having phone convo she hadn't wanted me to hear.

Uly was Zane's action item, but Zane was incommunicado. I'd like to know what was up with the dapper distiller. His being out of touch this way wasn't like him.

In the interim, I wondered if Tim had any information about Uly. They were both local bakers, after all. I'd see if I could find a time to ask my darling husband.

I popped in the last bite of granola, milk, and blueberries and cleaned my bowl and spoon. Coffee could wait until I got to Mac's Bikes. I stopped and listened to Belle. She was now humming an exact imitation of the theme song from NPR's *All Things Considered* evening news program. It was a show often on our kitchen radio while Tim prepared dinner. I supposed I should be glad Belle so far had never picked up car alarms to perform.

I stroked my bird's head. "Tim will be home this afternoon, Belle. You be good, now."

She let out a wolf whistle. "You be good, now. Tim will be home. You be good, now."

I smiled and locked the door behind me, pointing myself toward downtown and my livelihood. Before I reached Mac's Bikes, I made an important stop. I stepped into the fragrant kitchen of the bakery at about eight thirty, since it was directly on my way to work.

Amid swoon-worthy scents of yeasty loaves, crusty sourdough, and sweet pastry, Tim perched on a stool, leaning over the wide stainless counter with a hundred round loaves of bread in front of him. He was wielding a handled razor-blade holder to score the top of the loaves, one after the next.

I waited until he glanced up before speaking so I didn't startle him. Never surprise a man holding a sharp blade.

"How's my favorite baker?" I asked.

"Good morning, darling. I'm trying to stay off the ankle, but it's already much improved from last night. I'll be fine." He extended the hand not holding the lethally sharp blade.

I moved into the one-armed embrace and kissed his head. "Why does that thing make me think of homicide?" A shiver ran through me.

"Only you, Mac, would see a *lahm* and think about how it could be used to do harm." He shook his head, but his expression was a fond one.

"Is that what it's called?"

"It's spelled like *lame* but pronounced *lahm.*"

"Whatever the spelling, I can't help how my brain works," I said. "Listen, I don't want to keep you, but I thought I'd see how you were doing."

"Thanks." He continued slicing across the top of boule after boule. "I'm better simply seeing your lovely face. You were sleeping so soundly this morning, I didn't want to wake you."

"Yes, I completely missed you." I often woke for a good morning kiss when Tim slid out of bed in the early morning darkness. "Hey, Tim?"

"Hey, Mac."

"You know Uly Cabral, right?"

"I've met him, yes."

"Do you know anything about his past?" I asked.

"I don't know much of anything about him, actually. Yes, we're both bakers. I think he mostly bakes cookies and brownies for pub customers who want dessert, and he's a beginner. He inquired about a job here before he began working at the Rusty Anchor. But I needed a well-trained baker, an employee well-versed in both breads and pastries."

"Like Isaac."

"Exactly like Isaac. The United States Navy taught him well, and he had years of baking experience before I hired him, despite his young age." Tim glanced up. "Sorry I can't help, but I really don't know Uly at all."

"I hear you. Well, I'm off to open the bike shop."

"Takeout pizza for dinner tonight?"

"Sure." I remembered the "not happy hour" arrangement. "Except the book group is meeting at the end of the day to hash through what we know about the case. We're going to Jimmy's for not-happy-hour, and we usually end up eating, too. Do you mind if I miss dinner?"

"My dear wife, I am in my mid-thirties and fully capable of ordering a pizza for myself. I only hope the police will make an arrest and take all this off your shoulders."

"You and me both."

"And so you don't worry, Isaac said he'll bake the cake for your parents tonight. That way it'll be cool and ready for me to decorate tomorrow."

"Perfect. Let me know if you need help." I blew him a kiss and slipped out the door.

Chapter 44

I moseyed on toward my shop. I was so relieved Tim hadn't hurt his ankle worse than he had. He knew how to take care of himself, as evidenced by sitting while he worked. And I knew he'd ask for assistance if he needed it, as he had by requesting that Isaac bake the anniversary cake. I hadn't even asked him about flavors. The cake would be heavenly whether it was white with lemon or a super-triple-dark chocolate. Knowing Tim, he probably already knew what Mom and Pa's favorite cake was, or he'd asked my grandma.

Nearing Mac's Bikes, I slowed at the sight of Zane about to unlock his store across the street. Did I have time for one more detour? *Sure.*

I crossed over. "Good morning, Zane."

He jerked, dropping his key, and whirled. "Mac, you startled me."

"Sorry." He was not his usual dapper self. His bow tie was askew, and part of a shirttail hung untucked.

"What's bothering you, my friend?" I kept my tone gentle. "You haven't been around, and it seems like the last time we spoke, you were avoiding my gaze as well as my questions. Is everything okay?"

"Not at all," he whispered. "Almost nothing is okay." He fumbled on the ground for the key, but his hand shook when he tried to insert it into the lock.

"Let me." I held out my palm and waited for the key, then easily opened the door.

He stepped in. "Thanks, Mac. Come in, and please lock the door behind you."

I followed him inside, turning the dead bolt once I was in. He kept going, into the back, so I did, too. I'd only ever been in the retail section. Behind the Employees Only door were shelves and stacks of boxes with labels indicating all kinds of wines and spirits. Cases of beer paraded in rows, and the cool air was scented with hops. A counter against the wall appeared to be dedicated to shipping. Unlike many storerooms, in here the walls were painted a pale yellow, and framed posters from quilt shows decorated bare stretches of wall.

I joined Zane in a small office, where he sank onto a swivel chair at a desk.

"Have a seat." He pressed his hands together between his knees and rocked.

I handed him his bunch of keys, then sat on the other chair. "Is there a problem with the babies, Zane?"

"What?" He stopped his back-and-forth rocking. "No. As far as we know, the pregnancy is healthy. The twins have good weight gain and strong heartbeats."

"That must be a relief."

"Yes, naturally."

I waited, but all he did was rock. "Zane? Please tell me what's going on."

He raised his gaze. "The babies are fine. It's our friend, the mom, where the problem lies."

"Is she sick?" I hoped she wasn't an addict like Jamie.

"No. Leilani is fine," he said. "I mean, it's not her exactly, but you're not going to believe who her sister is."

How long was he going to drag this out? I loved Zane, but I also had a shop to open. I cleared my throat. "Try me."

"Her sister is Sita. Sita Spencer."

Whoa. I sat back. "Did you know that earlier in the week when we met?"

"No." He kneaded his hands as he gazed at me with troubled eyes. "Mac, what if our babies' auntie is a murderer?"

"That would be dreadful." I leaned forward and laid my hand on his knee. "But as long as the mom— what did you say her name was?"

"Leilani."

"What a beautiful name. Anyway, as long as Leilani had nothing to do with the homicide, everything will be fine for her and for the twins. But tell me, did you pick up some new information to make you think Sita was involved in Byrne's death?"

"Maybe." He wrapped his arms around himself.

"What does 'maybe' mean?"

"Yesterday Stephen and I went to Leilani's house to pick her up so we could all go to her midwife appointment together. Sita and Carl were coming out of her house together, and they were arguing. I couldn't help overhearing. When Carl realized I might have heard him, I tell you his glare could have nailed me to the wall. It was terrifying, Mac. Nobody's ever looked at me like that."

"What exactly did he say to her?" I asked.

"As far as I could hear, it was him saying they couldn't leave, that they'd be fine if they stayed, that nobody had anything on them. Sita seemed super worried, though."

"Huh."

"I don't really know why he was glaring at me. We didn't hear any details at all."

I thought the problem was that Carl didn't know how much Zane and Stephen had heard. He might have assumed they'd picked up more than they had.

"We waited until those two left. When Leilani came out of the house, she told me Sita was her older sister."

"She must be much older, if Leilani is of childbearing age."

"She is. I only hope Sita isn't doing anything to upset Leilani. We need her to be calm and happy so the twins don't pick up any bad vibes."

I smiled at him. "Don't worry, Zane. Those little ones are sheltered and cushioned in there. They're going to be fine."

"Thanks for listening, Mac." He sat up straight and relaxed his shoulders. "I feel so much better getting all that off my chest. Stephen thinks I'm fretting for no reason."

"And you probably are. But don't go walking through any dark alleys, okay?"

"Are you kidding me? I wouldn't venture into a dark alley under any conditions."

"Good. And keep your doors locked." I stood. "Now, I have to open my shop, and so do you."

A quick hug later, I was out the door and on the sidewalk. Except now I was the one fretting on Zane's behalf.

My destination was only yards away, across the street. The back of my neck prickled. *Why?* I glanced all around. It definitely felt as if I was being watched. I couldn't see anyone lurking. Tourists strolled past the shops holding covered cups of hot drinks. A cycling club whirred by in matching neon-pink shirts. A big pickup full of lobster traps clunked over a pothole. Was there a person clandestinely peeking around a corner at me?

I squared my shoulders and checked for traffic. As soon as I crossed and put a foot on the curb, I spun around. Nope. I still couldn't see the cause of my goose bumps. I was in somebody's sights, and I didn't like it.

Chapter 45

All the way through my Mac's Bikes opening check-list, my thoughts kept returning to Carl and Sita and the nonspecific conversation Zane had witnessed as they stood on the sister's front stoop. The mention that "nobody had anything on them" was particularly worrisome. It could refer to a lesser crime than murder, I supposed. But if they'd been talking about Bruce Byrne's homicide, it meant the two of them at least knew about it, whether they both had a hand in the actual deed or not.

Should I have urged Zane to tell Lincoln what he heard? Probably. Except that might freak out my friend even more than he already was. Me, I was still a little freaked by feeling I was being watched. I kept moving. Letting a nebulous worry slow me down was no solution.

I headed outside and stood for a moment, savoring this still-perfect summer morning. Westham was coming to life, with the smell of bacon wafting my way. Two Lycra-clad women hurried by toting yoga mats, while a family perched on a bench across the way nibbling pastries out of white bags. A van pulling a trailer full of brightly colored kayaks bumped along the road.

But my brain was distracted from being truly present in the sacred here and now by thoughts of homicide. As I fitted the Open flag's pole into the holder outside the door, it occurred to me that nobody was talking about how Byrne was poisoned, how the taxine had been administered. That is, nobody in the Cozy Capers group. I hoped the authorities already had those logistics figured out.

Did the toxin taste bitter? Many plants did as a protective measure against animals foraging on them. If so, the taxine would have had to be disguised in a sweet cocktail or a substance that was already bitter, like a drink with a heavy dose of bitters or a bitter liqueur.

I thought on. Maybe I was on the wrong track. Byrne had died in a bar, but he might not have ingested the fatal substance in an alcoholic drink. What if, as had occurred to me after seeing the pileated woodpecker, Byrne had been injected with the poison? Or had it been administered to him by another means?

Except the even more important question was, Who lured him into the bar after hours, and how did they manage that without being seen?

If Carl and Sita had been the murderers, they might have invited Byrne for a late drink to talk about old times under the pretense of forgiving him for ruining Sita's teaching career. Yvonne could have invented a story about wanting to finally apologize for her affair with his wife. Uly or Edwin might have made up an excuse about wanting to ask Byrne for career advice.

If I could find the time, maybe I'd pop by Westham Assisted Living and have a chat with Uly's grandfather, Al Cabral. Not to ask, "Do you think your grandson is capable of murder?" but to sound him out and learn more about Uly. That kind of excursion would require me firing up Miss M, though, and right now she was safe and snug in the driveway at home.

I glanced up to see a dark-haired, slender man wheeling a bike toward me. Ah, yes. I ran a bike shop, not a PI agency. I took another look and realized the man with the bike was Uly Cabral. Exactly the dude I wanted to see.

I watered the plants in the window boxes while I waited, then greeted him.

"Hey, Mac." He ran one hand through his thick hair in a frustrated gesture. "My car broke down, so I rode my bike to work. Except it has a wicked low tire. Can I leave it with you for the day?"

I squatted and squeezed the front tire, which was rough under my fingertips. The wheel wasn't only wicked low on air, it was cracked and dry. I stood.

"Sure, but you might need a new tire. That one's in bad shape." I peered at the back wheel. "So's the rear tire."

"But can you fix them today?" he asked.

"We should be able to, but I'll have to check with my mechanic when she gets in."

"Will it cost much?"

"I can't say until we assess the condition," I said. "I'm sure it'll be a lot less than getting your car fixed."

"That's the thing. The car was a junker when I bought it, and I can't afford repairs right now."

The bike was a bit of a junker, too, but I didn't say so.

He pressed his lips together and gave his head a slow shake. "I work so hard at the Anchor, and Yvonne pays me peanuts. I deserve a lot better."

"I thought Carl O'Connor owned the pub."

"He does. But Yvonne makes all the decisions, and he usually just rubber-stamps them. Except for this week, now that he's here in person. Man, he's got his finger in every single pie, no matter how small. It's infuriating."

"You sound unhappy there," I said. "Have you looked for work elsewhere?"

"Like at your husband's bakery, Mac? Brunelle wouldn't hire me, you know. He told me to go get experience under my belt."

"And that's what you're doing, right?"

"Sure. And now I'm working for a murderer, too."

"What do you mean?" Did he have information on Carl?

"I mean I think Yvonne had it in for Mr. Byrne from way back. She's a chef. It would have been easy for her to, like, poison him."

Whoa. I gave a slow nod. That hadn't been the answer I'd expected. And had he mentioned poison as a wild guess? If he hadn't, then something was fishy about him knowing poison had caused Byrne's demise. I didn't think the method of death had been made public.

"Why would she have it in for him?" I asked.

"I'm not quite sure. Stuff from their past."

Perhaps Byrne had been blackmailing Yvonne about her affair with his wife all this time.

"Does the pub have security cameras in the alley or out front, do you know?" I asked.

"Now you sound like the police," Uly said. "No, we don't. Carl's always been too cheap to install them. He said Westham is a safe place. Yeah. It wasn't safe for Mr. Bruce Byrne."

"It wasn't. You must have had him as a teacher at Westham High. Did you like him?"

"Nobody liked him, Mac, and that's a fact. He was unfair, manipulative, and a raging homophobe to boot."

"I hadn't heard that last part."

"You heard it from me, but you can ask anyone who has ever been associated with that school," Uly said. "They'll tell you. I don't happen to be queer myself, but I was in the Rainbow Club at school, as were several gay friends. Mr. Byrne did his best to get the club shut down. When he couldn't, he tried to make our lives miserable."

"He wasn't anybody's idea of a good role model, even when I had him," I agreed. "It's hard to understand why the district kept renewing his contract."

Orlean drove into the shop's parking lot and parked at the far end.

"Here's my mechanic now," I said. "I can ask her about fitting your bike into the schedule."

"Hey, Orlean." Uly raised a hand and smiled at her as she approached.

"Morning, Uly, Mac."

"Looks like you two know each other," I said.

"Yep," Orlean said. "Got a bike for me to make rideable?" She grasped the handlebars.

"Yes, please, if you have time." Uly shoved his hands in his pockets.

"Can do. I have your number." She lifted the front of the bike and wheeled it in on the back tire.

"I'm off to work," Uly said. "Thanks, Mac."

I watched him hurry down the street. I had no idea how he and Orlean were acquainted, but my mechanic of few words was a woman of many surprises. Maybe I should ask her about the homicide. She probably already knew who murdered Byrne.

Chapter 46

The shop got too busy for me to talk about the homicide with Orlean, which was fine. I doubted she'd be comfortable with the topic. Amid the chatter of shoppers and sounds of Orlean clinking tools and running the air compressor, I managed to send my grandma a text asking if she'd unearthed anything yet. She responded immediately.

Not yet, but soon.

I could live with that. I'd have to. Gin said she had one more resource to check out about Carl. So far she hadn't offered anything up. I was sure she was as busy with Salty Taffy's as I was with Mac's Bikes. A gorgeous summer day in July at the start of a weekend promised no less.

Still, even as I sold socks and pumps, helmets and tire-repair kits, shorts and lip gloss, my mind turned things over in the background. Three adults rented bikes. A family asked to extend their rental through Monday, now that the rain was over, but I had to break the news that their bikes were already reserved by another party.

Dealing with rentals reminded me that the party was tomorrow afternoon, and everyone who worked here was invited. When Edwin came in, I'd ask him to contact all the reservations for pickup and the holders of return-due bikes and let them know everything had to happen before 1 p.m. on Saturday. I always recommended using the handy phrase, "Due to circumstances beyond our control." That sounded better than "Gone fishing" or even "Must attend important last-minute party."

"When you get a minute, Mac," Orlean called to me.

I held up a finger and finished the credit-card transaction for two of our branded shirts, then made my way to the doorway of the repair area, which smelled of oil and rubber. "What's up?"

"Uly's tires were worthless. Had a couple lightly used ones I put on. Gave it a light tune, adjusted the brakes. I'm going to pay for this. Want me to write it up and stick the cash in the till?"

I stared, impressed with the number of words she'd strung together all at one time.

"What are you looking at?" Brusque Orlean was back.

"Nothing. You don't have to write it up, but the cash would be great. Thanks for doing that." I crossed my arms and one ankle over the other. "How do you know Uly?"

"Me and his mom are tight. I texted the kid that his bike's ready."

"Where does he live?"

"Has an apartment in North Falmouth." She turned her back and went back to the wheel assembly she'd probably started yesterday and had put aside for Uly's ride.

Orlean might not say much, and when she spoke, it was blunt and unfiltered, but she had a big heart and acted on it. I didn't need a glib, chatty mechanic. The one I had would do fine, and I needed to keep her happy.

By eleven the shop had cleared out, or I thought it had. The quiet didn't last. One more person strolled in. Not a bike customer, but a person in pursuit of justice. That is, Penelope Johnson.

"How can we help you, Penelope? I'm actually glad to see you."

She laughed. "Well, that's a switch. Few people are during an investigation like this one." She approached the counter and glanced right, left, and behind her. "It looks like you're not too busy at the moment. Might I have a few minutes?"

"Yes. Come around and take a load off." I pointed to the other stool.

"This won't take long." She stayed on the other side of the counter. "First, do you have information you might have picked up in your travels about town? You and your group, I mean."

"Possibly." I kept my voice low. "Zane King and his husband are having twins with a woman named Leilani."

"Zane King of the liquor store over there?" She pointed across the street with her chin.

"Yes. He discovered yesterday that their baby mama is Sita Spencer's younger sister." I related what

Zane had told me about overhearing Sita and Carl arguing in front of the house.

Penelope raised a single eyebrow. "Okay. Go on."

"Uly Cabral seems to think Yvonne might be the bad guy. You and Lincoln know about her affair with Byrne's wife, right?"

"Yes."

"Uly himself described Byrne as a homophobe of the worst order," I said. "Or something to that effect."

"Is Cabral gay?"

"He said he isn't but that he's an ally and was part of the Rainbow Club. I thought Gin sent Lincoln a photo of the Westham High yearbook that shows the club, including Uly as a senior, with Mr. Byrne glaring at them." Hadn't she sent it?

"I'll ask him," she said. "What else?"

"Let's see. My grandma happened to have a little chat with Sita Spencer. I'm sure you already know that Sita taught at the high school but didn't get her contract renewed." I waited, but Penelope neither admitted nor denied knowing, so I continued. "Sita told Reba she'd received good evaluations and peer reviews, but Byrne didn't like her, and he was apparently permanent chair."

"That is, czar of the English Department."

It was my turn to laugh. "Yeah. So, do you have anything to share with me?"

She gazed at the corner of the room and lightly drummed her fingers on the counter. Deciding whether to reveal a tidbit or two? Maybe. I could stay quiet as long as she could. It was a skill I'd been working on, and one that came in super handy in conversations about murder.

"I think you know about the taxine," she finally murmured.

"Yes. But I don't know how it was administered. Do you?"

"We're getting close."

"I heard a rumor that Byrne himself might have had a hand in his wife's accident. Do you know anything about that?"

"It's on our radar," she said.

"What about alibis for the time of his death, security-cam footage, all that police-y stuff?"

Penelope's phone buzzed. She reached into her blazer pocket and checked the display.

"Thanks, Mac. Talk to you soon." She turned and strode out the door.

So much for an actual exchange of information. Like the last time we'd had a chat, I hadn't learned one new thing.

Chapter 47

After Edwin had arrived and was settled, and Orlean had taken her lunch, I told the team I was heading out on an errand. This time I made my way to my father's office at the church. He usually had his finger on the pulse of the townspeople, even when they weren't members of his congregation. Maybe he could tell me about Carl's history with Bruce Byrne.

I smiled to see Abo Reba sitting in a cushioned armchair across from Pa. "Looks like I won the double jackpot."

Pa held out his arms for a hug. "Lovely as always to see you, my dear."

"Likewise, Father dear."

After I also greeted my grandma, I sat in the chair next to her upholstered rocker. Reba's feet rested on the small stool Pa kept in his office for her and her extra-short legs, because otherwise they dangled like a child's. He also had a water bowl in the corner for when my brother's dog, Tucker, came to visit. The office was filled with books and framed photographs and souvenirs from around the world, an atmosphere of comfort and welcome, with the air spiced by the chai Pa loved to drink.

"What brings you calling this fine afternoon?" Pa asked.

"Should I leave?" Reba asked.

"Please stay, Abo Ree." I gazed at my wise father. "None of us in the group can seem to dig up information on Carl O'Connor and any past dealings he might have had with Bruce Byrne."

"Why, we were just talking about him, weren't we, Joseph?" Reba said, eyes bright.

"You were?" I asked.

"He did have 'dealings,' as you put it, but it was years ago," Pa began. "Bruce confided in me once about Carl."

Reba nodded with an air of excitement, the chair creaking with her rocking.

"It seems the high school hired Carl mostly to coach," my father went on, "but he was also required to teach several academic courses, as all coaches are. The administration assigned him business English and a health-and-wellness class. He apparently did miserably at both. He made his students equally miserable. Bruce was particularly incensed about the business English class, and said the man deserved to be laid off midyear."

"He wasn't fired?" I asked.

"No, but as good as," Pa said.

"It can be a matter of terminology," Reba piped up. "The union rightly insists a teacher firing may result only after certain egregious behaviors are witnessed and proven."

Which I assumed included things like physical violence, sexual abuse, larceny, or conviction for possessing controlled substances.

"But principals have other ways of easing out faculty who are inadequate to the task," she added.

"Which Carl clearly was," Pa said.

"Do you think he held a deep-seated grudge for all these years and finally took Bruce's life?" I asked.

"I think it's possible." Pa tented his fingers.

"Pa, you need to tell Lincoln."

"He and I have spoken about the matter." His smile was a sad one. "I think Carl O'Connor has been a troubled man for quite a while. But my sympathy and pity cannot stand in the way of justice."

"Never," I murmured.

"Now that we've got that sorted out, shall we talk about the party?" Reba asked.

"No," I said. "Pa doesn't need to hash through any details. This celebration is for him and Mom. All they have to do is show up in casual party clothes and be ready to have a good time. Tim has the cake under control, and Derrick and I can surely—"

"We can what?" my brother asked from the doorway.

"Titi Mac!" Cokey, scooting around him, jumped up and down. "Abo Joe! Bizabo Ree! We're back! We came home!"

The next few minutes passed in a flurry of hugs and kisses and laps and more hugs. Derrick stayed standing.

When my favorite niece ended up on my lap for

the second time, I held on tight, kissing the baby-soft skin of her cheek.

"I missed you so much, sweetie," I said. "Did you have a super-fun vacation?"

"Yeth. Look, Titi Mac. I lost my tooth on daycation, and the tooth fairy flied all the way to our camping place in Vermont!" She stuck her little tongue into the gap in her top teeth.

"Wow. Did you put your tooth under your pillow in the tent?"

She nodded with all the seriousness of an almost-six-year-old. "She bringed me a whole dollar."

"Whoa." I mock-frowned. "Tooth-flation."

"I don't know what that means, Titi Mac. But I'm going to use my dollar money to buy a present for—" Her eyes widened, and she clapped her hand over her mouth. "It's aposta be a surprise."

"I won't tell," I whispered in her ear.

"Did Tucker have fun?" Pa asked.

"Yes." Cokey nodded vigorously. "But he was bad one time, and we had to shut him in the car."

Derrick, now leaning against the doorjamb, said, "He decided to chase a raccoon. It didn't go well."

"Where is the pooch now?" Reba asked.

"He's with Abo Astra," Cokey lisped.

"And your Neli?" Pa asked. "Did you leave her in Vermont?"

Cokey jumped down and put her tiny fists on her hips. "No, silly Abo. She wanted to go home because she's tired."

"Wonder why," Reba murmured.

Derrick opened his mouth. Glanced at me. Shut it.

Huh. What was that about? I rose. "I'd better get back to the shop."

"You don't need me today, right?" Derrick asked.

"No, we're good. Monday, though, okay? So I can let Edwin get back to whatever else he does."

Derrick nodded. "Let's talk later about tomorrow."

"Titi Mac, you can't leave!" Cokey rushed over and wrapped her arms around my knees. "I just got back."

"I know, Cokester. I'm going to see you soon and soon and soon. But right now I have to go sell bikes."

"Okay." She gave me a serious nod, as if she understood serious things like running a business. Then her face split in a grin. "See you soon, spoon."

"See you around, donut," I said.

"In a while, cockodile."

I didn't correct her. "See you later, alligator."

"See you there, square."

"In an hour, flower." I gave a little wave to the room and hurried out.

From behind me, Cokey said, "In a year, dear."

All the energy and all the love were back in town, exactly how I liked it.

Chapter 48

As the outer door closed behind me, I was still smiling at Cokey having returned. The smile slowly slid away as I remembered the still-at-large murderer. The obligations of being a business owner. Tim's strained ankle along with his worries about his sister.

Starting my walk back into a complicated reality, I let out a long breath.

"That doesn't sound good," a man said.

I glanced up. Snowy-haired Al Cabral climbed off a bicycle and wheeled it onto the sidewalk.

"Hi, Al. I didn't see you there." I caught a whiff of his signature Old Spice aftershave, a scent that always made me think of my grandfather.

"I just rode up." He studied my face from under still-dark caterpillar eyebrows. "Are you all right, Mac?" The eyebrows didn't match his white hair, which was thick and all there, combed straight back from his brow.

"I'm fine, but I confess to having a lot on my mind right now." I hadn't seen him since the business last winter. One of the residents in the assisted living facility Al managed had been connected with the murder of the poor skeleton Tim and I had unearthed behind a wall in our cottage, a wall now part of the new downstairs suite.

He stroked his thick, salt-and-pepper mustache. "Is it connected to this week's unsolved homicide?"

"Part of it, yes." *Huh.* Earlier today I'd thought about going to visit Al. Maybe I could take a minute now to accomplish the reason for that visit. "Do you have a minute to chat?"

He gave a look at the church, then gazed at me. "I do. I was on my way to talk with Joseph about a matter. But you're here, and so is a bench. Your father will wait a couple of minutes if I'm late. Shall we?" He gestured to the bench set to the side of the walkway that led to the minister's office.

After he perched at one end of the bench, I joined him at the other. A clutch of teens paraded by on the sidewalk, the girls in makeup and impossibly short shorts flirting with boys in baggy shorts and flip-flops. Three pairs of retirees on big, shiny motorcycles putted past, their machines blessedly well-mufflered.

"I know of your past experiences assisting the authorities, Mac," Al began. "Are you doing so again with this case?"

"Not in so many words. But my friends and I are trying to discover a few things. Several of the people the police seem to be interested in were taught by

the victim, who was a high school teacher. I had him
as a teacher, too." I glanced at Al. He must know Uly
was one of those people of interest.

"I see. You might have heard that my grandson has
been questioned."

"I have." I kept it at that.

"I cannot conceive of that young man hurting anyone," Al said, his voice slow and ponderous. "The authorities do not care for his grandfather's opinion,
however."

"Did you know Bruce Byrne at all?" I couldn't sit
here and quiz a grandfather about his grandson, but
Al had lived in Westham his whole life. He might
have a clue about the dead man.

"A little."

"Did he live in Westham?"

"No. In Falmouth, I believe. But I attend services
here at the UU church, you see, as did Bruce. He was
not the easiest man to be around, however, and I
chose to keep my distance, as I try to do with anyone
who projects negativity. I've long thought Bruce
must have had a difficult upbringing to have become
such an unhappy and faultfinding adult."

"My grandmother said something similar about
his past," I murmured, although her comment had
been about the tragedy of his wife and stepchildren's
accident and death. It was Hal who'd confirmed the
difficult upbringing both brothers had had, and the
opposite ways they'd chosen to deal with its repercus-
sions as they matured.

"Reba Almeida. Now, there's a fine woman." Al
smiled. "Like her son, she always opts for seeing the
best parts of even those who are the hardest to like."

He pushed up to standing. "And speaking of your family, I'd best get in there for my appointment with him."

I rose. "Thank you for taking a minute with me."

"Any time, Mac, especially if you think it'll help find who killed Bruce. I doubt I helped you at all, though."

"You might have. It was good to see you, in any case."

"You take care, now," he said.

"I promise."

Byrne lived in the next town but came to Westham for church services. Why? Falmouth had its own UU church. Certain teachers preferred to keep their personal lives well distant from their students and the students' families. Not Bruce Byrne, apparently.

Or maybe he'd alienated folks in the Falmouth church community so much that he was no longer welcome there, which was an entirely plausible scenario.

Chapter 49

In the short distance from the church back to my shop, I texted Edwin.

Things crazy-busy or quiet?

Pretty quiet.

K. Thx. Am going to stay out another half hour.

I was so hungry I was in danger of snatching an ice-cream cone from the hand of the next child I passed. Ordering a bowl of chowder at the Rusty Anchor would solve at least that problem.

If I also saw or heard anything useful in the pub, so much the better. Plus, it couldn't possibly be dangerous to grab a bite there, even if Carl were on the premises, even if Carl were dangerous. July was the height of the season, and the pub was a bustling establishment with employees and lots of customers. I certainly wouldn't go alone into a dark cellar at a time like this. Lunch among dozens of others should be a safe prospect.

Making my way along the sidewalk was slow going amid the throngs of visitors. I passed a family with a baby and a pink-cheeked, snoozing toddler in a double stroller, a white-haired couple enjoying ice-cream cones, three young women rattling along in Italian, and a half-dozen hip-looking Asian young people, all skinny pants and dyed, spiked hair.

I was surprised at Edwin's report that my shop wasn't busy. Maybe all the biking tourists had gotten their business at my shop done early and were now out enjoying the day.

I pulled open the heavy door to the pub. It was almost two o'clock, and the Friday lunch rush appeared to be in full swing, judging by the clatter of flatware and the buzz of conversation. I told the greeter behind the podium I was there alone for lunch.

"All the tables and booths are taken, I'm afraid," she said, "and we have a wait list, but you can grab a seat at the bar if you want. You can order from the full menu there, too."

"Perfect." I thanked her and climbed onto a stool at the end of the bar. I scrolled through my phone until the bartender, a woman I didn't know, laid a cocktail napkin down in front of me. High tourist season also brought plenty of seasonal hires. I wasn't surprised I hadn't seen her before.

Her name tag read Delia. She looked a bit older than I was, with a cap of dark hair cut so it stayed off her face and out of her eyes, and she was lean and wiry like me.

"What can I get you today?" she asked.

"I'd love a cup of chowder, please, with a side of coleslaw."

"You got it. Anything to drink?"

It was almost the end of the day, and I was on foot. A glass of chardonnay would be so nice. But I still had to close the shop, and I'd be meeting the Cozy Capers at the bar in a couple of hours. Better to abstain for the time being.

"I'll have seltzer with lime, please."

"Coming right up."

"I'm Mac Almeida, Delia. I own the bike shop down the road."

"You're Mac, are you?" She cocked her black-aproned hip and set her hand on it. "People have been talking about you."

Ugh. "Um, good talk or bad talk?"

Her laugh was an infectious warble. "Mostly good." She scanned the room until her gaze settled on a booth near the door to the kitchen. "And part possibly not so good."

I glanced in that direction. Carl sat alone, a half-empty pint beer glass on the table, with papers spread out around it. He did not look happy.

"I'm not surprised," I said.

"Vonnie didn't bad-mouth you, you know," Delia said, "But your name did come up."

"Vonnie? Wait, do you mean Yvonne?"

"The same. She and I were college roommates. I changed my last name when I married—not a smart move, as it turned out—and she didn't even know it was me applying to be a drink slinger here."

"Where did you go to college?" I asked.

"School of Hard Knocks?" She laughed again. "I'm kidding. UMass Dartmouth. Hey, let me get your drink and your lunch."

The flagship campus of UMass, the state university, was out west in Amherst. Boston's campus was mostly attended by commuters. Former mill city Lowell to the north hosted a campus, and Dartmouth, not far from the Cape, was the fourth undergrad location. And where, according to Delia, she and Yvonne had met and become friends.

Maybe I could figure out a way to gently question the bartender about Yvonne's potential for murderous acts. Or not. Delia seemed happy to be reconnected to her old friend.

She returned to set a glass full of bubbles with a lime wedge perched on the rim, plus a silverware roll in front of me without fanfare and turned away before I could thank her. I studied Carl from across the room for a moment, but glanced at my phone when I sensed he was about to look up and see who was so rudely staring.

Should I go speak with him? Maybe it was better if I pretended I hadn't seen him. He looked busy with accounts and whatever else those papers represented. And I needed to be getting back to the shop as soon as I'd eaten.

The immediate question was solved by Delia setting down a brimming cup of the best chowder on the Cape in front of me, plus a little dish of the tangy cabbage salad. I inhaled the delicious fragrances as Delia drew several oyster cracker packets out of her apron pocket and pushed them across the counter.

"Enjoy."

"Thanks. I will." I found my spoon and dug into the warm, creamy, seafood-laden stew, glad the cup rested on a small plate, it was that full. Several swoons later, I came up for air and a sip of seltzer.

To find Carl O'Connor at my side.

Chapter 50

Where had Carl come from? No, I knew that. The real question was how he'd snuck up so quietly without me noticing.

"Mac, isn't it?" He set his elbow on the bar, a bit too close for comfort. "Enjoying the chowder?"

I leaned away. "Delicious."

"You have quite the reputation for being a private investigator around here. How's it going? Are you getting close to ID-ing the killer?"

"You were given the wrong information, Carl. I own a bike shop. Like all the other business owners in town, I want to see this homicide solved and done for. Don't you?"

"Naturally."

Up close like this, the lines in his face were more obvious, as was a little patch of facial hair on his cheekbone he'd missed shaving. His hair, rather than appearing stylishly gelled, was nothing more than greasy. His breath smelled of stale beer. *Ick.*

"Good. Anyway, figuring out a murder is the responsibility of the police, not me," I added.

"Still, the police don't seem to be doing much, do they?" He leaned even closer into my space.

"Hmm." I scooted my stool back a skosh. "I'm not sure. I wonder if the authorities are looking for a person who had connections with Byrne through the high school."

He shifted his gaze away. His jaw tensed.

"It happened before my time, but I heard he might have laid off your girlfriend from her teaching position at Westham High School," I said. "Sita, right?"

He relaxed his shoulders. "Where did you hear that?"

"What, that your girlfriend's name is Sita Spencer? She told me herself, when she bought your birthday present. Oops." I covered my mouth. "Did I spoil the surprise?"

"No. I meant where you heard Bruce was involved in canning Sita."

I shrugged. "Can't remember." I sipped my drink. "Does she teach at a different school now?"

"After a fashion. She leads tours at an arboretum and gives workshops on plants native to the region."

"Sounds interesting. South Carolina, I think she said, right?" I savored another bite of chowder.

"North Carolina. Raleigh."

"You must have a whole different set of plants down there. What do you do for work, Carl? I mean, other than owning a pub."

He glanced away. "I'm also employed at the arboretum in Raleigh." He lifted his chin. "And I own several investment properties up here."

He sounded defensive about the arboretum job. Maybe he did maintenance or worked as a gardener. Nothing wrong with that, unless it conflicted with his image. Did I dare push him for more about his own connection with the victim? Probably unwise. It hadn't gone well the first time. But . . . what the heck? The days without a resolution to the case were piling up. "Educating kids can be a hard profession. I don't blame Sita for changing her focus. Did you ever do any teaching?"

"What's this, twenty questions?" The pseudo-friendly expression slipped off his face, including the smarmy smile. "If you're looking for the killer, you might want to look closer to home. I heard one of your employees had a pretty big beef with poor, dead Bruce Byrne."

"What do you mean?" I asked. He had to be talking about Edwin. What did Carl know about him? "Which employee of mine are you referring to?"

He crossed his arms and shook his head, smirking. "I'm sure you know exactly who I mean."

Delia slid down the bar. "Hey, no harassing the customers, boss." She kept her tone light.

I smiled at her and inwardly thanked her for her sense that this conversation needed a bit of intervention.

"Wouldn't dream of it," he said. "Enjoy your lunch, Mac." He strutted back toward his booth but veered into the kitchen before he got there.

To harass Yvonne instead of me, I expected.

Delia frowned. "I've been enjoying working here.

But if Carl's going to stick around, I might have to look elsewhere. That man has major problems."

"Seems like it."

"I mean," she lowered her voice, "he's a personal slob, for one thing. For another, he thinks he's God's gift to the ladies. Which he's totally not. And he's been trying to tell all of us, but especially Vonnie, how to do our jobs. For starters, the dude has zero idea about the art of bartending or keeping the customers happy. And cooking? Forget about it."

"Yvonne mentioned the micromanagement to me yesterday. Carl must be pretty insecure."

"Ya think?"

"Or maybe the finances aren't working out for him," I added. It was possible, based on that notice I'd seen about him owing back taxes on the pub property.

"So far we're still getting paid on time, but that's due to Vonnie's management more than anything he's doing." Without looking in that direction, she made a vague gesture toward Carl's booth. "Or not doing. Look at that, for example. During our busiest lunch service of the week, he sits alone occupying our biggest booth. Doesn't make sense, money-wise, plus he's robbing the waitstaff of hefty tips."

"I hear you." I doubted he cared about the tips, if he was even aware of the consequences of his actions.

Delia rolled her eyes. "I wish Carl O'Connor would simply go home and leave us to our jobs, which we know way better than him how to do."

A man at the other end of the bar raised an index finger and caught Delia's eye.

She let out a sigh. "Can I get you anything else, Mac?"

"Only the check, thanks."

"Be back in a flash with that."

She drew the man a second draft beer, then tapped into a screen for a moment. She laid the slip of paper face-down in front of me.

"It was so nice to meet you, Delia." I glanced at the check and laid a twenty and a five on the bar. "I don't need change."

"Thanks, hon. Good to meet you, as well."

"Can I ask you one quick question?"

"Hit me." She slipped the cash into her apron pocket.

"Please don't take offense," I began. She might not be so enthusiastic once she heard my question, but I had to ask. "Do you think Yvonne is capable of murder?"

She opened her mouth. Closed it. Blinked. Then spoke in a murmur. "No offense taken. The answer is absolutely, definitively no. I do not think Yvonne Flora would ever kill anyone, for any reason. Is that answer unambiguous enough for you?"

"Yes. I appreciate it."

"Mind you, she can have a temper on her. But that's all it ever is. Strong feelings that don't get expressed in any way except words."

"Duly noted." I stood. "Thanks, Delia."

"Hey." She slid a business card out of her back pocket and handed it to me. "If Vonnie needs a character reference or anything, please contact me, okay?"

"Thank you." I slipped the card into my own back pocket. "And you can always find me at Mac's Bikes."

"Come back soon."

"I promise." I was beyond relieved she hadn't gotten her back up about my inquiry. She also hadn't become defensive about her friend.

"Take care, Mac." She loaded up my dishes in one arm and swiped at the counter with the cloth in her other hand.

I would take care. No question.

Chapter 51

I drained my glass and hurried back to Mac's Bikes, again dodging the tourists as I went. At least now no children were in danger of having their cones stolen. The sidewalk seemed even more crowded than before, as were the thoughts in my busy brain.

I'd learned a bit more about Carl O'Connor from him, and from the delightful Delia. But he'd still refused to talk about being a teacher. Maybe he'd done so poorly at the high school because he'd been recently credentialed and unsure of his preparation in the classroom. Perhaps his smarmy behavior was overcompensation for poor social skills.

I was well aware I was channeling Pa with those thoughts. My father was the King of Kindness. He always offered the benefit of the doubt before moving on to any less-favorable criticism. In Carl's case, I was inclined to skip straight to judgment.

In the bike shop, business seemed to have picked up since I texted with Edwin. The place was packed. It hummed with conversation punctuated by the clink of tools in Orlean's lair.

I quickly stashed my bag and used the restroom, then waded in. At the retail counter, Edwin rather frantically rang up purchases while asking rental customers to please be patient.

I slid in next to him. "Want me here or with rental?" I asked in a near-whisper. I was the boss and owner, but he was the one who'd been managing the hordes for the last hour.

"Can you handle rentals?"

"Happy to." I headed toward the back. "Rental people, come with me, please."

Those eager to return, pick up, or inquire about rental bikes followed me like I was the Pied Piper of Westham. Not that I could play a pipe or any other musical instrument other than a kazoo, which didn't count.

A few parties asked to reserve rentals beginning tomorrow.

"That's fine, but we'll be closing at one o'clock for the day." I didn't need to give a reason. "You'll have to pick up your bikes before then. If you can't, we're always open on Sunday."

An hour later I glanced at the wall clock, which now read nearly four o'clock. Edwin was helping one last customer with their purchase. I'd dealt with the crowd of rental people. I drifted over to the repair area.

"Finishing up?" I asked Orlean.

"Yep."

"Thank you. I won't be in tomorrow, but I'd like you and Edwin to close at one o'clock, okay?"

She bobbed her head without looking up.

"You both need time to clear out and relax before my parents' party gets underway," I added.

"Got it." Now she gazed at me. "You okay, Mac?"

"Yes. Do I not seem okay?"

"You look fine. Just thought, with this homicide business, that mind of yours might be working at double time." She smiled.

It wasn't a broad beam, but for Orlean, it was a smile that connected us.

"Thank you." I smiled back. "I do confess to an over-busy brain this week."

She still looked at me. She hadn't dismissed our conversation and refocused on the bike at hand as she normally would. Something was up.

"I'm guessing you might have a piece of information for me," I murmured. "Yes?"

"Could be." She wiped her hands on a red grease rag, then returned it to the back pocket of her sturdy blue work pants. She spoke in a low tone. "Grapevine told me certain folks are putting it out that he's the guilty party." She gestured with her chin toward Edwin's back.

"Who's in your grapevine?" I kept my voice equally as soft.

"Doesn't matter. What does matter is this. That young man would never in any universe harm another being. He may be my ex-brother-in-law, but I know him pretty well. Can't possibly be the perp."

"Thank you. That helps." I smiled to myself at the term. "For the record, I agree. But for the investigation, did he happen to be with you Sunday night?"

She gave a definitive nod. "Yes. He's been renting a room from me, now that my sister cleared out. I don't sleep that good. I'm a hundred percent positive he never left the house. Not by car, not on foot, not by bike."

"Did you tell Lincoln or Penelope that?" I asked.

"Did they ask me? They did not."

"Orlean, if I pass along what you said, are you willing to confirm to Lincoln what you told me?"

"Obviously. I got nothing to hide. And if it takes that young man off their list, even better."

Whew. "Thanks."

The last customer slipped out the door, and I raised my voice to include Edwin. "Let's close and get out of here promptly at five today. That okay with both of you?"

Orlean gave me a look as if I wore a hat labeled Crazy Lady. "Who doesn't want to clear out a little early on a Friday night?"

Edwin laughed. "What she said."

"Sounds like a plan. Edwin, were you able to get in touch with the rentals due to be returned or picked up tomorrow?"

"All set."

"Thank you," I said. "I appreciate it."

"Had to send an email for a few who gave a landline instead of a cell number. I mean, who even has a landline these days?"

"Right? Plus, they're on vacation, so they're not even reachable that way." I stepped out into the sunny parking lot and pressed Lincoln's number. His cell number.

"Haskins." His tone was abrupt. "What's up, Mac?"

"I'll be brief. I'm sure you're busy. Orlean told me

Edwin Germain rents a room from her. She says she can attest to him not leaving the house by any means Sunday night. Thought you should know."

"Interesting. Thank you."

"She said the police never asked her about him. Didn't he tell you all that was where he's living?"

"It's been a full and difficult week, Mac. That's all I can say. Do you have anything else for me?"

"Maybe. I was having lunch at the Rusty Anchor a couple of hours ago. Carl O'Connor approached and leaned way into my personal space. I couldn't figure out if he was threatening me or trying to hit on me. Anyway, he said I should be looking at one of my employees for the murder. I assumed he meant Edwin."

Lincoln gave a low laugh. "What, you don't think Orlean is capable of committing homicide?"

"Actually, that would be correct. Like, no way." I remembered what Pa told me about Carl. "My father said he spoke with you about Carl's past and his association with Byrne."

"Correct."

"Good." I said I didn't have anything else to share. "But the group is going to not-happy-hour at Jimmy's Harborside at five thirty today. You're welcome to join us."

"Thank you. Don't hold your breath." He disconnected.

He might not be able to stop by and be happy with the group and me, but he knew where to find me if he needed to.

Chapter 52

The Friday afternoon bar scene at Jimmy's was rowdy and noisy today, but Norland had arrived early and snagged us a high-top table for six in the quietest corner. Because I'd walked over to the restaurant, I ordered a gin and tonic to indulge myself and celebrate summer. The windows of the bar area were open to the sea breezes, so the smells of grape, hops, and cocktails mingled with salty air in the best of ways.

By five forty-five, all the Cozy Capers were gathered around the table except Zane. Flo had a glass of chardonnay lined up next to her yellow legal pad and pen. Gin joined me in a G-and-T. Tulia sipped a ginger ale, while Norland nursed his pilsner.

Flo tapped pen on pad. "Where's Zane?"

Gin glanced up from her phone. "He says he's on his way."

The waitperson stopped by and asked about appetizers. "Special Friday half price ends at six, so you know." Discounted munchies were part of the not-happy-hour tradition.

"How about an order of the fried calamari for the table?" I asked, surveying the group. Jimmy's never-rubbery calamari were always crisp and sweet with a hint of lime, and the thin slices of jalapeño deep-fried along with the squid added a perfect touch of spicy.

Flo nodded.

"Yum," Gin said.

"Let's make that a double order of the calamari," Norland said, "And a plate of the stuffed mushrooms, please."

Tulia looked up from the appetizer menu on the table. "Plus an order of the eggplant crostini."

"That it?" the server asked.

"And six skewers of chicken satay with peanut sauce," I added. Anything Thai presented an irresistible lure for me.

"You got it." The server bustled away.

In her place appeared Zane, breathless and with furrowed brow. He slid into the only open seat, which was between Norland and me.

"Everything okay?" Flo asked him.

"I guess."

"Is it the business with Leilani's sister?" I asked.

"Yes," he said. "On our way back from the midwife, Leilani confessed she'd never been close to Sita and wished her sister hadn't come back to town."

"That's heavy," Tulia said.

It was. I couldn't imagine not wanting a sibling of mine to return to where we'd grown up.

The server set down the satay skewers and a plate of stuffed mushrooms that smelled so good my stomach growled out loud. Each was mounded with a delicious-looking filling of crab and sun-dried tomatoes, topped with bread crumbs and browned cheese. The waitperson took Zane's order for an Oregon pinot noir and left.

"Who's Leilani?" Gin asked.

At the same time, Flo said, "Sita Spencer has a sister?"

Right. Neither Zane nor I had shared with the group what he'd told me this morning. I pointed at him. It was his story to tell.

He explained about the mother who was bearing their twins, and how Sita and Carl had shown up at Leilani's house yesterday not long before he and Stephen had. "The two of them were on her front porch arguing. We stayed back and well away until they left before we approached the door."

The server brought the rest of our appetizers. I munched and savored a perfectly battered and fried calamari, dipping it in the plum tomato aioli. I chased it with a crostini. The eggplant topping had been roasted and whirred into a kind of baba ghanoush spread featuring plenty of olive oil, a bit of lemon, and a hint of roasted garlic. It tasted like heaven.

So did my sweet-and-bitter fizzy drink, with the wedge of lime adding the perfect flair. At least until I thought about the bitter tonic water. Had a G-and-T been the smoke screen for Byrne's dose of taxine? A little shudder ran through me.

Flo swallowed her bite of mushroom. "What else do we have?"

"I looked into taxine a bit more," Tulia offered. "You all know Sita works at an arboretum in North Carolina. An arboretum by definition grows and nurtures a wide variety of shrubs and trees. I happened to make a call down there, and they have a healthy specimen of the most toxic cultivar of yew."

Norland smiled at her. "I like that you 'happened' to call them. That's the definition of safe investigating."

"Or not. Did you use your real name?" I asked, suddenly worried. "What if Sita checks in, or they tell her a person named Tulia happened to call? You have as unique a name as she does, after all."

"Mac," Tulia scolded. "Of course I didn't use my English name. I considered giving my Wampanoag name, but that's unique to me, too. Instead I said I was Professor T. Alexander, a botanical substances consultant with the FBI."

Zane nearly snorted his wine, and his expression lightened for the first time since he'd arrived.

"They totally bought it." Tulia grinned.

"I did a little poking around last night, too," I offered. "I found a few highly negative review comments about Sita in her role as a tour guide. One said they were alarmed by how much she seemed to know about poisonous plants."

"I can understand that." Tulia glanced around the group. "Guess who does the pruning in the sector where that particular yew grows?"

No one ventured a guess, although I had my suspicions.

"Carl, that's who." Tulia's smile was grim. "Whether Sita was in on the deal or not, I'd say the information could be useful to the detectives."

"Have you told them yet?" Norland asked.

"Too busy, and now I'm here," she said. "I will soon."

"Good." Norland nodded his approval.

Flo made a note on her yellow pad.

Carl doing physical work for his pay didn't comport with what I'd seen of him. But maybe that was the only work he could find down there. Sita could have pulled strings to help him land the job.

"I can also share info about Carl," Gin volunteered. "Him being my action item and all."

I opened my mouth, remembering that I hadn't communicated what Pa had told me about Carl and Byrne at the high school. I shut it again. Maybe Gin had discovered the same info.

"I found Carl's name in the school faculty records," she began. "And I dug up the principal from those years, whom I spoke with only an hour ago, a Mr. Benvenuto." Gin related the same story Pa had told me. Carl had been hired to coach and to teach business English and a health class. He'd received rotten reviews and evaluations, and they laid him off midyear. Gin continued. "He apparently brought suit, but the school district was within their rights."

"And he's hated Byrne ever since," Norland observed.

"That's about the size of it," Gin agreed.

I had nothing to add about that . . .or did I? "My father found out the same information. He told me a couple of hours ago. I asked if Lincoln knew, and Pa said he did."

"Good," Gin said. "I was wondering if I should tell him or Penelope. Or both."

"Does anyone know if Carl and Sita overlapped at the school?" Norland asked.

"I don't," I said.

"Maybe they met there," Gin said.

"Or not," Tilia offered, "but if they met in North Carolina, they could have bonded over their dislike of Byrne."

"I learned a bit about Edwin that's important," I began.

Before I could go on, my grandma bustled up to the table. Her expression as animated as ever, she nearly vibrated with excitement.

"Abo Reba, what are you doing here?" I asked, astonished. I didn't think she was the happy hour type, at least not in recent years.

"Mrs. Almeida, won't you join us?" Norland slid off his stool.

She held her hand to the side of her mouth. "I've been tailing them," she said in a raspy whisper. She pointed at her hand in that thing people do when they want to hide the gesture from whomever they're pointing at. "Don't turn around, Mac."

It was all I could do not to swivel and stare. Instead, I gazed at Flo across the table, who was facing the direction in question.

"The couple we've been discussing have taken a table for two," Flo murmured. "The ones visiting from North Carolina, that is."

Reba nodded her head, fast. "Isn't that handsome detective with you? I thought surely he would be. He could apprehend them on the spot. I'm sure he's never without a couple pair of handcuffs."

I stared at her. "What do you know that we don't?"

"Well, aren't they the prime suspects?" Reba dropped her hand and gazed at each of us in turn.

I blew out a breath. "Maybe. But that's for the police to act on. To tail, as you put it. Not us." And specifically, not her.

Lincoln materialized at the table as quietly as my grandma had. "What's this about prime suspects?"

Chapter 53

"Hello, young man." Reba beamed up at Lincoln. Way up.

Lincoln smiled back, but only briefly. "Mrs. Almeida, I'm going to have to ask you to leave surveillance to the professionals."

Her smile faltered. But only for a second. "Why, all I was doing was moseying along the sidewalk. I heard my grandgirl was going to be here with her friends, and I thought it would be fun to stop by and join these young people in an adult libation."

"Yes, ma'am, and that part is fine," Lincoln said. "What is neither fine nor safe is you keeping within listening distance of two persons of interest in a case of homicide. An as-yet-unsolved case, I might point out. You paused when they paused, and you moved when they moved." He turned his focus on me. "I hope you didn't encourage your grandmother's participation in this, Mac."

"Absolutely not. In fact"—I shifted my own gaze to Reba, who wore her most angelic *Who, me?* face—"*in fact*, I asked her directly *not* to do anything that wasn't strictly online or by word of mouth. Didn't I, Abo Ree?"

"Where can a girl get a drink around here?" she asked, ignoring both of us, then headed to the bar.

"Haskins, do you think they know she followed them?" Norland tossed his head, signaling behind him.

"I don't believe so," Lincoln said. "I was actually surveilling them from my vehicle. But under no circumstance does Mrs. Almeida walk home alone. You all understand that?"

Every one of us nodded.

"You either, Mac," he said. "None of you, in fact, not until we have an arrest. Now, quickly before she gets back, do you have any news for me?"

"We were talking about Edwin before Reba showed up." Flo pointed her pen at me. "He was Mac's action item."

"Right," I confirmed. "He's renting a room from Orlean. She said she'll swear he didn't leave the house Sunday night or early morning. I already told Lincoln."

Flo jotted that down. "Alibi sounds watertight."

"Zane, have you found anything on Uly?" Flo asked.

"I'm sorry." He shook his head. "This week has been all baby stuff, all the time."

I doubted that situation would change anytime

soon for him. Would I be in his shoes in the near future? Knowing full well how I could obsess over details and how desperately I needed my life to be well organized, I could imagine barely being able to run my business and being pregnant at the same time, to say nothing of acting the role of an amateur sleuth.

"Don't worry about it." I only hoped I would remember not to worry if—no, when—the time came. "Uly brought his bike to the shop this morning. I took the opportunity to have a little chat with him."

Gin grinned. "As we do."

"Indeed. He seems to think Yvonne is the guilty party we should be focusing on."

"Why?" Lincoln asked.

"He didn't specify," I said. "Something from their way past. Maybe the thing with Byrne's wife?"

Lincoln bobbed his head without actually agreeing to anything.

"Uly also said that Carl is micromanaging all the staff in the Rusty Anchor this week," I said. "That includes Yvonne, who normally runs the place. Nobody who works there likes it. And Uly mentioned how much Byrne disliked LGBTQ people, and that he tried to get the high school Rainbow Club disbanded."

Gin nodded. "My daughter told me about that a bit, too."

"Orlean is apparently close to Uly's mom," I said, "but I don't know if he has an alibi. She did say he lives in North Falmouth." I spotted my grandma chatting up the bartender. "Tulia, tell Lincoln what you learned from the arboretum."

She repeated her information about the taxine

produced by the extra-toxic variety of yew at the arboretum, and about Carl doing pruning for the organization.

"Thank you," Lincoln said. "Mac, you should know that Carl O'Connor came to the station and attempted to file a complaint against you for harassment."

I peered at him. "He did what now?"

"It was a spurious complaint, and we did not accept it. Is there any truth at all to the story?"

"No, there is not. I've barely set eyes on him all week. I told you I was in the pub this afternoon for a cup of chowder. If anything, he was harassing me. You can ask the bartender, whose name is Delia, if you need a witness. She saw the whole thing."

Tulia's jaw dropped. She closed it. Lincoln blinked. And again. Tulia's gaze shifted to Lincoln and away, but she didn't say anything. What was that about?

"Understood," the detective finally said. "Please give his table a wide berth when you leave here tonight."

"Yes, sir," I said.

"Stay safe, all of you." Lincoln flashed another perfunctory smile and strode away.

Which was also away from wherever it was behind me that Carl and Sita sat.

"What's this about Carl in the bar?" Zane asked.

I spied my grandma about to return to our table holding a stemmed glass full of whatever drink she'd ordered. "I'll text it to the thread. I don't want her to hear."

Norland helped Reba onto his stool, then dragged over another one for himself. I ordered another drink when the server came by, as did Zane and Gin.

None of us breathed another word about the murder or any of the prime suspects for the rest of the evening. But I knew more brains than mine were rolling over information and thoughts on exactly that topic.

Chapter 54

Tulia dropped me at my front door a little before eight after she left Gin at her place. Norland had volunteered to drive Reba home. Dusk had fallen, and the sky was more dark than light, with deep shadows lurking in every corner and behind every tree. Even without Lincoln's caution, I would have asked one of the group members for a ride home. Plus, teetotaler Tulia was a permanent designated driver, a role she embraced.

"See you at my parents' party tomorrow, right?" I asked her after I thanked her for the lift.

"Wouldn't miss it for anything."

"Drive safely home," I called to her through the open window.

"Always, Mac."

The lights of our cottage were on inside and out,

and the sight warmed my heart. I'd called Tim before I went to the restaurant. He'd said his ankle was okay, and that he'd be home all evening. He might already be asleep by now, but I hoped not.

The best sight in the world greeted me when I walked in the front door. My wide-awake husband beamed me a gentle smile from where he sat, foot elevated on a cushion on the coffee table. Swing music played softly from a Wi-Fi speaker. He set down the book he'd held and extended his other arm wide open to welcome me.

I dropped my bag and slid into his embrace. I loved his scent, a mix of rainwater shampoo, bread, and healthy man. After an entirely satisfying exchange of affection, I sat back. "How's the ankle, husband of mine?"

"Tired, as is its human, but I think we're getting there. I know I overused it today, but I'm sure a good night's rest will work wonders." He stroked my hair. "How's my favorite PI? Did you guys crack the case?"

"Hardly. We learned a few things and stayed out of trouble—mostly." I giggled. "Except for the inimitable Reba."

"That woman is a pistol of the first order. What did she do this time?"

"She showed up at Jimmy's Harborside, saying she'd tailed Carl O'Connor and Sita Spencer there. She was all clandestine spy, whispering to us about them."

"Had she followed them?"

"She had," I said.

"And she was thoroughly delighted with herself, yes?"

"A hundred percent. Except Lincoln appeared right behind her. He'd been surveilling the couple from his car, and he saw exactly what Abo Reba did. He basically told her in no uncertain terms to quit it."

"Did she listen?" he asked. "Is she going to comply?"

"What do you think? I'm not entirely sure she will. At least tomorrow she'll be busy with the party." *The party.* "Shoot. I was supposed to get with Derrick and figure out last-minute stuff for the celebration. That didn't happen, and it's not going to tonight." Some daughter I was.

"It's all going to be fine, Mac," Tim said. "I checked with Astra while you were out. The members of the UU teen group have mobilized to make all the logistics happen. One of the kids is at the vocational-technical high school and is a senior with a focus on catering and event management. He's excited about managing the celebration, small potatoes though it is, and he'll get school credit for it."

I twisted to stare at him. "Seriously?"

"You bet. You know how much young people adore your father. And your folks didn't want you and Derrick to do any of the heavy lifting. The kids are going to decorate and set up tables and chairs, manage linens and dishes, serve and clean up food and drinks, the works. The music selection might end up pretty, shall we say, young. But your parents put in a few song requests. It's going to be awesome."

"That's incredible. I can't say I was dwelling on the party too much, even though I should have been."

"You've had a few things on your mind, sweet wife."

"Mmm." I nestled into his strong, warm arm again.

"I'm looking forward to celebrating our own fortieth anniversary." He squeezed my shoulder.

"Wow. We'll be in our seventies. That's kind of hard to fathom."

"It will be a rich and joyous path to travel with you, that's all I know."

I smiled at him, imagining us. Hopefully not ill or decrepit, but certainly life-worn, age-spotted, with skin creased by experience. And, hopefully, with grand-babies running around.

But we still had to navigate the here and now. "No more word from Jamie?"

"No." He fell silent.

"And that worries you."

"A lot. I tried to call her earlier. Today is when the older kids were supposed to move to their dad's. I wish I knew a friend of hers out there who I could ask to drop by and make sure she's all right. But my troubled sister has alienated more friends than she's made."

I squeezed his knee. I was the luckiest woman in the universe when it came to family and partner and friends, and I knew it.

He yawned. "I'd better turn in."

"You're not going early tomorrow, are you?"

"When I can make a lazy breakfast for my beautiful bride?" He gave me an adoring smile. "Not a chance."

"Good. I'm not working, either, and I told Orlean and Edwin to close the shop at one."

"Perfect. It'll only take me an hour or two to decorate the cake, and I'll have plenty of time after breakfast."

I swore softly as a thought occurred to me. "I don't have a gift for them, for Mom and Pa."

"They don't want material things, hon. You know that." He pulled me in close and engaged my lips in a most luscious kiss. "I bet they'd like another grandchild, though," he said in a husky tone that made me want to get to it right there on the couch. "What do you say we—"

His cell rang. He groaned. He looked at the display. He swore, and not under his breath. He disengaged from me and stood.

"It's Jamie?" I asked.

"It is. I'm sorry, my love. I have to take it."

"You do. Go."

He connected the call and disappeared into the bedroom, closing the door behind him.

Poor Tim. He was the most superlative person I'd ever been with, and he had the least-functional sibling in the world.

I wandered into the kitchen and ran a full glass of water. I sat at the table, sipping and thinking. Tim had called my mom about party arrangements. He'd cleared his work schedule for tomorrow. He had even put Belle to bed. And he'd been about to take me to our own bed.

It was true, I'd once again entered my ovulation window. But we had a few days yet this cycle. I was well aware my parents would love the gift of another grandbaby, or more than one.

Who knew, maybe Derrick and Neli would have a child. Granted, my bro was in his early forties, but

Neli was younger than me. Little kids keep you young, anyway. Plus, Cokey would be ecstatic to have a younger brother or sister, and certainly to have a cousin.

Pa would say it was in God's hands, whether Tim and I conceived a child or not. And I supposed it was.

Chapter 55

Water consumed, I grabbed a Tim-baked peanut-butter chocolate-chip cookie and headed back to the couch. Murmurs of conversation still filtered in through the bedroom door. I didn't want disturb Tim's call with Jamie. And I was too wired to go to sleep yet, anyway.

Before I settled in, I went around and made sure all the doors to the outside were locked. I closed blinds and curtains on any windows facing the street. A murderer at large left no room for carelessness.

Back on the couch with my feet up, I checked the group thread. Norland reported escorting Reba all the way to her apartment door and making sure she was safely inside with the door locked.

I thumbed a quick message to him.
Bless you.
Tulia had written that Sita posted on social media

a photo of her Jimmy's Harborside lobster salad.
Tulia added an interesting bit.

**Sita included a touch of snark in the post, saying
"Watch out for nosy Nancies in the JH bar."**

So, she'd seen us putting our heads together. As
far as I knew, she hadn't gotten close enough to hear
our conversation. I snapped my fingers, remembering I'd promised to text the gang about what had
happened in the Rusty Anchor today, because I hadn't
wanted to get into it with my grandma listening.

I outlined my late lunch in the pub. Delia's link to
Yvonne. The bartender's comments about Carl micromanaging and being bad for business. Him smarming
over me. Me backing away. Carl basically accusing
Edwin of the murder.

I ended with what I'd asked Delia.

**I grabbed a chance to ask Delia if she thought
Yvonne could have killed Byrne. Her answer was unambiguous NO. Then she mentioned Yvonne's temper.**

I sent that, then nibbled on my cookie wishing I
had a chaser of whiskey. It had taken me years to discover how well the flavors of peanut butter and
chocolate paired with single-malt Scotch. Now the
combo was often my go-to dessert after dinner. Tim
didn't understand the attraction, but he rarely drank
hard liquor in any case. Right now, with our trying to
get pregnant, it was better to abstain from too much
drinking. Once the test showed those two little lines,
I would lay off alcohol entirely.

Flo added to the thread.

**Delia notwithstanding, do we really think Yvonne
killed Bruce?**

I tapped out a response.

I hope not, but there's no real evidence either way, right?

Norland responded right away.

There is not.

Flo didn't add anything further. Gin, Zane, and Tulia were obviously off doing normal things with loved ones instead of obsessively thinking about homicide on a Friday night. I frowned, thinking about that bit I'd never followed up on with Flo. I wrote to her alone.

I'd love to know what that "one more thing" with Bruce was. I won't share it if you want to keep it between us.

I waited, but no text came back. Then my cell rang, and it was Flo herself on the line. I hurried to connect the call.

"All right, I'll tell you," she began without preamble.

I kept quiet. I didn't want to do anything to make her hesitate or rethink her decision, but I moved into the kitchen to talk so I didn't disturb Tim in the next room.

"I might as well," she said. "The cops know now."

Even over the phone I heard her bitter tone.

"One day a few years ago, I saw him in the teen fiction section," Flo continued. "Well, it was before you moved back to Westham, so maybe five years ago. Anyway, Bruce slipped a library book into his bag. I was talking to someone at the time and didn't question him. Mac, the youth librarian came to me a while later and said we had a number of books missing from that section. They were novels popular with the kids, the kinds Bruce hated. Science fiction. Fantasy. Urban dystopia. With characters that reflected ethnic and LGBTQ diversity. The books weren't checked out, but they were gone."

"And you thought it was Byrne taking them."

"I did. We have several security cameras inside the library. I got my facilities person to move one so it had a view of the teen section. Sure enough, we caught Bruce on video. Stealing books from a public library, Mac. Can you even?"

"Wow. I hope you reported him to the police and showed them the footage."

"I was about to when the whole thing blew up."

"Oh? What happened?"

"What happened is that the next time I saw him in the stacks, I asked him to come into my office and confronted him. I was furious. But I'd left the door open, and somebody heard me. They—anonymously, of course—reported me to the library board of directors, saying a person with that kind of temper shouldn't be in charge of a public facility. For all I know, Bruce himself called it in."

"You didn't threaten to hurt him or anything." I sure hoped she hadn't.

"Not exactly . . ."

Whatever that meant.

Flo continued. "The board sent him a letter asking him to return any books he might have inadvertently forgotten he'd checked out. He brought back a whopping two volumes. And the board turned the other cheek. They didn't do anything, Mac! It was if he had influence over them of some kind."

"That's strange."

"And get this. I got a note in my file saying next

time there would be disciplinary action against me. I was pretty furious at that, too, I'll tell you."

"I can understand that," I said. "I hope Bruce at least stopped stealing."

"He did." She let out a heavy sigh. "But the police know I had strong words with him, and then he goes and gets murdered, and I think they're still suspecting me."

"Having a key to the pub doesn't help, I'm sure."

"Not at all. Listen, I have to get to bed. I'm beat."

"Thanks for sharing that story with me, Flo. Do you want it to stay out of the group thread?"

"Please, if you don't mind."

"Not a problem. Good night." I sat back.

Stealing or defacing books was about the worst thing you could do to a lifelong librarian, especially when they portrayed marginalized populations. It was akin to banning books. No wonder she was upset. But a loud argument wasn't exactly grounds for killing someone. If it was, the world's population would be a lot smaller.

Maybe she'd kept some worse conflict with Byrne back from telling me. Otherwise, why would Penelope and Lincoln be so interested in Flo?

Chapter 56

Back in the living room, my tablet lay on the coffee table where I'd left it. Maybe I could learn more about Yvonne if I dug deeper. Or the library board might have filed a report with the town about the book thefts or the disciplinary action. Before I could pick up the device, replies to my texts to the group started rolling in.

Gin expressed her sympathies about the smarminess.

Zane chimed in.

I experienced Yvonne's temper more than once. She wanted a particular wine for a pairing at a special event. Didn't want to actually pay full price. The event was a rich lady's birthday, not a charity fundraiser. I refused to discount it. Got read the riot act up and down. Will never do business with her again.

He had direct evidence of Yvonne's temper. Come

to think of it, I'd seen her flare up, too. I wrote to the group.

Remember in spring? I came across Y in pub kitchen appearing to threaten Chamber director with a lethally sharp knife.

Norland added a note.

And she's a vet, trained by the Air Force.

Correct. Yvonne had been stationed at the Joint Base Cape Cod, a multi-military command training base not too far from here. Was that when she'd met Byrne's wife, or had it been later? I knew by this time that the police always gave a close look to the person who reported finding the victim. Neither Lincoln nor Penelope had been forthcoming about Yvonne's actions, whether innocent or guilty.

No new texts came in. Now I grabbed the tablet and settled back on the couch cushions, tucking my feet up. The bedroom had gone quiet. Tim was either lying there thinking or had fallen asleep.

He and I had been married for six months, but we had been seeing each other for about three years, nearly the entire time I'd been back in Westham. During those months and years, we'd figured out a few things about each other. If he wanted my company right now, he would come and find me. I let him have his privacy and his rest.

I took a minute to consider all the things my parents had figured out about each other over forty years of marriage. I'd never be able to list them all, and I was positive plenty of compromises had been reached I'd never known about, like the miscarriages and the reasons I didn't have younger siblings.

What I did know, and witnessed every time we were all together, was how much they still enjoyed each other's company despite maintaining rich lives separate from their spouse. Or maybe because of it.

An idea for a gift now burbled to my mind's surface. I had dabbled in writing various forms of poetry when I was younger. Maybe I could scribble a silly ode and read it at the party. Pa and Mom would love it, even if nobody else did, and I could print it and present them with a framed copy. It was a great project for tomorrow morning and an immediately available gift that didn't depend on a semi-random joining of egg and sperm.

I shifted on the cushions and felt a crackling in the back pocket of the jeans I'd been wearing since this morning. I pulled it out. *Right.* Delia had given me her card. I stared at it. The writing didn't list bartender as her profession. Instead, it featured a stunning but simple design, and had Graphic Designer under her name. But it was her last name—Haskins— that caught my attention. The same name as Lincoln's. The surname wasn't an unusual one. Surely this was a coincidence.

Or was it? Delia didn't particularly resemble him. I doubted they were siblings. She'd said she was divorced, and I knew he was. I nodded slowly to myself. He'd had a reaction when I mentioned her name at Jimmy's. So had Tulia, which made sense. She and Lincoln were both members of the Wampanoag tribe, which wasn't that large. Tulia would have known Lincoln's wife.

Lincoln had become a friend. I'd really liked Delia. How had two such congenial humans not found a way to stay in love like my parents had? No, that question was naïve. Nobody could ever really know what went on between two people in an intimate relationship. Things couples didn't agree on and got divorced over had to be myriad.

I could, however, try to find out a little more about Delia Haskins. I navigated to her graphic design website, which was visually attractive and featured a number of projects she'd worked on. But plenty of freelancers had trouble staying afloat, financially, which could explain why she was bartending on the side. I checked social media. She wasn't much in evidence on a couple of sites but did post photographs of intriguing angles of buildings and light on another one.

Nothing about a divorce. Nothing about kids. Lincoln had once vaguely alluded to an event in his past that had been emotionally wrenching. We'd never talked more about it.

My phone rang. I checked the display but didn't recognize the number. Still, it could be Jamie trying to reach Tim again, who might have turned off his phone or set it to Do Not Disturb for the night. I didn't know her number by sight, and these days the first three digits in a cell number—the area code—didn't necessarily tie that number to a specific region, so people didn't have to change their number when they moved.

I'd better get this, in case it was her. I connected and said hello.

No one spoke, but it wasn't dead air. The faint sound of breathing came over the line.

"Hello?" I asked. "Who's there?"

Crickets.

"Hello?" I pressed. "Who is this?"

Silence.

I jabbed at the phone to disconnect the call. The hair on my arms stood up. My neck prickled, and a shiver ran through me. I hoped the call hadn't been Jamie in trouble.

But if it wasn't, someone else had called me to say nothing. I didn't like that at all.

Chapter 57

By eight the next morning, I sat bleary-eyed in glasses, a T-shirt, and soft pants, nursing my first cup of coffee at the kitchen table. Tim chopped and sauteed, filling the kitchen with delectable aromas and the yummy sounds of someone making my breakfast. Both of us hiring reliable weekend help for our businesses had been a great move. I loved being able to relax on Saturdays and Sundays. Tim did, too.

He set a plate of warm blueberry muffins on the table and kissed my forehead.

"How was your call with Jamie?" I asked.

"Kind of nutty." He grimaced. "She was all weepy and despairing, saying she'd never see Timmy and his sister again." He headed back to the stove. "At least she was taking care of Ella. She said she had to go to make her dinner."

"That's good. Do you think she's taking care of the baby she's carrying, too?"

"If you mean not using or drinking, I honestly can't say. And this time I didn't even ask. She was having a bad enough day, but at least she didn't sound wired, dopey, or messy drunk."

"Glad to hear it. And then you fell asleep."

He turned with a soft smile. "I did, Mac."

"I did, Mac," Belle piped up in Tim's voice. "I did. Kind of nutty. Snacks, Mac?" She waddled over to my chair.

"Belle, you had breakfast," I said. "You can have snacks later."

"Snacks later." She switched to my voice. "Snacks later. Belle's a good girl." She finished off the repertoire with a wolf whistle. Belle could brighten anyone's day.

"Your ankle feels okay today?" I asked Tim. "I don't notice you limping this morning."

"I'm definitely on the mend. I have to be able to dance with my beloved wife this evening, don't I?"

I returned his smile. And sipped my coffee, admiring the view of his quite remarkable rear end as he returned to his cooking.

When I remembered last night's call, though, I stopped smiling. I found the number the breather had called from and read it out loud to him. "Does that ring a bell?"

"No."

"It's not Jamie's, right? I mean, could she have gotten a new phone and changed her number?"

"I'm quite sure she didn't," he said. "Why?"

"That number called me last night, but whoever the caller was didn't say anything. I heard breathing.

Not heavy, icky breathing, but it was the sound of a person on the other end."

"They never spoke?"

"No, even though I kept saying hello. In the end, I disconnected. But it gave me the creeps."

He folded over the omelet and flipped it in the pan with one deft move of his wrist. A minute later, he set a plate in front of each of us.

"Dig in while it's hot." He sat kitty-corner from me.

I reached for his hand and squeezed it before picking up my fork. "Thank you." The onions were sauteed until they were nearly caramelized, the sliced mushrooms were soft and aromatic, and the now-melted grated Manchego cheese added the perfect finishing touch.

"You're welcome," he murmured. "You know I love cooking for you, sweetheart."

How lucky was I? "So, I figured out a gift for my parents. I mean, one I can produce today."

"Yes?"

I described the poetic ode I had in mind. "I'll print it out and stick it in a frame. I think they'll love it."

"You've always said how much Astra encouraged you and Derrick to give handmade gifts," Tim said. "Are you planning to write a sonnet like the Bard's?"

"No, I have more pedestrian goals. I'm going to try making up a set of limericks." I bit into a perfect muffin. At home Tim made them with whole wheat flour and half the sugar, so it was nutty and not too sweet, plus juicy with fat blueberries. I rolled it on my tongue. "Cinnamon?"

"Exactly. I think it brightens the flavor." He tilted his head and tented his fingers. "There once was a baker from Bourne, who didn't like cooking with corn. He staged a revolt and caused quite a jolt, that crazy old baker from Bourne."

I snorted. "Yeah, like that."

"I once knew a girl from the Cape, who had the most luscious of napes. We snogged with the tide, I made her my bride, that beautiful girl from the Cape." He leaned over, pulled me close, and nibbled the back of my neck.

"Hey, you, I had a mouthful of muffin," I protested, even though I loved both the limerick and the nibbling.

We chatted and ate and enjoyed our quiet morning together, which ended up including a delightful dessert of prospective baby-making before he took off to decorate the anniversary cake.

Chapter 58

By ten o'clock, I was showered and dressed in respectable shorts and a top, in case I needed to run out for anything. My contact lenses were in, and I'd restored the kitchen to a food-safe, scrubbed-down condition. I grabbed my keys and my laptop.

"Come on, Belle. Let's go hang out in the tiny house."

"Home, Mac? We're going home, Mac?"

"Yes, Belle, the tiny house was our home."

She was so darn smart. She and I had lived together in my tiny house until last December, and I knew she still loved it as much as I did.

I unlocked the tiny house and left the door wide open. The screen door would keep the bugs out and let in the fresh air. Belle hopped from chair to table to floor. She made her way up the ladder-like stairs leading to the sleeping loft, chattering all the while.

I laid the laptop on the drop-leaf table—the one I'd never refinished—and wandered through the four-hundred-square-foot structure, remembering. There was the love seat where Tim and I had loved as well as hashed through our relationship goals. The empty space where Belle's cage and roost had sat, and where I had put her to bed every night. The bookshelf Belle's BFF and shopping gal pal, Alexa, had sat on top of. The window at the rear of the house next to where a small outside deck jutted out from the structure.

I glanced up to the loft. The way the light was right now, the wide, foot-high clerestory window reflected the parrot's image back to her. She preened and turned this way and that, apparently admiring her own reflection.

"Hello, gorgeous," she muttered in Tim's voice, then switched into Malik's. "Can you believe that flaming socialist? I wanted to throttle him. Son of a b—"

"Belle." I used my sternest voice. "That's not appropriate. Come on down."

She preened at her own image.

"Come down, Belle." I stood, fists on hips, pointing at my feet. "Now. Do you want to go back to the cottage alone?"

"Come down now. Come down now." She hopped down the stairs, one at a time, muttering all the way. "Cottage alone. Cottage alone, Mac."

"Good girl." I drew a zipped plastic bag of grapes out of my pocket and poured them into a small dish. "Here's your snack. Now, please be quiet. I need to write a poem for Astra and Joseph."

I sat at the table and fired up the laptop. Belle blessedly stayed quiet, even after she'd used her huge black curved beak to scarf down all the grapes. As a mockingbird outside ran through its borrowed repertoire of songs, I thought about my beloved subject matter.

My parents had met on the island of Nantucket, a ferry ride from here through the Atlantic Ocean and Nantucket Sound. Mom, already widowed for a year, and toddler Derrick were staying with her aunt and uncle there, who had kindly offered a rent-free suite until Mom figured out what was next for her life. She'd found a job managing ferry schedules for the Steamship Authority, and Pa had been interim pastor at the UU church on the island.

I could work with that. Tim had put the idea into my head of writing an ode comprised of limericks. I began typing.

> *There once was a pair on Nantuckey,*
> *Both young and ever so plucky.*
> *It turned into love*
> *As if sent from above.*
> *Their marriage is way more than ducky!*

> *A wedding came soon for the pair,*
> *A baby girl next for to share.*
> *With big brother too,*
> *The house was a zoo*
> *Still, love and much fun filled the lair.*

> *Our Astra and Joseph they raised*
> *Two siblings quite different but praised.*
> *A grandgirl named Cokey's*
> *A darling, no jokey.*
> *Even Reba declared, "I'm amazed."*

> *This couple they lead separate lives,*
> *And neither one breaks out in hives.*
> *Together they cook*
> *And plans they do book.*
> *Their marriage now marks eight times five.*

I sat back. "How does this sound, Belle?" I read through all four corny verses. I was no expert, but my goofy ode seemed to have the right rhythm and the appropriate number of syllables in each line. "I think I need one more verse, don't you?"

Hmm. Maybe one more in conclusion. Or another one about each member of the couple. I was sure I could write one focusing on Mom's profession as an astrologer, as well as her role as an artistic and loving mother, daughter-in-law, and grandmother. I could easily pen another about Pa's life calling to be a minister and his well-earned reputation as everyone's favorite confidant and sounding board.

Cokey would be satisfied the ode included her name, and I'd slid in Reba. But how much of this should be about the rest of the family? The spotlight should be squarely on the enduring marriage we were going to be celebrating in a few short hours.

> *To pastor became Joseph's calling*
> *Helping up those who find themselves falling.*
> *He listens and counsels,*
> *With grace—not a hard sell.*
> *Preaches peace to those who like brawling.*

Hmm. That one might need a bit of revision.

My fingers were poised to type a verse about Mom when a shadow crept across the side window. A human-sized shadow. Across the window where the deck was. The mockingbird went silent. A footstep sounded. The creak of a board. I froze. Here I was thinking I was safe in my backyard sitting in my own former home. Except . . . an unlocked screen door provided the only barrier between me and a murderer.

Belle cocked her big head, aiming a yellow eye in that direction.

I hauled my phone out of my shorts pocket. My sweating hand shook, and I nearly dropped it.

"Mac?" Yvonne called from outside the door.

Chapter 59

*Y*vonne. A chef I'd been friendly with. Maybe I didn't have to worry. But she was also a woman with a temper, according to more than one source, and a person with a possibly valid reason for causing Bruce Byrne to go away on a permanent basis.

I quickly slid my phone onto its Mute setting and tapped Lincoln's number. I laid the phone on the table where I'd been writing. I willed the detective to pick up the call and listen in. In case I needed him.

"Yes, Yvonne?" I stood, not wanting to be at a disadvantage.

She appeared at the screen door, standing a couple of feet back from it. "Got a minute? It's about the food for your parents' party."

Was it my hearing, or did her voice sound a little wobbly?

"I didn't know you were involved in their celebration. But sure, I can speak with you." I stepped closer to the door and extended my hand toward the handle, intending to step outside for the conversation. Something was wrong here, and I didn't want anything to be wrong inside my small but beloved sanctuary, especially not with Belle as my companion in the tiny house. That had happened once before. I couldn't have a repeat.

In a fast move, the door was yanked open. Yvonne stumbled toward me. I set my feet in a strong stance and caught her. The chef seemed high, or maybe she was drunk.

"I'm so sorry," she whispered.

She had nothing to be sorry for. "Why?" I asked.

In a quick move, Sita Spencer appeared behind Yvonne. *Whoa.* I swallowed. It was time to worry, after all.

"Hey, Sita." I mustered a bright tone. "What's going on?" No casual pro-forma question, this. I needed to know what the situation was, and quick.

"What's going on?" Her tone was sardonic. "This is all over, Mac Almeida. You and your little club of bumbling would-be detectives can't do anything right, can you? Your stupid grandmother included."

I inhaled, fast and sharp, and got a whiff of fear. It could be emanating from any of us, and it certainly was from me. Still, nobody dissed Reba Almeida, not on my watch.

"And then this idiot comes at me." Sita glared at Yvonne. Sita's short hair had looked chic and groomed the previous times I'd seen her. Today it stood out from her head and gave her a wild look.

"I didn't—" Yvonne protested.

"Shut up. I'm talking to your buddy Mac." Sita

gave me the evilest of smiles, her dark eyes glittering, then continued. "I made Yvonne show me where you lived. When we saw you and the bird come out to your shack here, well, that was as perfect as it gets." She grabbed Yvonne's left upper arm with one hand and slid a syringe out of her bag with the other.

No!

Chapter 60

Yvonne's face paled. She gasped and tried to pull away. In contrast to her usual attitude of being tough and competent, her apparent terror right now made her seem almost frail.

I tried to swallow down my own fear. "Sita, what are you doing?" I stepped closer, but she brandished the syringe at me. I took a step back. That thing likely held a lethal dose of taxine.

"She was on to what Carl did," Sita snarled. "I'm not going to have her ruining his life—or mine."

What *Carl* did?

"I'm not on to anything. You have to believe me." Yvonne's eyes pleaded with me.

"And you're next, Mac." Sita again pointed the syringe at me.

I kept out of reach. In my periphery, I spied Belle listening closely. And silently for once, thank goodness. She edged closer. I willed her not to come within Sita's reach. If there was such a thing as human-parrot mental telepathy, let it work now.

"What did Carl do?" I tried to keep my voice from shaking.

"Like you don't know," Sita scoffed.

"Believe me, I don't." I strongly suspected she knew he killed Bruce Byrne, though. Maybe Sita had even helped him do it. She seemed desperate for him not to go down for the crime. Her being desperate could work in my and Yvonne's favor. Maybe.

I figured dragging out the current conversation was one of our only hopes of surviving this horrible situation. The heroine often tried nudging the bad guy to keep talking in the cozies we read. It might or might not work in real life, but the tactic was worth a try, since our options were tiny in number. "Do you mean Carl killed that teacher?" I asked.

As I did, Yvonne bent her right elbow and brought her palm flat in front of her. She gave me an intent look and made a sharp movement with her left hand, pushing the fingertips into the other palm. She repeated the movement. I didn't know her meaning, unless that was an ASL sign. For what, I had no idea.

"You know what? I'm all done with this little chat." Sita fixed her thumb on the pump end of the syringe and yanked Yvonne closer.

Yvonne shrank into herself, lowering her chin. She flashed me a sideways gaze, as if she was sending me another message. Despite her apparent terror, I got the distinct impression she wasn't shrinking. Instead she was girding her core as she coiled to attack. Like a snake. Like a cat. She was a trained veteran in the armed forces, after all. If she attacked, I was all in.

"Alexa, call the cops!" Belle shrieked.

Sita lost her focus. Yvonne launched herself, butting the top of her head with full force into Sita's face. I smashed the edge of my flat hand on Sita's wrist. The syringe fell to the floor. I kicked it across the room. Yvonne struck at Sita's knee, dragging her foot down the shin to stomp on Sita's instep. Sita cried out and crumpled. She writhed, cursing, on the floor.

"Got any rope, Mac?" Yvonne asked, frantic. "Wire, duct tape, computer cables, anything."

All I wanted to do was grab Belle and run, but Yvonne was right. Sita could rally any second now and come after us.

"Yes." I yanked open a narrow storage closet where I'd stashed a hank of clothesline rope I'd hoped to string up for free solar laundry drying.

Sita screamed. I whirled. Belle stood on our attacker's head, and she wasn't being gentle with those talons. Blood dripped down Sita's face as her hands scrabbled at my parrot. She almost had hold of Belle's legs. I tossed Yvonne the rope.

"Belle, please get off her. Now."

Belle cocked her head, regarding me. "Belle's a good girl." She used her sharp, powerful beak to peck at Sita's hand, then hopped off. "Got any rope, Mac?" She waddled off, muttering about the cops and what a good girl she was. She included a few of Sita's swear words along with Malik's favorite "son of a . . ." phrase.

"Give me a hand, Mac," Yvonne said, her tone urgent.

Between us we subdued Sita enough to bind her hands and feet.

"You need to call nine-one-one," Yvonne said.

"A call to Detective Haskins has been open all this time." I grabbed my phone from the table. "Lincoln? Are you there?" But all I heard was silence.

"It's the fuzz," Belle yelled. "Let's blow this joint."

She was correct on the first count.

"Westham Police!" August Jenkins stepped into the doorway, pointing his weapon with both hands.

Directly behind him came Lincoln, also in a bullet-proof vest, holding his own police-issued weapon. He lowered it almost immediately. "Stand down, Jenkins."

"Yes, sir." August lowered his gun, shifting it to one hand.

"Hey, handsome," Belle hopped over to Lincoln. "Belle's a good girl." She finished with a wolf whistle.

"Would you tell that bird to shut its mouth already?" Sita whined.

"No, ma'am." Lincoln said. "Belle can say whatever she wants."

Outside a siren wailed closer until it shut off. Another two officers hurried up. They assisted August with handcuffing Sita. I watched them usher her out, with Sita hobbling. I told the departing officers I didn't need the rope back.

"But one of you should very carefully retrieve that syringe," I said to Lincoln. I pointed at the far corner of the room where it had ended up, nearly under the little refrigerator. "I expect it has a lethal substance in it."

"Got it." Lincoln gazed at Yvonne and me. "Nice job, ladies. You, too, Belle."

Chapter 61

Yvonne and I sat at my patio table on the deck behind the cottage with Belle. Lincoln had asked us to wait here until he'd gotten the crime-scene team in place in the tiny house. Yvonne had been keeping mostly quiet, scrolling on her phone, ignoring me. I didn't mind. I spent a little time on my own phone and wrote a quick text to the group.

Sita abducted Yvonne, brought her to my place 10:30 this AM. Belle and I out in tiny house. Sita had syringe. Yvonne, Belle, and I overpowered her, tied her up. THEN police came. Now waiting for debrief w/ Lincoln.

I sent the message but kept my phone on mute. I didn't want to be barraged by a flurry of reply notifications. I decided for the moment against letting Tim know what had happened. I was fine, and he'd get the scoop the minute he came home after finishing the cake.

Belle had finally calmed down from her frantic talking and pacing. I gave her a bowl of frozen cut-up carrots, one of her favorite snacks.

"Parrots are weird, aren't they?" Yvonne tilted her head, studying Belle. "Look at that tongue of hers."

"It is a little startling when you first see it," I said. Belle had a prominent black tongue to match her beak. She used the beak to pick up small bits of edibles, like the peanuts I'd spilled, and to crack food open, and her thick tongue swept the food back into her throat. I was used to the sight, but it was odd to watch for the first time. I also loved seeing her on her perch balancing on one leg while her other talon, serving as a hand rather than a foot, held something like a pomegranate to bite away at.

The snack calmed Belle, who now perched quietly on the arm of my chair. I had calmed down, as well, and could finally settle into my surroundings. Only a few light clouds floated by in the cerulean sky.

I remembered September eleventh. I had been a high school student that year, and we'd all heard at school about the terrible hijackings and deaths, although they hadn't let us watch the video footage of any of it. I'd come home, sat in the yard behind the parsonage, and wept. That day had been as beautiful of a day as today, and the death and destruction that had happened in New York—not very far south of here—made a terrible contrast, one my young mind had had trouble grasping.

Today's attack, on an equally lovely day, was minor

in comparison, with a blessedly different outcome thanks to my companions here.

I glanced at Yvonne and cleared my throat. "You were amazing in there. Thanks for getting us out of that jam."

"It's all in the training, Mac. Have you ever taken a self-defense class?"

"Unfortunately, no. Gin and I have talked about it."

"I recommend you find one. There are some pretty simple things you can learn to do. Most of the time all you need is to temporarily disable your attacker so you can break free and run."

"Sounds wise. That thing you did with your hands beforehand. Was it an ASL sign?"

"Yes. It means 'attack.' I was a bit hampered, with Sita holding on to my upper arm. This is what the sign should look like." She laid her phone on the table and repeated the sign a couple of times with sharper, more defined movements.

"I wasn't sure what you were doing, but I knew you were sending me a message."

"I didn't know if you signed, but it was worth a try."

"Where did you learn American Sign Language?" I asked.

"I had a deaf friend at college. He taught me some basic signs, and then I took a couple of courses in ASL. It's kind of fun to natter away in public in a secret language." She picked up her phone and returned to whatever she'd been reading.

I opened my mouth to ask about the woman she'd been biking with. Nah. Yvonne clearly had someone with whom to stay fluent in the language. Digging for any more details would be nosy.

Gin would be up for taking a self-defense class, even though I hoped neither of us ever ran into a murderous attacker again. I, at least, didn't have much of a track record for staying free of that kind of threat. I'd be better off being prepared.

Chapter 62

Lincoln, now sans bulletproof vest, finally trudged up the steps and took a seat. Not a minute later, Penelope Johnson appeared at the foot of the steps.

"Ah, Johnson," Lincoln said. "Please join us."

Belle perked up. "Alexa, call the cops. Call the cops! Hey, handsome." Predictably, the wolf whistle finished off the set.

Lincoln snorted. Penelope, who had met Belle last winter, only smiled.

I shrugged. "Alexa isn't here, Belle." I stroked her head. "You're a very good girl."

"She was a very, very good girl a little while ago," Yvonne agreed. "Jumping on Sita's head was a big help."

"Were you listening in, Lincoln?" I asked.

"I was. Smart move, Mac."

"It was the only thing I could think to do at such short notice," I said.

"Please run through the entire sequence of events for us," Lincoln said. "Ms. Flora, you can begin with how Sita Spencer happened to bring you here to Mac's."

"I was in the pub kitchen doing prep." Yvonne frowned as she spoke. "She must have had Carl's key, because she let herself in. She said I had to come with her to your house, Mac, that she had important information to tell both of us. And if I didn't cooperate, Carl would fire me."

"You believed her?" Penelope asked.

"I know she and Carl are a couple. So, yes, I believed her. I love my job, ma'am, and I need the money."

"Did she threaten you physically in the restaurant?" Lincoln asked.

"No, not until we got here. When we pulled up, Mac and the parrot were heading into the tiny house. Yvonne said we had to wait a little while."

Long enough for me to write five verses of goofy limericks. Which had actually happened pretty fast.

"Please continue," Lincoln said. "What happened next?"

"Sita told me to call out to Mac and say I wanted to talk."

"Right," I said. "I'm sorry, Yvonne, but I'd wondered earlier in the week if you might have been Byrne's killer. Yesterday I heard you talking on your phone in the alley, and it sounded, well, suspicious."

"It was that blasted Carl." Yvonne pressed her lips together for a moment, then continued. "He wanted me to cut a couple of employees from my staff. I refused."

Huh. Why had he called her about that? He'd appeared in the alley a couple of minutes later. Maybe he'd called Yvonne because he didn't want to make those demands face-to-face.

"Mac?" Lincoln nudged me out of my reverie. "Did you have a thought to finish?"

"Yes. When you showed up here, Yvonne, your voice sounded kind of funny," I said. "My danger radar went up. I now know it was valid but for the wrong reason."

"That's why you phoned me and left the call open?" Lincoln asked.

"Exactly. And I muted the cell's sound in case you said anything, so she wouldn't know you might be listening."

"Smart move," Penelope said.

"Anyway," Yvonne continued, "when you appeared at the door, she pushed me inside."

"You kind of fell toward me," I said. "I didn't realize she'd pushed you."

"Mac, you take the narrative from there," Lincoln suggested.

"Sita appeared behind Yvonne." I took in a deep breath and blew it out. "She pulled out a big old syringe and basically proceeded to tell us that she wasn't about to let us ruin Carl's life." I gazed at Yvonne. "She said you were on to what Carl did. Were you?"

"Kind of. Like you, I had my suspicions."

"Except yours were correct," I pointed out.

"The timing of him showing up seemingly minutes after I found Bruce's body was too strange,"

Yvonne said. "And then he was around all the time. Asking questions, mismanaging everything he touched, pretending he was totally shocked that anyone would commit murder in his precious pub. So, yeah. The whole business seemed off."

I glanced at Lincoln. "Tell me you have him in custody by now."

He pointed at Penelope.

"Yes, ma'am, we do." She smiled. "He did not come easily, though, loudly claiming his innocence over and over."

"Penelope and Jenkins picked him up in the pub," Lincoln said. "That part was easy."

"We simply walked in the back door," Penelope continued. "Cabral was in the kitchen, apparently desperate to get meal prep done alone but being interfered with right and left by the owner."

"Poor Uly," Yvonne murmured.

"Together with the detective here, we had enough evidence to charge O'Connor," Penelope said. "Lincoln really pulled some strings to rush through the DNA analysis, because the state lab is incredibly understaffed, not to mention overbooked."

"We're hoping Ms. Spencer will be willing to speak up about why she thought O'Connor needed protecting," Lincoln added.

Protection from bumbling would-be sleuths like the Cozy Capers, was what she'd said. I didn't care what Sita thought of us. Our group did what we could, and if it helped detectives like Lincoln and Penelope, so much the better.

"By the way"—Penelope gazed at Yvonne—"we have closed the Rusty Anchor again until further notice, just so you know."

Yvonne nodded. "I figured that would happen."

"Have you learned what pretense Carl used to convince Byrne to meet him at the pub after hours last Sunday night?" I asked.

"We have a witness who overheard a conversation at the place where Sita and Carl are staying," Lincoln said. "The witness says Carl spoke of letting bygones be bygones, and that he wanted to clear the air. He addressed a person named Bruce, and said they'd have more privacy if they met at the Anchor at eleven."

"A kiss-and-make-up that Carl had entirely opposite plans for," Penelope murmured.

"Wow." I sat back.

That crusty, unhappy man who had made so many others unhappy had thought he was going to reconcile a past wound. Maybe his heart condition had been making him hyperaware of his own mortality.

Chapter 63

I wrenched myself back to the present. "Did Carl give Bruce the poison in a drink?"

"Yes." Penelope nodded. "Mr. O'Connor apparently hadn't studied up on how to destroy evidence. He seems to have simply added the murderous glass to the restaurant's dishwasher, which is where we found it. He did wear gloves, which eliminates fingerprints, but not DNA. It took the lab a few days to analyze the trace contents, but they did discover taxine in the glass."

"But only today," Lincoln muttered.

Better today than never. I kept that thought to myself.

"And we found a small container of the stuff in the place where the two are staying."

"I'll bet Sita provided him with the poison," Yvonne said.

"We believe so, and we're close to nailing down

that information." Lincoln nodded. "A colleague of hers in North Carolina has been most helpful. If Ms. Spencer herself were to offer more information in exchange for a small token of leniency, that would help. And if she doesn't, we'll get there, only more slowly."

"I just remembered something," I began. "The first time I met Sita was Monday morning, when she came into the shop. She bought several bike items that she said were for her boyfriend's birthday. I said I hoped the weather improved so they could enjoy the trails, and she said things had already improved. At the time, I didn't know what she meant. Now I wonder if she was talking about Byrne being dead."

"That sounds about right," Yvonne said.

I glanced at the door of the tiny house, where a black-clad crime-scene tech was doing something with the door. My eyes widened, and I slapped my forehead, swearing under my breath.

"Lincoln!" My words tumbled out. I pointed at the techs. "How long are they going to be in there? I have summer rentals checking in this afternoon."

"Hmm," he said. "At what time?"

"Three o'clock or after. I can't tell them to go find a hotel." This was a disaster. Nobody could find a decent room on a Saturday night in July with two hours' notice.

"Let me have a word with the team." Lincoln ambled over to the tiny house and was back in two minutes. "You're all set, Mac. They said they'll be finished in about half an hour. You two were attacked there, but they don't have a corpse to document."

"Thank you." My relief was a fresh breeze washing away the worry. Having to wrangle an unavailable lodging for our very first customers was the last thing I needed today. As it was, we'd have to sweep through there and make sure the place wasn't mucked up with fingerprint powder.

Bicycle brakes squealed to a stop outside the fence. I stood to get a better view of who had ridden over here. My grandma climbed off her red adult tricycle—size small—and came bustling up the walk toward the deck.

"Excuse me," I said and trotted down the steps. "Abo Ree, what are you—"

"Mackenzie, my love, are you all right?" She opened her arms. "My police app reported a to-do at your address!"

I stepped in for a hug. "I'm fine. Belle's fine. And a bad person got taken away in handcuffs. You didn't need to ride all the way up here." Our place was up an incline, and my grandma mostly rode on the flat rail trail.

"It was good for the old ticker. Hey there, Lincoln." She relinquished me and marched up to the deck. "Now then, young man. Did I not instruct you to keep my grandgirl out of harm's way?"

He gave a helpless shake of his head. "You know as well as I do, Mrs. Almeida. There's no holding back Mac."

I jumped in, preempting Abo Ree's own words. "But all's well that ends well."

Tim hurried up. "Mac, sweetheart. Why are all these police cars here? Are you okay?" A smudge of purple icing graced his cheek.

"I'm fine. All is well." I stood on tiptoes to kiss him. I gently swiped off the decoration. "How's that cake looking?"

Chapter 64

Mother Nature smiled on my parents' party. Now at seven thirty on Saturday evening, not a single cloud marred the gentle, end-of-day Cape Cod light and the way it softened colors and caressed all the sharp edges. Even the mosquitoes were in hiding.

Joseph and Astra's backyard was filled with family and friends. Low music played in the background accompanied by conversation and the occasional shriek and yip from girl and dog playing together. The catering students were quietly busy clearing paper plates and tidying up the food table.

Mom sat chatting with Lincoln, Tim, Reba, and Orlean. Pa had been making the rounds, speaking with this person and that. I was pleased to see Al Cabral in the mix. He and Pa were now in an animated conversation across the yard from me.

Like everyone else, I'd feasted on ribs and crabcakes, potato salad and garden greens, and so much more. To start the party off, Tim had mixed anniversary cocktails for anyone who wanted one, the same drink my parents had served at their wedding. Featuring vodka, peach schnapps, and cranberry juice, it was a bit sweet for my taste, but I'd sipped it slowly. Tim had said he was happy to serve as bartender, since that was a job the high school students were too young to do. He'd also offered a nonalcoholic version of the cocktail.

I now sat with a plastic cup of wine in a small circle with the other Cozy Capers. I'd filled them in on everything that had gone down this morning.

"Do we have any loose ends?" Flo asked.

"My brother said he knew Sita years ago," Tulia said. "She was a piece of work even then. The woman can hold a grudge like nobody's business."

"I can vouch for the piece-of-work part," Flo murmured.

"Sounds like she and Carl were meant for each other," Gin said.

"I'm relieved I was wrong about Yvonne," I said. "She was pretty impressive, with acting terrified and then launching a full attack at Sita."

"And I'm glad neither Uly nor Edwin had anything to do with the death," Zane added.

"I am, too." I nodded. "Or Flo, although none of us ever really thought you did." I smiled at her.

"I wonder what will happen to the Rusty Anchor," Norland said. "Now that Carl is out of the picture."

"Maybe he'll have to sell the business, and Yvonne and the employees can buy it," Flo suggested. "I've heard of that happening elsewhere, but for different reasons."

Whether Yvonne bought the pub or not, she and all the staff would be happy not to have Carl breathing down their necks.

"Listen to this," Zane said. "We talked to Leilani. She said she's glad Sita is in jail. Her own sister. Isn't that sad?"

"Sisters usually know each other better than almost anyone else," Gin murmured.

"Any siblings do," I said. "When you grow up together . . ." I let the thought trail away. Tim knew Jamie on a deep level. What she was capable of—and what she wasn't.

I sipped my wine and sat quietly for a moment.

"Titi Mac, Titi Mac!" Cokey raced across the lawn and hurled herself at me, all pink dress and energy. "Guess what?"

I held my wine out to the side in the nick of time. "What, darling?"

Derrick and Neli strolled up, hand in hand. Neli's dark cheeks glowed as pink as the fuchsia sundress she wore. She extended her left hand, on which sparkled a small diamond set in a gold band.

"See, Titi Mac?" Cokey said. "Neli's gonna be my new mommy. And look, we have matching dresses." She twirled.

"You do, and you're both lovely in them. Even Daddy has a pink shirt on." I stood and hugged my future sister-in-law. "It's official? I'm so happy for both of you."

"You mean for all three of us," Cokey protested.

"Yes, *querida*." I focused on the grown-ups. "Have you set a date?"

Neli glanced at Derrick and gave him a little nod.

"We did," he said. "The last Saturday in August."

"That's soon." I hurried to add, "Which is awesome. Let me know what I can do, okay?"

"You can count on it," my brother said.

"And we're gonna have a baby, too," Cokey announced. "I get to be the big sister."

Oho. Thus setting a wedding date for next month. Now the way Derrick and Reba had reacted yesterday made sense, when Cokey had announced Neli was tired. My grandma must have already known the news about the pregnancy.

Neli's smile wavered. "I hope you don't mind, Mac. The pregnancy just sort of happened."

"Are you kidding?" I asked. "I'm delighted for you both. For you all." Tim might feel sad about the reminder that it hadn't happened for us yet. And sure, a tiny spot of envy pulled at my heart. But I was good. And maybe close proximity to a growing future niece or nephew would remind my own body to get with the program. "You've told Pa and Mom? And your mother, Neli?"

"Yes, to all." Neli smiled.

"After this one knew"—Derrick ruffled Cokey's angel curls—"we figured we'd better hustle over and give you all the news at once."

"I'm glad you did. I couldn't be happier."

Norland stood and shook Derrick's hand. "Congratulations to all of you."

The others in the circle offered their congrats.

"I suppose this means you won't be rejoining the book group, Derrick?" Gin asked.

Derrick had been a founding member of the Cozy Capers, but between caring for Cokey, going back to school some months ago, and then meeting Neli, he'd dropped out.

"Afraid not," Derrick said. "I can't fit it in." He slung his arm around Neli's shoulders, who leaned into him.

"You're always welcome back. Either or both of you." I glanced around the yard. "Should we do the cake and toasts soon?"

"Yes, I think so," he said. "I'll go ask the students to get the dessert service ready."

"I have a little presentation to make, too," I said.

He gave me a thumbs-up.

Chapter 65

Ten minutes later, Tim's sheet cake was out and ready to cut, its purple and yellow flowers bright against chocolate frosting. In the middle, surrounded by a yellow piped heart, was a photograph-in-icing of the happy couple looking impossibly young at their wedding forty years earlier. What a marvel that bakers could transfer pictures like that to an edible form.

The family flanked my parents, who stood holding hands facing everyone there. Reba, Tim, and I were on one side, with Derrick, Neli, and Cokey on the other. The catering kids had made sure everyone held a plastic cup filled either with bubbly wine or sparkling cider, according to their request. I'd asked Derrick to do the talking.

He lifted his cup. "Here's to Astra and Joseph and another happy forty years!"

Everyone raised their drinks and sipped. Pa gave Mom a big embrace and a long kiss, which garnered them applause all around. I grabbed my frame from the table behind me and stepped forward.

"I have a little something to share with you both, and with everyone," I said. "My apologies to real poets everywhere."

After the police, Yvonne, and Abo Reba had left at around noon, I'd again reassured Tim I was fine. We'd wiped down the tiny house, and I'd set up the lockbox for the tenants' self-check-in.

Then I'd managed to write the verse about my mom, her astrology, and her mothering. I thought for a moment and composed one last verse, then proofread and printed the gift. I even found a simple frame for it.

Now I cleared my throat and began to read, beginning with, "An Ode to My Parents." I read aloud and made it through the first five verses. I glanced at my mother, at my father, at the two arm in arm, beaming at me even while they each wiped away a tear.

I hadn't choked up yet, but that sight about did me in. I took a deep breath and kept reading.

> *A marriage to last forty years*
> *Doesn't come without strife and some tears.*
> *But Joseph and Astra,*
> *Their love's no disaster,*
> *Let us toast them with many a cheer!*

When I pronounced "disaster" as any good New Englander would—*disastah*—I got a laugh.

"That's lovely, honey," Mom murmured. Pa beamed with damp eyes.

Derrick stepped up next to me and lifted his glass. "To Astra and Joseph!"

Everyone echoed the second toast. Cokey clapped and chimed in with, "Yay to my Abos!" Tucker added a bark.

Reba held up her hands and waited until all were quiet. "I was a witness to the beginning of this long and joyous union. I won't be around for the party forty years from now, but that's as it should be. Astra dear, you've made my boy happy, all that a mother could wish for. And, Joseph? You've done me proud, son."

In the middle of the ensuing hugs and applause, Tim's arm came around me and squeezed.

"Nice doggerel, Mac." His smile was his usual adoring one.

I wouldn't tell him Derrick and Neli's news now. He'd find out soon enough. All I said was, "Thanks."

Pa and Mom both announced their gratitude to all who came.

"Don't leave after cake," Mom added. "This party's going to have dancing, and then some." She aimed a wink in Lincoln's direction.

"When are we having happy amivershree cake?" Cokey piped up, prompting a smattering of laughter.

"As soon as your abos make the first cut." Tim gestured to my parents to approach the cake and escorted them over.

Chapter 66

Lincoln materialized at my side. "I'd say you're as glad as I am that we have our coconspirators behind bars."

"The timing couldn't be better."

"You might be interested in what went down after we had both of them charged and locked up."

"You know I am." I gestured us away from the crush of celebrants heading for cake.

We ended up standing next to the hedge bordering a property at the back. It was the home of a woman who'd sadly been murdered a year ago. Hers had been the body Gin had found next to her taffy shop, the homicide Gin had been suspected of carrying out.

"Dish, Lincoln. What happened?"

"You've heard of a prisoner singing?"

I stared. "I'm going to take a wild guess and assume you don't mean a Johnny Cash singalong in Folsom Prison."

He threw back his head and laughed. "No, I certainly don't. Although the film of his performance in a prison yard is something I'll never tire of watching."

"Then it has to be that either Sita or Carl is blaming their partner for the murder and the assaults and all of it."

"How about both of them? They've turned on each other, big-time. It was like musical jail cells in there a little while ago."

"Wow."

"She said he put her up to all of it. He claimed she was the mastermind. The poison, the plan, everything, and that he had no idea Sita would go after Yvonne and you. He put on quite the air of being shocked."

"What, like, 'I'm shocked there's gambling going on in Casablanca' kind of shocked?" I asked, referring to one of my favorite lines from the vintage movie.

"Exactly."

"At least it's solved and over. You must be a lot more relieved than I am."

"It's always satisfying to bring a homicide case to a close, yes."

I smiled at him. "You're sticking around tonight, I hope."

"Are you kidding? I wouldn't miss a dance with Astra MacKenzie."

I could ask him about Delia, if her last name was linked with his. But I decided not to. I didn't want to do anything to spoil tonight's happy mood, which Lincoln seemed to be sharing, and rightly so. He headed over to snag a piece of cake.

Me, I felt a contentment that had been elusive all week. Murderers were behind bars, right where they belonged. And the rain had stopped. All was well in the world again.

Recipes

Chicken Salad

A curried chicken salad is perfect for a summer evening. Tim put this together for a meal with Mac.

Ingredients
2 cups cooked chicken, shredded or cubed
½ cup red seedless grapes, halved
½ cup pecans
1 tablespoon capers, drained
½ cup mayonnaise
1 teaspoon curry powder
Salt
Pepper

Directions
Toast pecans in a dry, cast-iron skillet (or other dry frying pan) for about ten minutes or until fragrant, shaking frequently. Roughly chop.

Mix mayonnaise and curry powder in bottom of serving bowl. Add other ingredients, plus pecans, and mix thoroughly. Increase mayo if you like and curry powder to taste, and add salt and pepper to taste.

Serve over salad greens with a sliced baguette or a side of potato salad.

Fresh Corn Salad

Tim makes this salad with fresh sweet corn from the farmers' market, the first cukes and cherry tomatoes of the season, and plentiful basil leaves.

Ingredients
3 cups lightly steamed, fresh corn kernels cut from the cob
1 cup gold or red cherry tomatoes, halved
1 cup peeled cucumber, cut in ¾-inch cubes
2 tablespoons olive oil
1 tablespoon rice vinegar
1 teaspoon fresh lime juice
4 (or more) fresh basil leaves, slivered
Salt and pepper to taste

Directions
Toss all ingredients and serve with grilled chicken or fish.

Chicken Pad Thai

Mac tried to learn to make one of her favorite dishes to surprise Tim, but it didn't go entirely as planned.

Serves four.

Ingredients

8 ounces dried flat pad Thai noodles or stir-fry rice noodles

¼ cup tamarind juice concentrate (or 2 tablespoons Thai tamarind paste mixed with 2 tablespoons water)

3 tablespoons dark brown sugar

2 tablespoons fish sauce

2 teaspoons chili-garlic sauce, such as sriracha, plus more for serving

¼ cup hot water

3 tablespoons vegetable oil

4 large eggs, beaten

2 cups shredded cooked chicken (omit or replace with tofu for vegetarian version)

2 bunch scallions, thinly sliced, separating green from white

2 cups mung bean sprouts

⅓ cup roasted, salted peanuts, chopped

Lime wedges (for serving)

Directions

Place noodles in a medium heatproof bowl. Add boiling water to cover and let stand, tossing with tongs frequently, until soft and pliable but not tender, 7–10 minutes (depending on brand). Drain and rinse with cold water, then drain again.

Whisk tamarind concentrate, brown sugar, fish sauce, chili-garlic sauce, and hot water in same bowl you used to soak noodles.

Pour oil in a large skillet (at least 12" in diameter) and place over medium-high heat. Add eggs and cook, stirring constantly, until dry curds form, 1–2 minutes.

Add chicken, scallion whites, fish sauce mixture, and noodles. Cook, tossing often with tongs, until sauce is mostly absorbed and noodles are well coated, about 3 minutes.

Add scallion greens, bean sprouts, and half of the chopped peanuts. Cook, tossing constantly, until heated through, about 1 minute more.

Divide noodle mixture among four plates. Top with chili-garlic sauce and remaining peanuts. Serve with lime wedges for squeezing alongside.

Ode to Summer Fruit Tart

The author learned this delicious dessert featuring summer fruits from her good friend Jennifer Yanco in the late 1970s. The recipe is a classic and needs no updating. Tim whips up an Ode for an easy summer dessert.

Ingredients
1 cup unbleached white flour
¼ cup butter
2 egg yolks
1 whole egg
¼ cup sugar
Pinch salt
8 ounces softened cream cheese (not whipped)
Grated rind of one lemon
Summer fruits such as blueberries, raspberries, strawberries, peeled and sliced ripe peaches
½ cup fruit jelly

Directions
Line a baking sheet with parchment paper and set aside.

Cut butter into flour until the consistency of coarse salt.

Beat together yolks, whole egg, sugar, and salt. Mix into flour and butter until well combined. On a floured surface, pat into a disk and wrap in plastic wrap. Refrigerate for at least one hour.

Preheat oven to 350° F. On the lined sheet, roll out the dough to about 8" x 10" (not too thin).

Bake the pastry for ten to twenty minutes. Watch carefully for browning. Cool on a wire rack.

Mix the cream cheese and grated lemon rind together. Spread all over the cooled pastry.

Arrange the fruit in any kind of pleasing motif.

Melt the fruit jelly in the microwave or a small saucepan and paint on the arranged fruit with a brush.

Slice into squares and serve for dessert or with brunch.

Pain au Chocolat

Tim makes his own pastry for these chocolate-filled croissants, but you can go the easy route and buy a box of puff pastry dough.

Ingredients
Puff pastry dough
4 ounces good quality baking chocolate, cut into skinny pieces
1 egg
2 tablespoons whole milk
Powdered sugar, sifted

Directions
Line two baking sheets with parchment paper.

Remove the dough from the refrigerator. On a lightly floured counter, roll the dough out into an 8×20-inch rectangle. Use your fingers if you need to. The dough is quite cold, so it will take a lot of arm muscle to roll. The dough will want to be oval shaped, but keep working it with your hands and rolling pin until you have the correct size rectangle.

Using a pizza cutter or sharp knife, slice the dough in half vertically into skinny rectangles 4 inches wide. Cut 3 even slices horizontally, yielding 8 4×5-inch rectangles. Cut each rectangle in half lengthwise so you have 16 2×5-inch rectangles.

Work with one rectangle at a time. Using your fingers or a rolling pin, stretch it to be about 8 inches long. Do this gently as you do not want to flatten the layers. Place a few small pieces of chocolate in a single layer at one end and tightly roll the dough up around the chocolate. Make sure the end is on the bottom.

Repeat with remaining dough, placing the shaped croissants on the baking sheets, 8 per sheet. Loosely cover with plastic wrap or aluminum foil and allow to rest at room temperature for 1 hour, then place in the refrigerator to rest for 1 hour or up to 12 hours.

Preheat oven to 400°F.

Whisk the egg and milk together. Remove the croissants from the refrigerator. Brush each lightly with egg wash.

Bake until croissants are golden brown, about 20 minutes. Rotate the pans halfway through baking. If croissants show signs of darkening too quickly, reduce the oven to 375°F.

Remove pain au chocolat from the oven and place on a wire rack to cool for a few minutes before serving. They will slightly deflate as they cool. If desired, dust with confectioners' sugar before serving.

Anniversary Cocktail

Astra and Joseph enjoyed this cocktail at their wedding forty years ago. Tim re-creates it for their anniversary party.

For each drink, serve over ice in an old-fashioned glass with a lime wedge garnish.

1 ounce vodka
½ ounce peach schnapps
2⅓ ounces sweetened cranberry juice
2 shakes orange bitters

For a nonalcoholic version, substitute peach juice for the schnapps and replace the vodka with lime seltzer.